His Father's Footsteps

A Novel

Enrico Downer

"How far would you walk in your father's
footsteps to find the one who killed him?
"To the ends of the earth," he answered.
And the fire in his eyes said he meant every word.

For my son, Troy

Contents

1 - The Letter

He remembers where he was standing, what he'd been doing, even what he was wearing the moment he learned his father was killed in America. He was standing in the kitchen-shed of his mother's three-gable wooden house, warming his dinner over a stove of flaming red-hot coals, wearing the same college uniform he had worn all week and the week before.

"Mark, sit down, son." Her voice over his shoulder was calm but firm, yet he continued stirring the frying pan assuming his mother was offering to take over the chore while he sat and waited to be served. She was always the motherhen at dinner time, always making sure her brood was fed. Her brood consisted of himself, his younger brother, Earl, and his adopted sister, Ermajean, who had been taken into the family since her parents had died the year before.

"Sit down for a minute, please!" This time he sensed the insistence in the pitch and the tenor of her voice. He spun around to see his mother, one hand on her hip, the other holding a letter limply, looking into his eyes, her own eyes brimming with tears.

"It's your father," she said, without further elaboration.

Still standing, he grabbed the letter and scanned it line by line. His father had been shot dead on a sidewalk in Richmond Borough, a borough of New York City. The letter said a search was underway for the killer; the NYC police was on the case; further details would be forthcoming. Judging from the wild and frenetic scribbling, the letter had been written by a nervous hand. It had taken a week as was customary for mail to reach Barbados and another two days to St. Lucy, the remotest parish on the island. He collapsed, held onto his mother, his head cushioned in her bosom and, shaking like a maraca, he cried his heart out while his fish dinner burned to an inedible char. He wanted to scream out loud like a child letting loose in a temper tantrum, but decided to channel his rage into a finely honed weapon of revenge.

His parents had been estranged for years but, from the far-off look in her eyes, she was no less stricken with grief than if he were still in her life. After all, he had fathered her two sons and she always boasted he was the only man she ever "knew". He remembers she never shed a single tear but pinched her lips and suddenly seemed to grow older. Then she plunked herself in her favorite cane-backed rocking chair and rocked faster and faster, closing her eyes and fanning herself furiously as she always did in church when the Spirit seized her.

It was no secret or source of resentment that his father had been living with another woman in New York, the one who it was natural to assume had written the letter, which bore the return address of a street in Harlem and was signed by a Maria. Neither was this woman blamed for the separation of his parents, for their common-law marriage had been falling apart long before he left the island. In the postscript was an invitation for one of the boys to come and stay with her in the aftermath, to say goodbye to their father, collect his belongings and preside over funeral arrangements while the search for the killer proceeded.

Being the older brother, he volunteered.

"I'll go, Ma."

"You t'ink you should …"

"Yes, I'm goin' leave tomorrow."

The grit in the tone of his voice told her he was not just going to preside over funeral arrangements. His voice told her he was determined to get to the bottom of why his father was killed, who was the killer and whither justice would be served. Whatever was the relationship between his parents, he adored his father. His early education, his street savvy, his unwavering pride as a young black man in a colonial society; all these things he had owed to his father. Suddenly, even the most mundane of memories came flooding back from the past with all of life's lessons he had been taught by his father, lessons now embodied in the person he had grown to be. In the beginning he was traumatized when his father left, but in time he had learned not to resent him for it: it was not a decision he had taken lightly. His brother, on the other hand, internalized it as abandonment.

"I am goin' find who killed 'im," he said through clenched teeth.

She heard the stridency in his voice and cautioned: "Be careful, son. Don' take de law into yer own hands, son. Let de police do their duty and if they don' find who kill yer father leave whoever it is in God's hands".

Ever since the day he picked up and moved to America, she always referred to him as "yer father" in the presence of the children. To friends and neighbors he was always "dat man". But to strangers he was Mr. Maynard and she Mrs. Maynard joined in a common-law marriage for umpteen years. She was a simple Christian woman with never a dark thought, one who was prepared to leave the wicked and the righteous in God's hands, and though he shared neither his mother's religion nor her dispassion for the things of the world, he knew it was her way of surviving the storms.

He remembers his younger brother, Earl, of a more impetuous temperament, coming home from school and, on hearing the news, flinging his schoolbag into a corner and flying into a howling, violent rage. He had to pin his brother's shoulders to the plywood partition until he simmered to a whimper lest he destroyed every piece of their humble possessions in their two-by-four living room. Afterwards Earl grew uncharacteristically ill-humored and moody.

Little Ermajean, the adopted one, home from school, was at first riveted in the doorway when the news was blurted out like a bolt of thunder and inadvertently reached her tender ears, when she slumped into a chair and, reining in her emotions, sat staring into the abyss silently without moving for over an hour.

He remembers an invasion by the neighbors as the news was eavesdropped by Mrs. Wilkinson next door and, in the blink of an eye, leapfrogged from house to house all the way down the street, and before long everyone in the family was engulfed in the arms of the solicitous as well as the inquisitive.

First came the narrow-minded Celestine Bradshaw. "Lucille, what a t'ing! You dependin' on de few Amurcan dollars de man send home every mont' and now he gone and get heself kill." As far as she was concerned, his father had selfishly done it to himself.

Then came the kindly Priscilla Carrington, mindful of the children. "Now dese thrildren don' have a father. I always did know Amurca wuz a dangerous place. He wuz better off stayin' home. Even though you and him wuz like cats and dogs, he would be livin' today."

Gertrude Thompson, never the shrinking violet, was unapologetically prurient and pecuniary. "Who is de wuthless Yankee woman he gone and live wid? Some piece o' jail bait? She cyant be no prettier than you, Lucille. Now she goin' get every cent that rightfully belong to he family." With that, she snatched from his mother's hand the plastic fan that advertised funeral parlors, and took over the fanning of his mother's face without missing a beat.

"Good God, Gertrude!" said Priscilla, "De man *dead!* You should never criticize de dead. De dead not here to defend heself. He should really come back and haunt you fer true. Leh de man res' in peace."

But Mrs. Brathwaite, a Christian woman, had brought to the house a grand bouquet of biblical blessings that shamed all the sentiments and blandishments showered on his mother that day. She began with, "Blessed are those who mourn, for they shall be comforted, Matthew 5 verse 4". She whispered softly in his mother's ears.

But he himself would not be comforted; he was ready to move heaven and earth to find the killer and the truth behind his father's murder. And to think he had not heard a single word of compassion for the dead but only for the living, he was truly saddened.

He remembers hurrying to Taylor's rum shop at the corner to apprise his father's friends and elicit some measure of sympathy for himself. They had already heard and were hoisting their glasses in a posthumous toast to his father, in remembrance of a dear friend and loyal patron of the shop. Taylor's establishment was where his father found peace and quiet away from all the fussing and confusion at home, whereas his wife always said it was where he sold his soul to the Devil.

The shopkeeper greeted him with an embrace. "Yer father wuz my right hand man, a good friend." The other men nodded in accord. "Never said one unkind word about yer mother all de years I know him. Never ever bring a woman in dis rum shop. Except f'r one time when Whilomena had a fight wid she man and he bring she in de shop f'r a drink to sooth de nerves. That wuz de kind o' man yer father wuz, always helpin' people."

Another of his friends, Malachi, chimed in with his own retrospections and remonstrations. "Listen to me. I warned your father a hundred times not to go to Amurca, that they killin' black people in Amurca like cockroaches. I told 'im if anyt'ing go to Canada or even Inglund. But de man would not listen. Talkin' 'bout how he met some Yankee woman and she wuz goin' help 'im get his green card. He told me he just had to get away, poor fella."

"Cornmeal" Carrington, another dedicated patron, who was an admiral in the St. Lucy Landship, pulled him aside to whisper in private, breathing his alcoholic fumes in his ear. He offered another perspective on the reason his father had gone to America.

"Son, yer father had to get away from home. Yer mother was drivin' 'im batty. That's de gospel truth. Lucille wanted perfection and ent no man on this God's earth dat is perfect. If he had his outside women it was yer mother dat drive de man to womanize. So de Yankee woman wid she pretty self come along and save yer father from de madhouse. Now he gone and get kill and yer mother is to blame."

But Mark could not bring himself to lay the blame entirely on his mother. She was a Christian woman who went to church, often two or three times on Sunday, read her bible "morning, noon and night" and basically lived her life by the dictums of the Beatitudes. It was clear his father had the sympathy of his peers and was understood and beloved among his own kind, for in Mr. Taylor's rum shop, as in rum shops all around the island, men could always be trusted to bare their souls and spill their innermost secrets over a bottle of rum.

He was told, long afterwards, his brother spent his days listlessly moping around the house, and at school in a world of his own, grieving for his father. And when his teachers came by to comment on Earl's moodiness, his mother told it was on account of his father having died and that he had died of natural causes. Afterwards she said it was not a lie; she always knew it was natural the tragic way he would leave this earth. And every night from his mother's bedroom he could hear his father's name murmured over and over in her prayers, for she was a forgiving woman and she forgave him for all his wrongs, as he hoped his father absolved her of all of hers before his last breath.

Next day he took the bus to Bridgetown, to James Street, to the garage where his father made his living as a car salesman before he turned in his keys and, without notice, walked off the lot. He wanted to inform his father's former coworkers before malicious gossip reached their ears from the street. Mr. Miller, the sales manager was effusive in his recollection of Dan Maynard but with an unfortunate choice of words.

"Your father f'r years was our top performer with a charisma salesmen would die for."

That his father had been held in such high esteem at work was enough to buoy his spirits at least for a while.

He had witnessed firsthand his father's proclivity to persuade. On an off-day from school he and his brother had accompanied him to his job. A working-class family of four, mother, father and two wide-eyed kids walked onto the car lot and approached his father about purchasing a used motorcar, price and affordability the only criteria. He had watched his father from a distance engaging the adults in a long, intimate and largely one-sided conversation while the children gawked at all the shiny vehicles driven by the rich and the middle-class.

It was his turn to gawk when half an hour later the family drove off the car lot with a spanking new 1956 Jaguar. He and his brother stood there in awe. Such were the charm and powers of persuasion his father possessed to have broken the man's resistance to an awesome car he likely could not afford.

Though Lucille Osborne taught her boys to always do the right thing, their love for their father would overlook his flaws as they continued to love him with all his shortcomings. He had no other trade or profession or education to propel him forward in life, so he traded himself, his gift of conversation and scintillating presence. And everyone bought. His formal education ended at fifth standard in the public system before he was thrust into the workplace to make a living, doing what he did best, selling himself. Selling himself meant wearing the best clothes, comporting himself with exceptional social graces and treating everyone equally whether rich or poor. He was adamant in seeing his boys acquired the education that had eluded him in his early years and he never failed to support them financially as best he could.

Earl was the favorite son in the eyes of his mother. He was dark of complexion like her with the same sensitive eyes and slightly pouted lips. He had his mother's hair, short and nappy and her non-nonsense disposition, a tendency never to stray from the straight and narrow.

He, on the other hand, took after his father, fair-skinned with silky-soft hair. He was told he had his mother's stubborn forehead but inherited the rest of his features from his grandfather on his father's side.

He had learned from his father that his own father descended from a long line of hardworking coal miners from Tylorstown, a little known mining town in Wales. Daniel Tennyson Maynard was his name, an infirmed

Welshman with a chronic respiratory condition commonly known as "black lung" that was exacerbated by cold weather. As a bachelor he moved to Barbados in the late 1800's in search of a cure. History books had taught him that the ailing half-brother of George Washington, a hundred years earlier, had done the same for the treatment of his tuberculosis and had fallen in love with the island. So he wisely left behind the dampness and the insalubrious climate of his native Wales and made his home in sunny Barbados in the rustic parish of St. Lucy. He came with little money, all the Maynards were of moderate means. Being poor he was shunned by wealthy expatriates from England who ruled the island. He was also avoided by most of the natives for the same reason.

The exception was Ursula Gibbons, a young entrepreneurial village girl, who ran a modest hairdressing business out of her house in Lamberts Village not far from where he lived. It was said she was the blackest and most beautiful girl in the whole of St. Lucy and for years she had caught the eye of every warm-blooded Bajan man within miles, though she had never returned their affections. However, she befriended the Welshman on the occasions when he would call on her for a haircut and their friendship eventually blossomed into a steamy romantic affair. All the people in the village thought the white man was merely looking for a body to keep his bed warm at night until the day he showed up at her house with a serious bouquet of flowers and got down on his knees to the bewilderment of Ursula and her entire family.

Nine months into their marriage Daniel Cuthbert Maynard was born and for another two years the old man rallied with the affliction of pneumonia brought on by his years working in the coal mines of Tylorstown. Then he succumbed.

The boy was raised by his mother and as a single parent with a single child she did the best she could to prepare him for a colonial society in which a man was measured more by his color than by his character. He was soon to appreciate the wisdom of her words. In school among his peers he reaped a heap of ridicule: they nicknamed him "white boy" and "high yellow"; moreover he was the first to be summoned to the blackboard to prove a theorem or conjugate a verb, not because he was set upon by his teachers but because he was the first to catch the eye as they turned to face the class.

He resented his father for this predicament in his youth. Then his fortunes reversed as he made his way into the workplace and found his whitish skin was a valuable social and marketable asset in a colonial society where the white minority ruled. Faced with this dichotomy of mixed blood and mixed race, he decided to explore his chances in America where he thought he might fit somewhere on the favored side of the color spectrum. Who would have guessed that when he went to America he would eventually become a black man?

In 1941 on one fortuitous Sunday morning, he met Lucille Osborne as she emerged from the fellowship of early morning mass at St. Lucy's Parish Church where her father was the deacon. They fell into a relationship which they both believed to be love and though the Church and society all frowned on cohabitation, they wasted no time in starting a family. Mark came first and Earl a year later.

But from the first day of their courtship, Lucille's heart and mind had been set on the sacrament of holy matrimony. However, as the years unfolded, Dan became more and more calcified in his ways as their union defaulted to common-law. And though she rarely admitted it, her desire to be properly married was continually at the core of their bickering and contentiousness until the day she realized he was unbreakable.

And so, she said her vows to another; she became wedded instead to the Church, St. Lucy's Parish Church, where she attended every service on the church's perennial calendar, practiced with the choir twice a week and voluntarily took charge of their continual fund raising. She had little time for her children.

However, it was fair to say his mother by example was her children's moral compass, whereas had they followed in their father's footsteps they would have learned to live a life of debauchery and waste. However, in his defense, he had always cautioned them with the words, "Do as I say, not as I do," and while he was the one who taught them to survive in a harsh world he also disciplined them with an unsparing rod.

Mark had never faulted his mother for wanting that enviable band of gold and that traditional piece of paper, but neither did he fault his father. As far as he was concerned, the matter was none of his or his brother's business; they had suffered no detriments being born out of wedlock. Some of his friends were in the same boat and all seemed oblivious of their having been conceived without the approbation of the law.

Now their father was dead. He could see in his mother's eyes that the marriage she had yearned for no longer mattered, and that in fact she might have unwittingly driven him away; it was time for forgiveness and compassion. She would look past the disappointments and broken promises and the feuding and fussing and come to see at last she had never ceased to love him.

In a day or two she would pack his father's valise and send her son off to find the one who killed his father. It was her son's wish. She couldn't deter him even if she tried.

2 – Maria Townsend

August 1958. Three days after receiving Maria's dreadful letter, he was in New York, standing at the curb outside the BOAC terminal. In the midst of an anxious crowd awaiting their loved ones, he waited to be greeted by a stranger, his father's friend, who was kind to have sent him the fare and some travelling money, though neither had been asked for. He was holding in his right hand his father's wooden valise which, like him, had never before left the island but which had been crammed with every inch of his entire wardrobe from pajamas to cricket whites. He flipped up the collar of his college blazer and dug his left hand in his pants pocket, for to him the air was freezing though New York was in the throes of a sweltering summer. He looked first left, then right, then left again repeatedly for someone he didn't know, who was at that moment looking for someone she had never seen. Neither he nor his brother had been sent a photograph of her, which would have been an awkward, if not unlikely, addition to the family's album. In his mind's eye she had to be more or less his father's age, somewhere in her mid fifties.

He always thought his father was the handsomest of all the fathers he knew, fair-skinned, svelte and ruggedly masculine. It was rumored he had melted a few hearts in his time until the day he met Lucille Osborne, a dark-skinned Bajan beauty; and from that point on, his wanderlust was stopped dead in its tracks. It was reasonable to assume, then, his father's friend was no less easy on the eyes, so scanning the multitude milling around outside the terminal, his eyes rested only on those women who he thought would have been worthy of a second look by his late father. So craning and squinting he picked out two or three likely brown and ebony faces but his gaze was not returned until ...

"Hello, is that you, Mark?" The voice and the tooting of a horn came from behind the steering wheel of a motorcar pulling to the curb with a blaze of chrome and flashing lights. It was a convertible, the kind he had only seen in magazines, while the image of the woman he had thought her to be all this time vanished into thin air.

"Yes, is me ... Mark Maynard."

"Hop in then. Throw your stuff in the back," she hollered, her blond hair flying in the wind.

In that instant he realized he had prejudged the color of her skin, and less meaningfully her age, and that his mind had pigeonholed her into the same race as his father's. But he knew his prejudice was innocent, for his mind had been conditioned by the society in which he lived and not by any primal preference that Maria should be any other than who she was.

Her voice was chirpy unlike the somber voice of the grieving mother he had left behind. As they pulled away from the curb he glanced over at her profile and, for the first time, was moved to forgive his father's foible, though, on behalf of his mother, he could not bring himself to overlook his infidelity. In any case, he had no reason to indict her for who she was, a younger woman, white, perhaps his own age, with a face and body he found exquisitely charming. Perhaps feeling his eyes upon her, she threw out a nervous flurry of disjointed sentences and questions left in the air unanswered.

"How was your trip? My name is Maria Townsend. How is your family taking it? Are you hungry?"

On the way across the bridge, on the Bronx Parkway to Harlem, she filled his ear with a steady stream of desultory conversation, most of which flew over his head, for he was more interested in her filling in the blanks about his father, the blanks left dangling in her letter.

"Your father was shot and killed outside a bar in Richmond Borough. The newspapers said he had stopped for a drink before heading home. It happened at the Hard Nuts Café, a name that is misleading because they only serve drinks. There was only one witness, a homeless man, a wino. They said he was huddling under a blanket on the sidewalk. Your father was made to kneel while the killer fired three bullets directly into the back of his head. He would've pumped three more holes in his skull if the gun hadn't jammed." She looked over at his face and seemed to pause for the weight of horror to register with its blood-soaked vividness in his imagination.

"What was he doing in Richmond Borough?" he asked. "I thought he worked in Brooklyn. He said so in his letters."

"You're right. He was a car salesman in Flatbush working for Giuseppe Motors. Made a good living.

"They said a month earlier another African American, a gay man, had been shot as he walked out of the Ramrod Nightclub on the West Side. Same execution, same description, six bullets."

It seemed the fires of racism and homophobia were raging in tandem all across the city. The homosexual had two counts against him. Therefore he had to be exterminated.

"Did the homeless man give an account of what he looked like, the man who shot my father?"

"He said there were two of them, and their heads were covered with hoods like ghosts."

"Do the police have anything to go on?"

"The old man said they left a white sheet behind perhaps as a memento, but everyone said the gunman was a copycat, and there was no KKK in this part of the country. One officer joked that the old wino was seeing ghosts, there was just one killer. Some didn't believe he saw anything, that he was just hallucinating or drawing attention to himself. Y'see, he was half drunk at the time, a flask o' something or the other sticking out of his pants pocket."

"Where is he now, my father?"

"In the city morgue."

"Let's go see 'im."

They decided to detour from the way home and go directly to the mortuary.

After his father flew the nest, his face and everything about him had lately been vengefully expunged from his son's memory, even though his father continued to support them financially from a distance, writing often, taking care of their school fees and books and satisfying their wants for the latest clothes, toys and fads from America. But as the cotton sheet at the morgue was lifted, he saw a man whom he had never forgotten, a father whom, in the deep recesses of his subconscious, he had never ceased to love, a man whose lifeless, piteous body could cause a torrent of tears to fall from his eyes. His head had been partially bandaged to mercifully obscure the damage, but his lips were exposed, tightly clenched in his last excruciating grimace. He bent down and kissed his lips, then he fell to his knees and cried his heart out.

No, he was not the perfect father but his mother was not entirely guiltless either in their fractious marriage. Nevertheless, he was reluctant to assign blame for their undoing, for who knows which thoughtless word or careless rub on either side had turned out to be the final straw? And so his tears were not just for his father but also for his mother, for he knew they loved each other in their own peculiar ways. Like a rose garden taken for granted, unkempt and uncared for, the love they once shared was bound to eventually wither and die.

Maria, emotionless at his side, placed her hand on his shoulder. He could only assume she had no more tears to shed. They drove to Harlem and parked next to a rental brownstone on 135th Street where she and his father had been living. The brick house was linked to a chain of like houses, in stark contrast to the weathered clapboard house he had left behind sitting on a quadrangle of rock-stones. He followed her, two steps behind, valise in hand, and though unable to remove his eyes from the slow, sensuous swaying of her buttocks as she climbed the steep entrance to the front door, he was nevertheless acutely aware she had been his father's lover. That she seemed no older than the Maynard boys should be none of his business.

She turned to him. "Make yourself at home." Then she added: "Everything in this house belonged to your father. It's all yours now." He ignored the ambiguity in these welcoming words.

It was a spacious bi-level house in which they could separate themselves for hours should they crave to be alone; separate bedrooms, one on each floor. It was a convenient arrangement that likely served as a virtual wall between her and his father during their spats — common to all affairs — until they could cool their tempers and resolve their differences separately in one night of quiet contemplation. The single tiny bathroom, however, he found less accommodating when he went to pee and found her underwear hanging on a line from wall to wall causing him to duck while relieving himself as her panties flapped around his face.

In this enormous house, at a time like this, they could well have benefited from each other's solace. His mind wandered back to that cramped wooden house in which his parents often quarreled and sparred and their angry voices rose to competing crescendos and bounced off the walls and there would be no escape for either Mom or Dad in that insanely tight space. Mom would flee to the church and return from the company of angels all blessed and forgiving and his dad would come back that night from Mr. Taylor's rum shop all mellow and pleasantly agreeable. They would close their bedroom door and, before long, the rhythmic creaking of bedsprings would tell a story of love and forgiveness.

Maria ushered him into the master bedroom in which the air was redolent of his father's Old Spice cologne and Captain Black tobacco while a bevy of his suits hung forlornly in the closet. While he unpacked his valise, placing a portrait of his dad on the dresser at eye level with his bed, he felt himself in the presence of his father.

Later that night she came to his bedroom dressed in a light-pink negligee that gaped at the waist revealing more of her skin than he cared to see. He forced himself to believe she was innocent of any other design than to make him feel a part of her family, as a sister would, thinking nothing of partially disrobing in the presence of a sibling. While he stood at the window wrapped in his father's night robe hanging loosely from his shoulders like a Roman toga, she sat on the edge of the bed, her eyes moving to the photo of his father, and recounted how the two had met.

"It was during spring break from Mercy College when me and some girlfriends chose Barbados for our first vacation out of the country. The other girls were one white and one black and we all fell in love with him but I was the lucky one. Or the unlucky one, depending on how you look at it. We were sitting in the lounge at Sam Lord's Castle where we were staying when he walked in alone and all eyes latched onto this handsome man all dapper in a pinstriped three-piece with matching fedora and two-toned shoes. He came over and offered to buy us girls a friendly drink and after an hour of drooling and giggling, I was smitten. But behind his charm and wit there was a sadness and vulnerability in his eyes. Mark, your father was not a happy man. The following night he returned to the Castle. We sat in my room and he chatted about his life, his work, his boys. He told me how he loved his boys. He was so proud of you two.

"I was living with my folks in Boston and commuting to New York weekly where between waiting tables I had a bit part in a soap opera on TV. He called me and said he was in the city and looking for a place to live. During the week I shared a loft in SoHo with a girlfriend, not a pleasant experience. I spoke to the Russian landlady about a vacant studio apartment on the top floor but she said her quota of minorities had already been filled. I needed to help him and we agreed to split the rent on someplace affordable, which is how I ended up here of all places, the only white person on the block at the time, with the exception of a pasty-faced Yugoslavian woman who promptly moved away.

"I was just fond of him in the beginning and then I fell in love. He had that … I don't know … certain sexual magnetism, I guess. What can I tell you?"

She sounded sincere. There was a tear on her cheek as she finished the story and he marveled at her obsession with the man who, all his life, he had never seen in the company of any other woman but his mother.

"How far would you go to find the one who killed your father?" she asked him.

"To the ends of the earth and beyond," he answered.

The fire in his eyes showed her he meant it. Whatever the reason his father was killed he made up his mind to find the truth. And so he wrote to his mother to say he was staying in America until he found that truth. He couldn't say when he would be back but surely not before the murderer was caught and brought to justice. He told her he was invited to stay as long as he wanted but omitted to say his father had been living in relative comfort for fear of dredging up past grudges.

That first night in America, in the bed in which his father slept with Maria, he stared all night into the dark, seeing his father's head against a blood-spattered ceiling, his eyes clenched tightly waiting for the end, hearing his father's voice pleading for mercy. He closed his eyes and pressed the palms of his hands to his ears, but to no avail. Tossing and turning well into the wee hours, he turned on the little transistor radio across the room and listened to the insipid voices of a late night show for no other reason but to rid his ears of the nightmarish screams and the staccato sounds of a gun, popping, popping, popping endlessly in the night, into his head, drilling deep into his brain.

3 – Rude Awakenings

In the morning she brought breakfast — tea, eggs and toast — to his bedroom and set the earthenware tray before him with a smile and a cheery "good morning". For a moment he imagined he had fallen asleep again and was lost in some fantastical dream. Such attentiveness he had never known in all his young life. Back in Barbados for breakfast he was always on his own. He would have to scramble under the house, fight off a rooster and deprive one of his clucking hens of freshly laid eggs.

She left the room and returned a minute later with slippers, a pair of Japanese babouches, which he took to be his father's. She placed them perfectly aligned at his feet. She moved to the window and tugged open the blinds admitting a shaft of bright sunlight to suffuse the room. Then she walked over to his bed, fluffed up his pillows and turned them over. Before the words "thank you" could come to his head, she was gone, leaving him transfixed with the notion that overnight he had become his father.

From that moment on, he made up his mind not to be sucked into his father's world of dependency nor in Maria's of servitude. From now on, he would do whatever he could for himself. Back home in his other life, his father had never known such deferential services. Had a request for breakfast in bed ever crossed his mind and left his lips, he would have been the recipient of a severe tongue lashing that might last the whole day. He could hear his mother now: "Yuh better catch yuhself. You en ha' no slave in dis house".

He had a pressing thought to visit the police station he had been told was in charge of the investigation. He closed his door and sat for an hour with a fold-out map of the New York transit system and studied the color-coded maze of tracks, transfers and crossings until he had committed to memory the circuitous route and multiple trains that would take him from Harlem to Richmond Borough. Then he dressed, donning one of his father's jackets, and headed for the subway.

He arrived at the Richmond precinct minutes away from where he exited the train. The precinct was a fortress of a building, ringed by razor wire and patrolled by rookies, while the interior was like an office of querulous disgruntled employees complaining to their superiors, a panel of dispassionate policemen sitting at their desks fielding questions and deflecting the abuses hurled at them by the complainants. These were the citizens of the surrounding area who had come laden with their burdens of unfairness to lay them at the feet of the officers and were pleading for justice and compassion, their plaintive voices echoing a litany of troubled cases, of burglaries, beatings, robberies, police brutality, parking tickets, stolen goods. No one was there to report on a life taken except for himself, a foreigner about to lean on an unfamiliar system of investigators, attorneys, judges, juries, the whole American system of purported justice.

He remembered as a young boy, at the age when local events of the morbid kind tended to intrigue, that he read in the local newspaper, *The Advocate*, the story of a white farmer on the island who had shot and killed a native boy caught filching a few potatoes in his vegetable patch. The farmer was given a sentence tantamount to a slap on the wrist while a native, who had taken the life of an English settler the year before, was hanged one morning without mercy at Glendairy with the concurrence of judge, jury and the people at large.

He quickly learned that what had pierced a hole in the hearts of him and his brother was a blip in the annals of murders committed every year in this vast metropolis and that, before long, the case might be consigned to the pile of unsolved murders that clog the passage of justice in this city of millions.

He remembers approaching the desk sergeant and chief investigator politely enquiring about the delay in capturing his father's killer. Sergeant Kaufmann, a stiff-necked officer with a surly demeanor and an unvarnished manner of speaking, took exception. It was clear the officer was riled by the affront to the reputation of New York's finest, not coming from a taxpayer but from a foreigner who had no prerogative to come to his country to criticize how his Department went about its business.

"What else do you want from me, pal?" asked the officer. "We put our best fellas on the case. So much we can do without a decent lead. We had our fair share o' stiffs that night. Your father was not the only one. People get shot up in this town every night. Some survive, some die."

He remembers retorting: "Well, my father was the only one to *me*."

And the officer snarled: "Look, mister, we can't solve every single damn crime. Some we win, some we lose. So we came up empty in the case of your father. There was only one witness and he was drunk as a fish that night."

The sergeant shrugged his shoulders and threw up his hands.

"Did your men interview the barman," he asked, "and the people in the bar that night?"

"What do you expect?" he answered brusquely. "And what duh hell was yer father doin' in Richmond Borough anyway when he worked in Brooklyn, huh? And besides, in a white section o' town, in a white bar, hangin' out in the Hard Nuts Café f'r Christ sake? You mean to tell me they ain' t no bars in Brooklyn?"

In his short time in America, he had not yet become aware that there were indeed bars for different colors. Then he remembered that back home rum shops belonged to the public regardless of color while some clubs were exclusively reserved for whites under the guise of "members only".

As he walked despondently back to the train station someone called his name. The person was an African American police officer, broad shoulders, thick neck, big arms. He had seen him at the precinct during the heated exchange with Kaufmann. He had been sitting with another complainant, his back turned, assumedly paying no attention.

"Might as well give up, brother. We don't get that much priority when it comes to Kaufmann. Your father was just another black stiff to him. Heard yer accent. Where're you from? Jamaica?"

"Barbados."

"Sure came a long way to run into a dead end. I was one of the fellas on the case. It was a hot night, ninety degrees in the shade. We had two other shootings that night and we were hustling to get your father off the street. Didn't even wait f'r forensics."

"What's your name, officer? Can I call you if I need you?"

"Malcolm. Yes, you can call the station, ask for Sergeant James." They exchanged phone numbers.

In the days ahead, the investigation ground to a halt. It had garnered a few groundless leads from some publicity seekers and had earned him some unneeded exposure in the *Daily News* and the *New York Times*. The *Post*, renowned for its glaring and sensationalistic headlines, topped the story with: *"Boy travels a thousand miles seeking justice for his slain father and finds none."* He still has a clipping of the press release featured in the *Richmond Borough Review* when the police spokesman stood before a cluster of microphones to assure New Yorkers he had good reason to believe the perpetrator would be apprehended in a matter of days. Then he asked the son of the man who was so callously slain to come forward and say a few words to the citizens of New York, so all would see in his face and in his words the fate that should never befall any man's son. Mark had declined.

He pondered the wisdom of retracing his father's footsteps to the scene of the crime. Even now he shudders at the thought of having done the unthinkable. Knowing what he learned later about the vicinity and its criminal elements he should never have given it a thought. It was possible that the killer with an egoistic feel for the dramatic might just as well have replicated the crime learning that the dead man's son was in the area.

He found his way to the borough one early morning when the environs would be bustling and early drinkers would be walking in and out of the club. He stood across the street in the dappled shade of an elm and contemplated the spot where they had killed him. In his mind he reenacted the sequence of the killing as he had envisioned it. Suddenly an awful tightness flew to his chest and a fluttering churned in the pit of his stomach. He saw his father stepping out from under the awning of the café and being startled when the masked assailant crept from the cover of the tall hedge that skirted the sidewalk. The man blocked his way. He heard the killer's voice, low but commanding. "Turn around! On your knees!" He heard his father's voice at first seeking an explanation, then pleading for his life, then doing as he was told. *Pop! Pop! Pop!* His father slumped forward, his hands and the shoes on his feet quivering with the last dregs of life oozing from his body, and his blood pooling next to his head before seeping into the earth. He saw the masked shooter fumble with his gun, unconvinced that the job was done, but the three bullets had found their intended mark before the weapon jammed. The killer vanished from the scene as quickly as he had appeared. In his mind's eye he witnessed the commotion as customers abandoned their tables and rushed to the door. They all stood around staring and whispering among themselves, some laughing, some bemoaning another crime in their fair borough of Richmond.

His ruminating came to an end as he walked boldly to the entrance under its green awning. He pushed past the swing doors and took a seat on one of the steel and chrome barstools at the counter.

With his hands upraised, he saluted the drinkers with a friendly greeting. "Hi folks!" The men sitting on both sides of him picked up their drinks in unison, withdrew from his company and retreated to tables in the rear. Left alone, he decided to strike up a conversation with the bartender, who with his muscular build and a face slightly misshapen, had the look of a retired prizefighter. A shamrock tattooed in bright green on his left bicep proclaimed him a proud Irishman.

"What'll it be, mister?" asked the barman, sliding a coaster, an ashtray and a bowl of stale peanuts in front of his nose.

"Nothing for me, just a few answers if you don't mind."

"You another detective?"

"No. I'm the son of the man who was shot and killed in cold blood outside your door couple weeks ago." He tried not to sound tense and combative.

Apprehension flickered in the man's eyes as he must have thought the stranger had come to settle a score.

"You got any children?" he asked the barman.

"Yeah, I got two."

"Well then you should know what I'm going through. A father might forget his children but a son never forgets his father, whatever his sins."

"That's true."

His face softened and, forcing a smile, he reached out to shake his hand.

"Sorry about your father but I already told the police everything I know."

"Did he come here often?"

"Yeah. Couple times a week."

"What did he drink?"

"Rum and coke. Nothing but Mount Gay. Had to order that specific brand through Miami just f'r the dude. He wasn't a big drinker but he never failed to leave a ten on the counter before he walked out the door. Yeah, yer father was alright."

"Do you know who killed 'im?" Just for the record the question had to be asked. The answer was predictable.

He just shook his head. "All I remember, it was the hottest god-darned night of the year."

"Was he alone that night?

He pursed his lips, picked up an empty mug, began wiping the rim furiously with a soiled rag, held it up to the light inspecting it for smudges, placed it back on the counter and took a deep breath.

"Well, as I said in my statement, they used to drop in around six, once or twice a week, had a drink or two between them, dropped a few coins in the jukebox, did a couple jigs on the floor, never got drunk, never gave any trouble."

"Did you know her?"

"Nope."

"Mind telling me what she looked like?"

"She wore her hair in dreadlocks, Rasta style, that much I remember, yeh man," he answered with a phony Jamaican inflection.

The next question crippled his tongue with fear, for the answer could lead him to anger and shame for his father. But the question needed to be asked in the interest of full disclosure of everything that happened that night in the club.

"So you think they were lovers?"

It was obvious he did not want to answer. He turned around, diverted his attention to rearranging empty glasses from one end of the shelf to the other, chucking empty bottles, fetching fresh ones from the cupboard, emptying ash trays.

But Mark prodded. "Were they?"

With his back turned, he muttered, so one else could hear, "You tell me! They were smothering each other with kisses all night."

He turned around, switching back to business mode. "I got no more to say, man. Want a drink? It's on the house."

"Rum and coke, in the name of my father."

With this latest revelation he found the image of his father evolving from the unfortunate victim, who happened to be in the wrong place at the wrong time, to the philandering father, who should have stayed at home with his family. But what had he done to be deserving of death? Was he a party to his own demise? In spite of it all, though his love for his father would be forever blemished, it would remain undiminished, for his love had been rooted in all the earlier years he had been a good father. He eased down from the stool, thanked the bartender and walked away without a second drink. Tears were welling in his eyes, his heart filled with shame.

Back on the sidewalk, he heard a rustling behind the juniper hedges. In his peripheral vision he caught a man emerging from the alleyway next to the café. A curled finger beckoned him to come closer. The man stepped away from the foliage and with his arms upraised revealed himself to be unarmed and unthreatening. Mark was looking at the gaunt white-bearded face of an old man, his head protruding from a sheet that doubled as a poncho which likely had once been white but now brown and mucky, having seen many nights lying on the bare clayey earth. He had the appearance of having emerged from a coal mine, his face smeared with coal dust, but under the dirt, his nose, his lips and his hair showed him to be a white man, a derelict no doubt. He walked towards the man but the pungency of his alcoholic breath forced him to keep his distance.

"Look man, is none o' my business but I seen you standin' under the tree yonder starin' f'r a long time at the Hard Nuts 'cross the road like if you tryin' to make up your mind 'bout a drink. I got my own here under this poncho if you care to join me f'r a swig with a seventy-year-old geezer who could use some comp'ny. Know what I mean?"

"No, it wasn't that," Mark started to explain.

"Reason is," the old man said, "I never seen no colored folks goin' in there, y'see. You is the first since the fella got shot right there, look right there, coming out o' the club." He pointed.

"You mean you were here and you saw when it happened?"

"Damn right I was here. They shot 'im in the back o' the head like he was a damn horse that broke a leg in a race so the animal wouldn't suffer no mo'. I saw it with my own two eyes."

"They? Was there more than one?"

"It was dark, man, and I was drunk as a skunk that night, if you know what I'm sayin'. They coulda been one or they coulda been two but the police say I was full o' shit, that I was seein' double with the liquor in my head." He took a step backward, stumbled and grabbed at the hedges.

"What did he look like?"

"Damned if I know. He had a hood over his head like one of them executioners from the French inquisition."

"Did he see you?"

"Damn right, the summabitch looks me straight in the eye through two tiny lil holes in his mask. But he don't worry about no ol' man plus I can't see his face anyway."

The old man reached under his poncho and produced an unlabelled flask of clear liquid. "Wanna swig o' my Gordon's?"

"No thanks. How about the man that they killed? You seen him before that night?"

"Shit yes, I seen him many times befo', going in and out o' the Hard Nuts."

"Alone or with someone?"

"Always with a woman. Yes sir. Dreadlocks hanging down her back, man, dreadlocks like long tails. I seen her runnin' down the sidewalk that night, clackety, clackety, clackety, in her high heels after the shootin'. She take off like a witch on a broom with all that Rasta hair flyin' in the wind." He chuckled at his own joke.

"And then I find this poncho, this white sheet in the bushes that I been wearing ever since to keep the wind off my chest. I guess they had to get rid o' it to make their getaway in regular clothes."

"What's yer name?"

"Joe Butts, Sergeant First Class, Serial Number 065587, first cavalry division, Korea."

"So where is home now f'er you?"

"Right here in the alley. Couple empty cardboard boxes. Some Salvation Army beddin'. Got my gin. And best of all, no taxes to pay. Livin' the life of Riley. Know what I'm sayin'?"

"Where was home before now?"

He tipped the bottle to his mouth, cocked his head back, emptied the contents and tossed the bottle into the hedges.

"I was sharin' a mobile home in New Orleans with some friends o' mine that I met in the war. Until they kicked me out. I was complainin' day and night 'bout the way they treat the negro race down in the South. I was gettin' on their damn nerves."

Mark wished him well, thanked him for the chitchat and walked away with the evidence from the lips of an old drunk who remembered his serial number in the war but could not remember if he had seen one or two gunmen that night. It would never stand up in a courtroom.

Questions remained. According to the barman, he had told the police about the mysterious woman, yet Sergeant Kaufmann never mentioned it. In addition, was she the motive or even a party to the killing? Was the killer present in the club that night and had followed his father to the exit? If so, why did the barman not think it newsworthy? He mulled over these puzzling fragments and came to the conclusion his father's death had been shrouded under a cloud of connivance and secrecy.

He, too, would be secretive in withholding from Maria the details of his visit to the scene of the crime, for how could he be the one to tell her there was another woman and then stand aside and witness the pain in her face.

He couldn't wait to get home, so in the privacy of a phone booth he telephoned the precinct.

"May I speak to Sergeant James?"

"This is he."

"Mark Maynard. Who was the woman with my father the night he was killed?"

The phone fell silent for a moment.

"Hold on a sec, I have to change phones."

Another moment of silence. Then the officer's voice lowered almost to an imperceptible whisper.

"She was in the original report but the boss didn't think she was relevant."

"How about the old man outside the café who said he saw everything?"

"Mark, he was drunk."

"But I just spoke to …"

"Mark, I can't say anymore right now. Call me later." The phone clicked off.

As he boarded the El back to Grand Central, the words "didn't think it was relevant" were buzzing in his ears like a million cicadas until he felt a rage rising inside him, for he knew that in the view of the police the irrelevancy of a witness to his father's death also implied the irrelevancy of his father's life as well. Once again the specter appeared of his father lying face-down on the walkway outside the café with his blood oozing into the earth from the three craters in the back of his cranium.

He found a seat on the train — on one of those hard ergonomic-defying seats designed for the commuters' discomfort — and found himself sizing up the passengers, the working class of this suburban borough heading to the city, their faces hard and expressionless, white faces, brown faces, black faces, all the same on this train of the racially diverse, faces reflecting neither love nor hate, just plain indifference, with one purpose, to get to the end of the line on time, to where a hundred trains every hour emptied themselves into that swirling, churning mélange of humanity that was Grand Central Station, and thereafter each person heading to his and her calling in the big city; then eight hours later the picture reverses and the train in which he now sits will be chugging back to the outskirts, but in the process the load of integrated commuters will separate into constituent sections of black, brown and white to return to homes in segregated sections of the borough. He had been in the city for just a week and already knew the melting pot was a lie.

♦ ♦ ♦

The funeral service was held at the Church of Divine Intervention in Harlem, a timeworn edifice at the corner of 116th and 7th. The pastor, Glenmore Sheldon, wearing a black Nehru suit, was a six-foot-five African American, a behemoth of a man who wore a mop of sheeny-black hair. He appeared to be given to the things of this world, judging from his regalia of jewelry, but he also spoke the language of the Apostles. A thick link chain of glistening gold hung from his neck and rested on the cliff of his stomach. A woman's teardrop earring dangled from one ear. Later he learned that the Reverend was also a civil rights activist, one beloved in the community, one whom it would be wise to befriend, and that he was sometimes inclined to bestow favors, a godfather of sorts. He came down the aisle swinging his clanging pot of frankincense and seemed to glare at him sitting next to Maria, and when their eyes met he mouthed the words "I have to talk to you".

A spattering of white faces dotted the congregation overwhelmed by a sea of blacks who had come to honor his father, lying in an unopened coffin next to the chancery.

After the minister had extolled the virtues of Dan Maynard, the congregants took turns stepping up to the lectern to lavish praises on his father and to share stories of a generous man who had meant so much in their own lives. It was a measure of redemption and he was gratified to hear their testimonials.

One man, who introduced himself as Mr. Ginsberg, wearing a yarmulke, took the stage to say he had been a trusted friend of the departed and that he had been a man of spiritual faith, though Mark knew his father had never been known to cross the threshold of either church or synagogue in his entire lifetime.

In the back of the church, a young woman, visibly in the advanced stage of pregnancy, her face veiled in black, raised her hand but preferred not to reveal her name. She said shyly and tearfully, "I just wanted to say, he was the kindest man I ever knew. I met Mr. Maynard after I had lost my husband and when I was going through a period of deep depression he came to my bedside almost every evening and told me stories of his life in Barbados and about his family, especially about his boys. Mr. Maynard rescued me during that dark time in my life. I truly loved him."

One by one, they stepped forward with their oratorical endorsements of the life his father had lived. Yet at the end of the service when they poured out of the pews, no one bothered to follow his father to his final resting place, except for the minister, Maria and himself. Instead they all made a dash for the church hall in the basement to feast on free hors d'oeuvres, rum punch and wine.

He pictured his father's horse-drawn hearse at the head of a mile-long procession back home in Barbados, his friends, family and acquaintances from all over the island present for the sendoff, women from the St. Lucy Landship resplendent in white, weeping and singing *The day Thou gavest, Lord is ended* ... Men lining both sides of the road would be doffing their hats as the mourners made their way to Westbury Cemetery.

Along with Maria and the Reverend in his sleek black Cadillac, he followed his father's hearse to Trinity Cemetery a few miles away. There, he found the grave was no ordinary sodden mound of clayey earth like most of the others. She had ordered for his father a mausoleum built of the finest marble and granite, the size of a small bungalow, the kind in Barbados that stood aloof from quaint decrepit chattel houses. He knew that had he been buried on the island, his resting place would have been indistinguishable with a stone marker half-buried in the earth.

He remembers that at the burial site, after his father had been lowered into the earth, the minister pulled him aside and, bending low from his enormous height, whispered in his ear.

"Listen! I have to talk to you ... alone ... very important!" His face was taut, his expression grave as if he were aware of some apocalyptic disaster.

He swiveled his head over his right shoulder, then over his left, though the only other person present was Maria standing at some distance away alongside the diggers, supervising them as they went about their work. He cupped his hands to his mouth.

"Son, that woman is trouble."

"Who?"

"Maria. She is what is known as a black widow." Then he added ambiguously, "in more ways than one".

"What do you mean, Brother Sheldon?"

"Your father was not the only one. They got rid of another close friend of mine. He was fooling around with Mr. Hasselberry's, the solicitor's daughter years before your father's time. Someone blew his head off with a Winchester in broad daylight. These women are dangerous, they have a predilection for the brothers and they are sweet on men like you from the Caribbean. I officiated at his funeral, the one who was banging the solicitor's daughter, and put him in the grave like I just did your father."

"Who's they?" he asked.

"The Ku Klux Klan. Ever heard of the KKK?"

"Vaguely."

"Well, they ain't just down south below the Mason Dixon. They're all around you right here in New York."

"Well, what's that got to do with me? I'm just livin' in my father's house, at least f'r now."

"It don' matter, son. It's the perception, see? They don' like to see black and white too close like that together. Take my advice. Get away from her as fast as you can, or sure as hell you goin' be next. Stick with yer own."

Mark dismissed the warning as a self-serving invention in the fanciful mind of the minister, perhaps to steer him into the arms of one of his love-starved female constituents. And as it turned out, he was right, for the next words whispered in his ear were, "I'm goin' introduce you to one of my sisters in Christ back at the chapel; she's an African princess."

HIS FATHER'S FOOTSTEPS

He saw Maria approaching and reassumed the image of the sorrowful consoling father priest. In any case what did he, Mark, have to fear? He wasn't sleeping with her, which in itself was perverse, an almost incestuous thought that had never entered his mind. Well, only vaguely, if he should be honest with himself.

They returned to the church, to the reception in the basement where he found himself the new guest of honor now that his father had been removed from their midst. They queued up like a band of groupies to introduce themselves.

First came Mr. Kenneth Holyfield. He was the publisher of the local community newspaper, *The Renaissance*. He was a corpulent man in his advanced years and walked with the help of a folded umbrella, which appeared to double in its utility as his walking cane in all kinds of weather. He whispered, "Son, you can have a job at *The Renaissance* anytime you want. Come see me when you're ready and show me what you got and I'll arrange for your working papers so you can stay in America. Anything for my friend, Dan."

He had written some impressive essays for his school paper at Harrison's College and was made aware of his aptitude as a journalist. He thanked him for the offer.

A dapper man, slim, low haircut, thin mustache, likely about his father's age, approached and threw his arms around him. He said he was Barbadian, Carmichael Codrington from Dayrells Road, St. Michael, seven years in America. He revealed himself to be an educated man; he worked in a bank in the city. Dressed in all black from hat to shoe, he spoke the Queen's English, but in the company of his newly found countryman he was all relaxed and resorted to a spattering of Bajan here and there. Exultant over his new discovery, he nudged him to a quiet corner away from the muted buzz of the crowd to speak in private and in confidence.

"Dan wuz my good friend, my best friend in Amurca. I wanted to say a few words on his behalf but I wuz all choked up, if you know what I mean."

It occurred to Mark he was never mentioned in his father's letters.

"I used to work part-time with your dad at Giuseppe Motors on Flatbush in Brooklyn, keepin' de books, pickin' up some extra cash on weekends. He wuz a jolly good chap, absolutely charmin'. I orchestrated a small loan at de bank so he could get himself situated when he first came to dis country. I loved de bloke dearly. He had a stellar reputation as a used car salesman. Used to push seven or eight cars off de lot every day. Made a lot o' money f'r himself and de owner, a Eye-talian named Bruno Giuseppe. But, soon after, your father had a stroke of bad luck."

"What d'ye mean, bad luck?"

Carmichael took two gulps of his rum punch and paused for a pensive moment as if something unmentionable had become of his father's association with Mr. Giuseppe.

"Something terrible happened." He took another sip.

"Y'see, over de years Mr. Giuseppe had mastered the technique of rollin' back odometers. Giuseppe Motors came under investigation by de FBI."

"How'd they find out?"

"I would have to say it was a perceptive buyer who made de arithmetic calculation that there wuz somethin' wrong with de equation of age and mileage. They just didn't jibe."

"So?"

"So the FBI got a hold of Dan Maynard who happened to be the salesman in question. They made a deal with Dan. They gave him a choice. He could either rat out his boss or be put on a plane back to Barbados. They gave him ten days to decide."

As Carmichael painted a picture of his good friend sitting in a windowless and sparsely furnished FBI interrogation room, being pumped day and night for company secrets, being threatened with deportation and weighing his options, Carmichael's face contorted with pain.

"Well, why did they pick on my father and not the owner, Giuseppe?"

"Dan was the fall guy."

"So what happened next? Did he talk?"

"No, but afterwards everyone thought he was the snitch."

"Well, guess who turned up next day with a high profile lawyer who happened to be the consigliore of the Altovese family. Maria had her contacts too in the Eye-talian community."

"You mean the Mafia?"

He didn't answer.

"The lawyer sprung him loose. The FBI had no grounds to detain your father. Problem is your dad had a falling out with Bruno. You didn't hear it from me but, soon after, your father received two thousand dollars from Mr. Carlo Altovese. It was a gift for not singing to the FBI, which, sure as hell, would have sent Bruno Giuseppe to jail and God knows whoever else in the Altovese family, who were the real owners of Giuseppe Motors. And still Bruno came to hate your father's guts, and jealous of him too, getting involved with Altovese."

"So where is Bruno now?"

"Back in business rollin' back odometers."

It seemed his father had his fair share of fans but also a few foes here and there. Should he pay a visit to Giuseppe and confront the Italian boss who might have been sufficiently vengeful to want to see his father removed from the face of the earth? Or should he just let sleeping dogs lie? As time dragged on he could not rid his mind of Bruno, the car dealer, his grudges and possible link to the murder. The notion of paying him a visit released a wave of cold tingly fingers that ran up and down his spine. He stole away to the vestry next door in search of a telephone and dialed the Richmond Borough precinct. He had committed the number to memory.

"Sergeant James? It's Mark Maynard."

"Found another rock for me to overturn?" he quipped.

"You didn't tell me about Giuseppe and his Mafia connections and his motive to kill the man who almost put him in jail."

"A Mafioso didn't kill your father, Mark."

"How do you know that? The man had a motive."

"The New York Mafia don't wear those stupid hoods. Y'see, it's below their dignity. They kill their man and all the witnesses same time like the old man who said he saw everything. We know their *modus operandi*. They don't hide their faces, the Klan on the other hand is a bunch o' cowards. Giuseppe would've dropped a coin and ordered a hit but the Klan got to 'im first. Leave Bruno out of it."

He hung up the phone and rejoined the throng of sympathizers, newly found friends and bearers of condolences. No one seemed to have a clue, no one except the Bajan would break away from the crowd to whisper in his ear a name or a motive or even an educated guess. They stood around feasting, talking and laughing. No one seemed to care or speculate about the one who might've taken the life of his beloved father. They had come to celebrate his life, not to bewail his departure. The ephemeral shadow of death had already passed.

As promised, the Reverend pursued him, held his hand in his and ushered him to a far corner of the capacious reception hall, away from the lights and the din where a gorgeous woman of jet-black complexion was swallowed up in the shadows. She wore a sari and a tiny ring in the side of a nostril. Their eyes met and for a few seconds of pure rapture he was unable to see anyone else.

"Brother Maynard, meet Sister Nakeisha Okonjo."

Towering awkwardly above them, the Reverend placed her hand in Mark's as in a wedding ceremony, then turned and walked away leaving him in the company of the Nigerian. He was to learn that she worked at *The Renaissance* as proofreader-*cum*-secretary and was there accompanying her boss, Holyfield. She was the only one who didn't know his father. At any other time and on a more propitious occasion, their meeting might have seen the dawn of a serious romance but the last thing on his mind was to become romantically entangled when all his emotions were attuned to one single goal. They exchanged phone numbers and promised to meet again.

Maria, visibly nervous, came over and abruptly tore him away to meet someone standing next to the punch bowl, waiting anxiously to be introduced.

"Mark, I'd like you to meet Angela. She said she was with your father that night in the club."

He was taken aback but, unlike Maria, was careful to conceal his surprise. His calculating mind had envisioned a woman with dreads, a black woman more likely. He had cloaked the mysterious woman in a cloud of suspicion after the bartender had been reluctant to say she was in the café at the time of the crime.

Angela was brunette, sultry, moderately attractive in his opinion, with a nervous habit of going through the motion of tucking her hair behind her ears when no hair was there to be tucked. Her choice of dress for the occasion was out of place: glaringly white cotton blouse, blue skirt, purse and shoes the color of oxblood. She extended a gloved hand.

"Um, I've been anxious to meet you. Your father was a dear friend."

"Yes, thanks. So you were with 'im when he died?"

"No."

"But Maria said you were with 'im," he countered, hoping not to sound accusatory for no reason.

"You asked if I was with 'im when he died. I *wasn't*," she answered.

"But you were with 'im that night."

"Yes, but I was retrieving my coat and my scarf from the closet in the back o' the club when I heard the shots and ran outside to see 'im face down on the pavement. He was already dead. It was awful!"

It was a technicality he could not debate, for he was forensically inept to make a judgment on the clinical detail of when a man actually dies. But one thing was crystal clear: the crime took place in the middle of a hot and humid summer when one would've been more inclined to shed the last piece of clothing before deciding to don a coat and scarf.

"Did you go to the Hard Nuts often with my father?"

"First time," she answered. Then her brow furrowed a trifle at his questioning on one persistent theme as if he implied she had been involved with his father's death. "He was just a dear friend," she said and, bidding goodbye to him and Maria, she turned and quickly walked away.

He wanted to hear more from the lady and followed her through the crowd, up the stairs, through the nave to the main exit, where from the top of the steps he spied a tuxedoed chauffeur standing alongside a black limo parked at the curb, holding the door open and ushering her into the back seat. He called to her but he was a trifle too late. As they drove away he could swear he saw her face through the rear window smiling and waving. She was the last person to see his father alive and he thought she knew much more than she was prepared to say in Maria's presence. She was his last hope to find the man who killed his father.

He turned to the wooden stand at the entrance to the church where an opened book lay inviting attendees to log their names and addresses for the benefit of family and church. She had signed her name, Angela Santana, her abode, New York, no street address.

He returned to the reception hall where the imposing Reverend Sheldon towered over the crowd gesticulating with his huge hands stabbing the air. The reception was drawing to a close. Everyone was riveted in place as he thundered a call to arms. The chattering ceased.

"My brothers and sisters, tomorrow morning at nine o'clock we assemble right here at the Church of Divine Intervention. Our church bus will take us over the George Washington to the Verazzano to Richmond Borough to the street across from the Hard Nuts Café where our dear brother was slain. We will march up and down the street, stopping traffic, blocking doors, disrupting business and bringing this Godforsaken borough to its knees until we get some answers. We will take our hymn books and sing as we walk. *We shall overcome* will be our rallying cry. The police and the politicians don't give a damn — Lord, forgive my choice of words — about the Dan Maynard case. Let's get together and light a fire under their feet. Who is with me? Let's see a show of hands!"

No one raised a hand.

4 – A Call in the Night

May 1961. Three years later, Mark Maynard was still in America living in his father's brownstone in Harlem. Every letter from home would begin with the same hopeful question, *Anything new?* Though his father's killer had not yet been found, nor had a motive been determined or declared to the public, he always felt that lurking behind his death was the deep-rooted fear of miscegenation, a phobia that was real in America long before his father's time, the fear that commingling between two persons of the opposite gender, one black, one white, would inevitably lead to interbreeding and eventually to the end of civilization as they knew it.

He answered each letter with the same cautionary note, that after all this time there was little hope. Barring a last minute confession by some old died-in-the-wool racist approaching the gates of Hell on his dying bed, there was little chance the truth would be known. No dedicated detective or persistent prosecutor or overly concerned citizen haunted by the sheer savagery of the killing was being driven today to unearth the evidence that might lead to the guilty. He advised his brother to get on with his life, his sister to do the best she could, his mother to cherish the few moments she and his father shared. But deep in his subconscious lived a kernel of hope that the killer would one day be found, as he had promised himself and his mother he would not return home until that day. He wrote home every two weeks, enclosed whatever money he could afford. Lately, Ermajean had been the one responding; his mother's arthritic fingers could no longer hold a pen.

It hadn't taken him long to plant his feet firmly on this side of the Atlantic and, true to his word, he never returned home, not even on holiday. His Barbadian friend, Carmichael, who went home two or three times a year, called him a hyphenated American and chided him with an old Bajan saying, "Boy, don't bite de hand dat feed yuh".

Even *he* was amazed at how fast he was becoming so culturally American, like a man who wanted at first to swim close to the shoreline and then finds himself sucked into a vast ocean by some irresistible wave. His accent had unconsciously become American. The Queen's English no longer rolled off his tongue as it once did. He substituted "zee" for "zed", "zero" for "naught", "lawr" for "law" and other myriad Americanisms. He learned how to smile with people he didn't know, or didn't care for, by crinkling his eyes and puffing his cheeks. He never understood the astonishment, sometimes terror, in the faces of strangers when he said "Hello, how you?" in his Bajan intonation. When he returned the smallest of favors with a generous "thank you" they seemed in awe. Yet he found himself accepting America with a greater understanding of her idiosyncrasies and afflictions; he also warmed to her worldliness.

Indeed, Harlem had become his home away from home, the heart and soul of black America, the oasis for those beleaguered souls who arrived *en masse* in 1905 during the Great Migration. He learned that they had transformed the formerly Dutch outpost into the Negro capital of the Nation and was inspired by this beacon of the African American diaspora, the inspiration for generations of renowned musicians; Duke Ellington, Ella Fitzgerald, Fats Waller, Miles Davis; charismatic leaders like Father Divine and George Wilson Becton; some of the greatest writers, Wallace Thurman, Langston Hughes and Zora Neale Hurston; the integrationist W. E. B. Du Bois; all those great minds that had been forged in the crucible of the South before heading North. Though he had found Harlem to be riddled with crime and the streets unsafe, he kept telling himself that running away from Harlem would be running away from himself before the mission that had brought him to this land was complete.

He had made good use of these short years, pursuing a degree in Creative Writing at Columbia U. and had learned to navigate the traps and landmines in that treacherous terrain that every man of color traversed on the way to success.

Maria, still living in the house, also had her occasional bouts of success as a fledgling actress, successfully auditioning for a role in a soap opera, *The Witches of Salem*. "You really ought to watch it someday," she told him. "I'm a regular witch".

Between classes, he went to work part-time at the weekly *Renaissance,* a name inspired by the Harlem Renaissance of the forties. He and Ken Holyfield, the publisher, had become friends. The newspaper included on its masthead the name Mark Maynard, Columnist, but he had also put pen to paper in his spare time to creating a compendium of fictional stories with critical political undertones.

Just for the fun of it, he had penned two books that had met with moderate success. Though he had not become, by any measure, famous as an author, neither was he unknown. A year back, he had been nominated for a National Book Award for a salacious story about politicians. *Le Jardin d'Eden* was a satire about a brothel in the District of Columbia situated close to the White House. The work might have succeeded had he heeded the suggestion that he cut back a tad on the eroticism, but he had insisted to the end that the integrity of the story would be at risk, which spoke to the principled stubbornness of his nature.

Then a few months after, his *Bowery Boys*, a novel depicting homelessness in the wealthiest city in America, was favorably reviewed in the *Times* and, among the ultra-liberal literati of the NYT, climbed instantly to the top of their list before it was dethroned by an eminently more established author.

At Columbia U he was never a rabble-rouser, simply a writer on the side who put on paper whatever injustice he perceived in the world around him. In the beginning he was just an outsider from the Caribbean looking in, somewhat abstracted but with a singular goal in mind, to find his father's killer. Then out of the blue he found religion, not the religion of the Church but the religion of "causes". First he protested against Jim Crow in the South, then the Vietcong in the East, then the CIA *vis-à-vis* Lumumba in the Congo, then against apartheid in South Africa … so many causes, so little time. But he had drawn a line at destroying campus property or joining rebellious students locking themselves into faculty quarters until demands were met, never extreme in his protestations, whatever the causes. Now at twenty-three, the old civil rights heroics were reawakened like the war stories aroused in the minds of veterans.

The course of his life was about to change dramatically when, in the middle of the night in late summer, he received a telephone call. Fearing some dire news from home, he rolled over and grabbed the receiver on the second ring.

"Hello."

"Are you Mr. Maynard?" It was the wispy voice of a young girl.

"Yes, I am Mark Maynard. Who's this?"

"Well, I know who killed your father."

"Who's this?" he asked again.

"My name is Rosyln Webb and this is not a prank call."

"Well … who … what … where did you hear this?" he stuttered.

"Trust me, I know who killed him." Her voice mellowed into a plea.

"Well, who *was* it?"

"I can't say on the phone."

"Well, send me a letter, tell the police, whatever." Incredulity and irritation crept into the tone of his voice.

"Mr. Maynard, I need to give you the evidence in person, okay?"

"Well, where're you?"

"I'm in Montgomery in Jackson County.

"You mean in Alabama?"

Now, why would anyone be phoning him from Alabama at two in the morning, disrupting his slumber, creating concern for his family and then proceeding to taunt him with a promise that had eluded him for years? Nevertheless curiosity and desperation combined to press the receiver to his ear. He was compelled to listen.

"I'm down here with the Freedom Riders. I myself am overnighting in downtown Montgomery at the YWCA. It's the only one in town. Meet me tomorrow in the lobby around six before sundown.

"One more thing, Mr. Maynard. I think you're being watched." She hung up before he could respond.

He rolled over and tried to sleep but sleep deserted him from that moment on. But as morning broke and he felt the warmth of sun on his face, sunlight through the open window flooded the room and pulled him back from the dark of the unknown and the unproven. The mysterious phone call drifted away into the ether like a dream.

He was about to peel off his pajamas to change when he looked up and saw Maria in her night robe standing in the doorway, one hand on her hip, the other holding a coffee mug.

"I heard the phone ring late last night. Anything wrong?"

He told her all about the mystery caller and her claim to hold the key to his father's murder, in addition about the proposal that they meet in Alabama.

"I'll buy you a ticket," she said coolly. Then she said, "When you return I'll be gone for a while. Going to see my Mom and Dad in Boston, they're getting down in age and he's not doing well. Your father met my folks once. We had dinner together one Thanksgiving. Was an awkward occasion."

There was a pregnant moment of silence between them when she came closer and sat on the edge of the bed.

"Mark, I have a confession to make. Then I'll tell you about my life's dream that was shattered in one night of envy and spite. I'll be right back."

She disappeared and he heard her footsteps retreating to the kitchen. And while she was gone he said a silent prayer. *Please God, don't let her confession in any way be connected to my father's death,* for if he should be honest with himself he was growing quite fond of her in the short time he had known her, though he insisted to his conscience it was a brotherly affection, nothing more.

She returned. She had dispensed with the coffee and in her hand instead was a glass of red wine. This time she stood at some distance in the doorway.

"First the confession. Remember I told you I met your dad in Barbados, in the lounge at Sam Lord's Castle with two other girls? Well that was the truth. What I didn't tell you was that one of the girls, who is no longer a friend, showed up at your father's wake. We both pretended to be strangers but we recognized each other right away. She said she was with him the night he was killed. Her name is Angela Santana."

"Yes, I remember. She said she was retrieving her coat from the coatroom when he was shot."

"That was a lie," she said dryly. "I believe that jealous, back-biting bitch was involved."

"Can you prove it?"

"No. But don't deny me my intuition. 'Hell hath no fury like a woman scorned.' You'll see what I mean."

She reached into her pocket and in her hand was a sparkling pear-shaped diamond set in a band of white gold. "Was supposed to be a June wedding, small ceremony, no fuss, a few friends. Carmichael was gonna be your dad's best man. Guess who was to be my maid of honor."

"Angela Santana?"

"You guessed it."

As far as he knew, all his life his father regarded legal marriage an impediment to his independence. Had he changed or was she under some blissful delusion?

She finished the wine in one gulp, turned and walked back to the kitchen, presumably to refill her glass, though she did not return and never again did she mention her traitorous friend nor her life's dream that never came to pass. In the larger scheme of things what did it matter to him? Her life would go on and, as young and pretty as she was, she would dream again and a diamond ring would be dazzling on her finger as it was meant to be.

He just wanted to know who killed his father. Nothing else mattered.

5 – A Different World

He remembers alighting next day from an interstate Greyhound bus at the Montgomery central station and finding himself in an unfamiliar world. The marquee high above the station said with a smiley face, "Welcome to Montgomery". But now, looking around him, he was just another colored man with his own colored restroom, colored water fountain, colored waiting room, colored this, colored that. And on the other side were the "white only" signs. On his side all the facilities were drab and sparing while on the other side they were modern and spacious. He had been born and raised in a colonial society where color lines had been assumed. They had been drawn by the colonizers, but more subtly, never spelled out, never written on walls, never painted on doorways, never enshrined in the laws of his country. The boundaries were nevertheless demarcated in people's minds and on the road to opportunities. If a person tried to cross the lines he would feel the rebuke from the other side but never was he hauled off to jail or, worse, beaten to death. But here all around him, the demarcations of black and white were right smack in his face, dead serious, no circumventing allowed, and for the first time he felt that everyone's eyes were upon him, watching his every move, seeing him for who he was, a nigger in the Deep South.

He approached the information desk where an official wearing a green visor was handing out bus schedules and street maps and answering travelers' questions.

He asked, "Sir, could you tell me where I could find the nearest hotel?"

The man, startled, looked up from his pile of papers and, peering over his spectacles with contemptuous eyes, he drawled, "Nigga, you'd better get back on that bus and keep moving. Ain't no hotel from Mon'gomery to Mobile goin' put you up in one of their beds."

He had never been called a nigger before and his first impulse was to reach through the information window and grab the transit official by the scruff of his neck, then stuff his papers down his scrawny throat. But reason prevailed; he was in a strange place; he was in another America.

He ran back to the curb and enquired from an old black porter carting luggage to the platform, where could he find a place to stay the night.

"You don' have much of a choice, son. Is only the Cobbler's Inn, ol' Bates place in Lincolnville, not too far, few yards south o' the railroad tracks down by the AME church."

He remembers following the tracks, lugging his rucksack a half a mile away to the Cobbler's Inn, which was more a hovel than a motel, and being welcomed by a leathery-faced man of average height, who looked to have spent his whole life in the sun. He was old and what hair remained on the sides of his head was gray but his sprightly movements, as he darted from his desk to the door, belied his age. He introduced himself as Mr. Bates, owner and manager of the establishment.

"Welcome to the Cobbler's Inn, young fella. Fifteen bucks a night. You one o' them Freedom Riders?"

"No."

"Well, eighteen f'r you."

He dropped a twenty on the counter for one night, two dollars for the room key.

The motel was situated between a liquor store and a ramshackle barber shop, just inside the city limits in the lowlands in a district they called Lincolnville, named after the Emancipator. On the other side of the road was a shoe repair shop from which he assumed the motel had derived its name. Apart from these places of business, both sides were lined with decrepit shacks sitting on cinder blocks, paint peeling away from their clapboard sidings like dead skin; old dilapidated houses frozen in time and sagging like old men under the weight of history. Old people were sitting out on their rotted porches whiling away their grey anonymous lives, poverty written on the faces of their half-naked, pot-bellied children already resigned to their place in the world, running up and down the narrow unpaved streets. Even the lush poplars, shiny green magnolias and oaks dripping with Spanish moss, in their effort to redeem the landscape with its turbulent history, spoke hopelessly of hangings and torture. Lincolnville was a desolate place.

It was true he was no stranger to poverty, for he had lived it in his own homeland but had never seen it so bleak, so naked and beyond recall. Back home, living within the constraints of a colonized society, he had always seen a certain glimmer at the end of a long tunnel and the shimmer of hope on faces looking forward with certainty to a new day. But not in this place; optimism, like the last migratory birds of autumn, had taken wing and seemingly flown away, for there was no promise left in Lincolnville.

He learned from the motel manager that Lincolnville was populated by descendants of slaves now serving the descendants of former slave owners. In the morning the black folk crossed over the tracks to work in the heart of Montgomery and withdrew before nightfall to their safety in numbers in their own neck of the woods. He remembers that the motel that day was filled to capacity with the people who called themselves "Freedom Riders" and who had descended on the segregated South in hopes of confronting Jim Crow and winning over a few Confederate hearts.

But he was there on other business, to meet with the mystery person who had managed to convince him she had irrefutable knowledge of his father's killer. He remembers finding his way to the YWCA across town long before sundown. She had told him to come early, before dark. As he entered the nondescript lobby of the nondescript residential building which historically housed young white Christian women of moderate means, all eyes were upon him. He made himself comfortable in one of the soft-cushioned cheap-looking sofas that reflected the antiquity of the institution and immediately felt hostility in the air as palpably as if he had entered a lair of lionesses. The middle-aged wide-eyed receptionist approached him with terror in her eyes. She called out, "Can I help you, boy? You are not allowed …"

"He's with me!" someone interrupted. The peremptory words came from a tall, sinewy woman, likely in her twenties, her hair swept back in a chignon, her chin in the air, descending the spiral staircase and walking directly towards him. She wore faded jeans and riding boots, a black cape hanging from her shoulders and trailing behind her. No wonder the clerk retreated like a sheepdog to her place behind the counter. He was hard-pressed to reconcile the voice of this woman to the wispy voice he had heard on the phone in New York.

Sitting beside him, she whispered in a less imperious tone, "This is what goes on all over the South, separating black and white is what they do best. Hello, Mr. Maynard. First, let me get something out of the way. My name is not Roslyn Webb, it's Paula Schroeder."

"And you can call me Mark."

"I had a good reason to lie. Y'see, my father is Senator Schroeder from Arkansas, well-known all around the South. Dad's been running f'r Governor ever since I was fourteen. He's running again this year, poor fella. But here's the problem, he's a Klansman, and if the word gets out, his chance of defeating Governor Faubaus is worse than a snowball in hell. This is where he and I part ways. Ever heard of the KKK?"

He nodded. He had gotten an inkling from Brother Sheldon.

"Well they already launched a chapter right up there where you live in New York. People think the Ku Klux Klan is only in the South but I got news f'r y'all."

She looked up, her hazel eyes panning the room for some malicious eavesdropper, then staring back at the women in the lobby, everyone mortified at the sight of the unlikely couple sitting in close proximity, talking, whispering like two lovers in the sanctity of the Y. The presence of a male at the Y was enough to boggle their minds and that of a black man bordered on the insane but then to see him with one of their women was unfathomable, enough to pop their eyeballs right out of their sockets. Returning their stares she commanded them to avert their eyes and in that moment she reached into her handbag and fished out a wad of papers folded many times over. With the dexterity of a pickpocket, she thrust the lot into the pocket of his jacket in one quick smooth motion. She was a fast talker like an auctioneer, poking the air with a finger, leaning forward and looking him straight in the eyes.

"You are now in possession of some dangerous stuff that some men will kill for. They were stolen from my father's files. Not by me, but that's neither here nor there. Guard them with your life. If you lose them or certain people get a hold of them, people will die. Including me. Including the person who passed them on to me. We're talking about secret names of the knights of the Klan that at this moment are recruiting more knights up north. One of them killed your father."

"Who?" His eyes widened, his heart pounding. He had already eased to the edge of the sofa.

She leaned in closer. "His name is Hamilton, a friend of my father. Came to our house years ago. Had dinner with my family, he and three other members. You'll understand why I didn't think it was safe to put this stuff in the mail or mention any of this on the phone."

"How do you know it was he? And why would he want to kill my father?"

"Family gossip. Whispers behind closed doors. I heard it with my own two ears. They were goin' to put 'im down. Your father was in the wrong place." She stopped short of saying he was with the wrong person.

"So why are you telling me this … giving me all this inside information?"

"To explain that, I would have to tell you my life story. But we don't have time. Where are you staying? You got to get back before dark."

Then she launched into the story of her life anyway.

6 – Little Rock, AR

She told him she was born in Little Rock in the state of Arkansas, the bedrock of separate institutions, black and white. The second time she had come within arm's length of a non-white person who was not a servant in the Schroeder household — a gardener, a chauffeur, a fieldworker, or Tess, the house servant who wore a hundred different hats — was when she joined the Freedom Riders. The first time was in September of 1957 in her sophomoric year at Little Rock Central High when a commotion erupted across the classrooms, in the lunchroom and up and down the hallways. On one hand there were cries of jubilation throughout the school but disappointment silenced some of the more aspiring students because Governor Orval Faubaus, champion of the segregationists, was going to shutter all the high schools in Arkansas and liberate the students for the rest of the year. Few knew or even cared to know what on earth had entered the Governor's mind.

"I remember that historic day," she told him. "I was standing between Dorothy Wellman and Lucy Paine."

She and her friends were in the locker-room corridor, across from the wall of lockers, when the nine black students strode down the aisle, their book bags clasped to their bosoms like roman shields. Their faces were blank as the walls, looking straight ahead, proceeding to their classes, as they were instructed, as were their right. At the precise moment when two or three were passing before them, Dorothy hawked up a prodigious gob of saliva, reared back her head, jerked forward and shot it like a projectile in the direction of one of the colored girls. She missed and the glutinous spit splattered on a locker and slid down the door.

Dorothy Wellman laughed. Then the two girls ran down the hallway like laughing hyenas in pursuit of their quarry who were the black students, leaving Paula behind wondering how her sweet-natured friends in the blink of an eye had become little beasts of prey.

"Even today I am haunted by my silence," she said to Mark, "'cause afterwards when my friends joined in the jeering and catcalling up and down the halls and in the lunch room, I never voiced a word of disapproval. Neither did I utter a word of compassion for those girls. Never!"

The matronly Mrs. Campbell, the mild-mannered Assistant Principal, was heard yelling at the top of her voice: "Get those nigras out of here!" It wasn't that she didn't know the word "nigger" but to say it correctly would be unbecoming and undignified, and since "Negro" had the ring of legitimacy she chose a more pejorative pronunciation to proclaim her displeasure that the complexion of Little Rock Central High was about to be forever changed.

"All the time a tiny voice was saying in my head, there is something wrong with this picture. I tell you, for a long time the guilt by association kept gnawing at my insides like an ulcer day and night."

It appears that up to that moment she had been blind to − or had chosen not to see − the barbarity of her own people, for she was born into that legacy of the slave master. Her grandfather, the late Eustace Schroeder, Dixiecrat and owner of three hundred and fifty slaves in his heyday had sold his last slave three years after the Emancipation Proclamation, according to city records.

So when did she awaken from that dark and oblivious depth of denial, to open her eyes and see a ray of truth and had decided on her own to lift herself up from that dark place? She, too, rolls back the years to tell the story of her own moment of transformation.

"I came home from school that day, on the bus reserved for children of my own kind, turned on the little black and white TV in my bedroom, and there it was, my lil ol' Central High was on national news for the first time. And the National Guard and the Federal troops were surrounding the black students as they climbed the steps to the door that had been shut. Then the camera turned and panned the white mob that had been awaiting the arrival of the students and their escorts — children, mothers, grandmothers, shouting, screaming, cursing the negro students, cursing the soldiers, cursing President Eisenhower.

"Then I looked closer and I could not believe my eyes. In a corner of the screen I saw someone who looked exactly like my mother in her favorite blue dress that she wore to church every other Sunday morning. Yes, it *was* my mother. I had never seen her that way before; she was always a gentle soul, never raised her voice at home, at her children, at her husband, not even at Tess, our maid. But *there* she was, joining with some of our neighbors who were also mothers, looking as fierce as a pack o' she wolves, taunting, hollering, raising their fists at the students, at the guards. And as they proceeded past them and up the steps to the school door, I saw the hate and fright in the eyes of the women, my mother among them, and I even saw her mouth the word "niggers" like all the other women did right there on TV for all the world to see. Yes, my own mother!

"But, come to think of it, it was not the N-word itself but that it burst forth from deep down in my mother's gut like bilious vomit. I myself used the word like any other, over and over ever since I learned to talk. It was just another word in my limited vocabulary. Family, friends, our minister, our Governor, hell, even our renowned writers, Steinbeck and Faulkner flung it about in their famous *Grapes of Wrath* and *The Sound and the Fury* and not a soul in the world ever said a blessed thing about it. But the hate, the visceral hate, ugly, mean, my mother's face and all the other faces, dark, twisted with murderous rage. I had never seen this side of my mother before. After the day that Little Rock was integrated, she was a changed woman; she started to hit the bottle and hasn't stopped. It was as if everything she believed in was shattered; that she was betrayed by God and mocked by the Devil; that the supremacy of the white race would be proven irremediably false.

"Whose side was I on? I had to choose a side. Should I deny my conscience? Should I side with my family, my friends, the people I knew all my life whether I thought them in the wrong or in the right? I asked myself 'was I no better than Dorothy Wellman and Lucy Paine and Mrs. Campbell and all the rest? Was I no better than my mother?' "

It was the best she could do to explain her rebirth as a bleeding-heart liberal and now a Freedom Rider born and raised in her own Deep South.

She recalled that later that evening in 1957 there were guests at the dinner table. "Dad had invited four of his friends to break bread with the family. It was a social get-together that evolved into a business meeting of sorts. After he introduced my mom, me and my brother Brad, and said the customary prayer — the prayer was always 'Father in Heaven, thanks for our daily bread and bless the Confederacy' — he introduced the men. The Murphy brothers needed no introduction. Peter was the well-known fire chief in Marietta and his brother, Clarke, worked for my dad on the wheat farm. The other two, a man named Hamilton whom they called "Hammie", blond-haired, likely in his mid-sixties, and another named Albert, much younger, whom they called "Al", were clearly not Southerners. Their Yankee accents gave them away.

'Let us welcome our former Yankee foes to our lovely state of Arkansas.' That was my father attempting to be funny. 'These gentlemen are here to help us take back our country. Just goes to show New Yorkers ain't all that bad.' They all laughed."

She remembers one of the New Yorkers rejoining with a quip of his own. "Well, it was all you crackers down here that chased the darkies up north, ain't it?" More boisterous laughter rippled around the dining room.

The other northerner, in deference to her father's political aspirations, stood with a dollop of froth from his beer clinging to his mustache. "Let us drink to the next Guv'na, the Honorable Gilmore Schroeder."

"And let us lend our moral support to our courageous Guv'na Faubus," said Mr. Schroeder. "And may our nigger-loving Prez'dent Eisenhower go to hell."

Tess, their servant, had just come in from the kitchen and rolled her big brown eyes at the mention of the segregationist Governor Faubus. She dared not say a word. She was invisible as a ghost until her hand, gnarled by years of hard labor, reached forward to serve a course, retrieve a dish or refill an empty glass, after which she would slink back to her place in the kitchen while the men gorged on her delicious cooking, chomping on her tasty southern-styled fried chicken, all the while fulminating against integration with her people.

Tess was close to Paula and Paula loved her like a mother for all the years she had known her as her nanny, the maid, chief cook and bottle washer. Paula never knew her last name; the last names of colored folk were not relevant to their work; she was told that last names engendered a level of importance which should never be conveyed under any circumstances. Yet all the years she had been their house servant she was free to come and go and, except for a seat at her master's table, she had the run of the house.

She had known that Tess's husband, back in the fifties, on his way to work, had been ambushed by two Klansmen intoxicated with moonshine and white power, and had been hogtied to the hitch of their pickup truck and dragged for miles down a back road while his body disintegrated like thistledown in the wind. The men were caught and later set free for lack of a single witness willing to step forward and put his neck on the line. It was a mystery down in Pine Bluff where she lived that she had cooked for white folk all those many years and not poisoned a few. But jobs for blacks in Marietta came down to the choice of toiling in the field for peanuts with no barriers against the elements or toiling under a roof for better pay plus a free meal.

The house was a typical plantation-styled ranch with multiple porches, heavy columns and arched dormers all reminiscent of the antebellum years, the Confederate flag and Stars and Stripes waving side-by-side. The interior was adorned with pictures depicting the war between North and South but deep within those walls breathed the fumes of hatred and little did the people know that the Schroeders' home was an incubator for the evil Klan.

Before the men dug into their shredded pork, sweet potato pie and collard greens, her mother slyly joked in her charming high-pitched drawl: "Thank y'all for leaving yer robes and yer hoods in yer trucks. You wouldn't want to scare the young 'un, would ye!" There was another round of riotous laughter.

None of this made sense to Paula, the young 'un, who had not been heard from at the dinner table and yearned to join the grownup conversation with a piece of her own. She began innocently to tell the story of her day at school, of the colored students and the federal marshals and the taunting and the protests and the spitting and the ...

"That is not your concern, my dear," interrupted her father. "Eat your supper and go to bed!"

Her mother nodded. "Yes, darling."

Brad chuckled and also drew the wrath of his father.

"You too, Brad!"

The two tromped upstairs to their bedrooms, Brad muttering along the way, commiserating with his sister. "Is nothing you said, sis, they just want us out o' the way so they can plan on what to do about the Fed."

"You mean about the President sendin' in troops?"

"Uh-huh."

She went to bed that night convinced of her parents' complicity in the fight against desegregation, and she felt no less complicit than them on account of her own silence. But she was not about to go to sleep. From her upstairs bedroom, she crept to the door and pressed her ears to the jamb to hear them talk. In between the bursts of laughter and the clapping and the clinking of dishes and beer bottles, she pieced together snippets that said the New Yorkers were about to be initiated into the Klan. The initiation ceremony was to take place next day.

"Clark, you gonna take Hamilton and Al deep into the woods tomorrow since you already know the lay of the land," her father was saying. "You know where that clearing is, back o' the silos."

"You comin' with us, Mr. Schroeder?"

"Oh no! God forbid someone see me sneaking off with you fellas. Next day I'd be in the news, the Republicans would have a feast with that story." The remark brought forth great amusement.

"How 'bout your boy? He is old enough to see how it's done."

But his father by his silence objected. Then one of the men from the Northeast reined in the frivolity and redirected it to the more serious business at hand.

"Seriously, we have a great potential in New York ... we have people back home waitin' for us to deliver ... 'specially in the burbs ... people lookin' f'r some organization ... some decent representation ... politicians cannot be trusted ... colored folks movin' out from Brooklyn, South Bronx and even lower New Joicey with the help o' dishonest, slick, greedy real estate salesmen and saleswomen ... decent hard-workin' people seein' their property values go to hell ... runnin' scared ... don' know where to live next ... leavin' all their good houses, properties and stuff behind. Gentlemen, I tell you, it's not right."

Their voices fell silent at the sound of Tess's heavy footsteps tromping in from the kitchen with her desert tray laden with pecan pie, peach cobbler, bread pudding ...

"It was good ol' Tess who stole the documents, bless her heart!" she said. "She was cleaning my father's study and saw the files sitting out in the open. Poor Tess didn't know how to read but she damn well knew the letters of the alphabet. A folder on his desk was marked KKK and that was all she needed to know. She grabbed it and snuck it into my lingerie drawer. Before the files went missing she was clean out of Arkansas ... somewhere down in New Orleans, according to her folks in Pine Bluff. Tess finally got some revenge from the Klan for her husband that they dragged to his death on a deserted cart road away from anyone's eyes. Now it's up to you, Mr. Maynard, to get some revenge for your father that they killed in cold blood."

The papers now tucked away in the inside pocket of his jacket was like a secret cache of war plans: minutes of private Klan meetings, names of recruiters, target locations, propaganda, plans to spread their web of terror beyond the South to the North to New York and beyond.

As much as he wanted to hear about the knighting of the New Yorkers and how they had recited their oaths deep in the woods behind the wheat farm, and how they had knelt to be anointed with sacred waters under the Confederate flag, and about the laying of a sword on their shoulders, he had to get going, it was growing late. He remembered the advice he had been given by the motel manager; he should be back before sunset.

As a parting gesture of gratitude, he promised to see her again at the Rider's meeting next day at the AME church in Jackson County, and took leave of her with an embrace while the YWCA women in the lobby glowered at the "signs and wonders" that had taken place right before their eyes.

A veil of darkness had already descended on Montgomery. The evening sun had already disappeared, dragging its remaining rays of red like fingers of blood across the clouds that lingered over the town. The minute he set foot on the sidewalk outside the Y he sensed a foreboding. He quickened his pace, focusing his mind on retracing the short route that would take him safely across the tracks and into Lincolnville. He found himself tapping the inside pocket of his jacket reassuringly as if by some witchery the contents might have been snatched away.

Then as he was about to leave the city lights behind, where the shops dwindled in number to one or two sleepy bars on the edge of town, he heard a voice.

"Hey you!"

He kept walking, his eyes straight ahead.

"I am talkin' to you, nigga!"

He had been called that name only once before, back in the bus depot when he had approached an official for information. He had heard it flung at his American brothers but never at him; after all, he was a West Indian, a man from the Caribbean, feeling in his heart equal to any man, whatever his color, whatever his race. The sound of it was like a sword plunged deep into his being, intended to destroy every shred of his humanity, to gut all inkling of pride, to reduce him to nothingness.

"Hold it right there, nigga!"

He heard that word again and his whole body stiffened, ready to fight, ready to defend himself, his name, his race, his honor. But in the pocket of his jacket were papers he could not afford to lose in a struggle, so he kept walking. Then in his peripheral vision two men appeared over his right shoulder, their heads bald and shiny in the pale-yellow glow of a street lamp. He quickened his stride to a trot, then to a gallop, then he felt a sharp blow to his right temple that sent him sprawling, knocking him to his knees; then the sound of shattering glass from a bottle that ricocheted from his head to the pavement. He sprang to his feet, started off at full pace. The world was spinning as he felt the blood trickling down his cheek to his neck, and heard their feet pounding the surface, their voices spouting hate, cursing like the yelping of scent hounds. He gave it all he could until his pursuers surrendered the chase and their curses waned in the distance. Only then did he slow to a brisk walk, clutching the pocket of his jacket, then feeling for the wound on his head as blood trickled through his fingers. Reaching the crest of the hill that overlooked Lincolnville, his breathing finally returned to its normal rhythm as the lights of the Cobbler's Inn loomed no more than a quarter mile ahead.

The motel manager was livid. He was standing in the doorway with his hands on his hips, peering into the dark, as he saw one of his overnighters approaching. He braced to chastise him as if he were one of his unruly children.

"Boy, you *must* be crazy! You knows no colored man be walkin' 'round these parts at night. Where you bin, boy?"

"In town … northside," said Mark.

He stared at the one he called "boy" for half a minute as if he were contemplating a moron. Then he saw the wound, a two-inch gash deep enough to now release a pulsating stream of blood, blood steaming hot from his running to save his life.

"Hold still! I see Mr. Charlie got you good," said the old man rushing back to his quarters, then reappearing with a bandage and cotton swabs soaked in iodine, which he pressed against the cut to stanch the flow. Mark winced and trembled with every dab of the cotton.

"Am I gonna need a doctor to get this thing stitched up?" The pain was tearing through his head like a knife.

"Ain't no colored doctors this side o' town, boy. Plenty white ones in northside but they ain't goin' touch you or me. You don't need no stitches. But you goin' have to live with a scar a mile long that you goin' take to the grave. Yes, you never goin' win no beauty contest now. But better than hangin' if you ask me."

At that precise moment he saw his father, Dan Maynard, and remembered when he was twelve or thirteen playing cricket in his backyard with a hard ball on a hard gravelly pitch when his brother bowled a short-of-a-length bouncer that reared up and caught him flush on his forehead. And when his father from his window saw when he fell, ran out and lifted him in his arms and ran four and a half miles all the way to the clinic of Dr. Goddard, who dropped the whiskey he was drinking and clapped a handful of ice to his forehead to reverse the swelling, then administered a generous sip of his Johnny Walker to ease the pain. The doctor was a white man.

"What you doin' in town anyway?" asked the motel manager.

"Went to see my friend at the Y," Mark explained, though he knew he didn't have to tell him his business but he figured his kindness deserved the courtesy of an explanation.

"A white girl?" asked the old man assuming the obvious. "Now I knows f'r sure you soft in the head, boy. You lookin' for a lynchin', boy?"

"I didn't know …"

The old man stamped his foot, snatched his hat off his head and flung it into a corner of the reception office, a two-by-four cubicle befitting this one-floor broken-down motel.

"Well you damn well need to know in this town you can't be lookin' at no white woman in duh face, boy … much less lookin' to get yerself some white jelly."

"She's not that kind of friend, Mr. Bates."

He snorted, "It don't matter, boy. You jest thinkin' you back in New Yawk. You in duh Deep South now … different laws."

"We still in America, aren't we?"

"Yes, you got that right. But is two Americas, see? And you and me in the other one. So if you lookin' f'r some booty tonight you can get it right here this side o' town. It ain't much different, different color, different hair, that's all. Take two steps 'round the corner to the Good Times Tavern. Ask f'r Madame Toulouse and buy yerself some comp'ny."

After he had wrapped the bandage three laps around the bloodied head he walked around behind his desk, reached up to the rack and handed Mark his room key. Then he grabbed his own key, locked the door and secured the place since everyone was in for the night.

"Did they see where you stayin' at?

"No, I lost them on the other side of the tracks."

"Well, you lucky 'cause dem crackers would sho' as hell burn this damn motel down to the ground." He lowered his voice to a whisper. "Who she be anyway, she from 'round these parts?"

"She is not a hussy, Mr. Bates, her father is a senator in Arkansas."

"You talkin' 'bout Senator Schroeder?"

The old man shook his head in either utter disbelief or fear for the boy's future.

Mark realized he should have known better. Or perhaps he knew better but didn't care, for his mind was locked in that phase of stoical indifference, crossing over to the other side for the answers he sought. He had been forewarned. For him in the sixties to be walking the streets of the Deep South after sundown was dangerous enough. To be thought he was wooing a white woman in the state of Alabama was more than foolhardy, it was downright suicidal. But the two of them had chosen to cross the racial line that defined separate worlds in the South to join hands. He was a young man from New York with Caribbean roots desperate to find his father's killer; she was a Southern gal from Arkansas, the daughter of a state senator with ties to the notorious Klan. She wanted to help. Was it in atonement for the sins of her father and his forefathers? he wondered.

"Let me tell you sump'in, boy," the old man continued, "didn't mean to be hard on you like that, but I have my reasons, y'see?" His voice had softened; he had seemingly ceased to reproach. "I had a son just like you … except better lookin'." He laughed for the first time revealing a quadrant of missing teeth. "Strappin' young man like you, his whole future ahead o' him, y'see?"

He reached into his wallet, extracted a tattered photograph and held it to the light. "That was my boy."

Mark was anxious to retire to bed to rest his aching head but felt humoring the old man with his storytelling was the right thing to do. "So, what happened?"

"Well, I'll tell you exactly what happened." He held onto the back of a chair as if he needed support to continue with a story that would weaken his knees. "My son, Luther, was in town one day and let his eyes rest on a white girl f'r two seconds too long. All she had to do was complain 'bout this young nigger buck raping her with his eyes. Same night my boy was hanging upside down from a branch of a live oak back o' the general store with his organ in his mouth. Yes sah!"

Mark found himself gasping, his hand to his mouth. The old man let go of the chair, took two steps forward and wagged his finger in Mark's face.

"D'ye hear me? That's why I'm sayin' you don't mess with their women, stay with yer own, otherwise you could end up just like my boy down in the AME graveyard."

He was done with his scolding, his disobedient "child" had been chastened, so his voice mellowed to a pleasant conciliatory tone.

"You from New Yawk?"

"Yeah, just passin' through."

"Well, you just pass on through 'cause ain't no reason f'r you to be stayin'. Bin thinkin' o' catchin' one o' them Greyhounds meself and headin' north."

"You mean to Harlem?"

"Don' matter where, son. Gonna ride that hound 'til the conductor say 'last stop'. Yes sir, I be headin' north, ain't fixin' to die in this hellhole."

"What about the motel?"

"Ain't no more Cobbler's Inn after this 'cause ain't no more Freedom Riders. They ain't never comin' back to Alabama. They say Gov'na Faubus too tough a nut to crack. So this is the end f'r all them nice people that lookin' f'r a miracle." He chuckled.

He wondered how the old man had come to own the motel in the first place. He must have read his mind and sought to explain.

"This here motel used to be a whorehouse. Twelve rooms, twelve beds, fifty bucks a night. Had a piece o' sharecropper land down in Mobile growin' spuds. After the missus left me, sold it at a loss and moved to Jackson County. Bought me the whorehouse and chased all the whores out on the street. Always had an eye f'r business. Yes sir! I looks into the future and sees all these black folks comin' down from up north and can't find no place to rest their heads 'cause Mr. Charlie don' want no niggas comin' aknockin' no matter how much money they have, and black folks up north do have some serious money to pay big bucks a night and never complain. So y'see, I put aside a lil cash ever' now and then so I can pay f'r that ticket on a Greyhound to wherever when all you black folks leave and gone. Know what I'm sayin'?"

"Whyn't you come take that Greyhound with me tomorrow," he asked the old man jokingly. "I could use the company. I'll even let you take the place of my daddy that they killed. But that's another story."

"Say, who killed your dad, boy?"

"A Klansman killed him."

The old man laughed, his shoulders heaving. "Now why you wanna joke like that? You know ain't no KKK up there where you live. The south is Klan country. But I'll tell you what, soon as them riders leave, I'm a goin' close up this joint and meet you in New Yawk. That a deal?"

"It's a deal," he answered.

He was in a good mood when he turned around, said goodnight and returned to his private quarters in the rear of the motel. Mark went to bed and the more he thought of the old man's story the less pain came from the incision on the side of his head. He wondered what his own fate would have been had he stumbled and fell or not outrun his skinhead attackers earlier that night. Would he now be hanging from one of those southern poplars or live oaks for having been in the company of a woman from the other side?

In the short stay at the motel he had felt a fondness growing for the motel manager. He was one of the despised but not one of the despairing. He was a businessman with an eye for the future, with a vision of fleeing the past. And with his greatest loss, the loss of his only son, he seemed to hold no rancor in his heart for his despisers, only lessons to be imparted to the naïve like Mark, who wandered into his neck of the woods not knowing the ways of the South.

By some miracle of faith, the pain subsided by morning and he could remove the unseemly wrapping leaving the Band-aid in place. After breakfast the church bus pulled up alongside the door of the motel and the roomers climbed in for the ride to the local African Methodist Episcopal Church where they would unite with a congregation of young Freedom Riders from every state north of the Mason-Dixie line. He had promised Paula at the Y he would see her again at the riders' meeting, so he decided to hitch a ride on the bus, partly on account of his promise and partly to satisfy his intellectual curiosity, but on no condition would he join the integrationists, for he was not of a mind to submit himself to abuse, to be spat on and beaten on the head and humiliated for trespassing on one of the segregated Woolworth lunch counters or crossing one of their ignominious color lines.

But not this woman, not this unlikely of Freedom Riders, a woman born in the Deep South and raised in a household of rank racists, affiliates of the Ku Klux Klan. She sat beside him in the back of the Negro church and told him how she awoke one morning, rode to DC, enlisted with the Core of Racial Equality, joined Mr. Farmer's caravan and never looked back. And how she had escaped, bruised but undaunted, from an earlier stop in Alabama, where the Freedom Riders were ambushed by a band of savage beasts, wild men who came out of nowhere, attacking the bus with rifle butts, hammers, clubs, bats, clawing at the windows and pounding on the sides. One of the hooligans set the bus on fire, smoke overcoming the riders, old and young, black and white, as they made their escape from the suffocating smoke, until they lay sprawled on the grass, burnt and battered and terrified, rescued from a town of rabid racists, a town named Anniston that for its infamy would likely go down in the annals of racist towns as a example of the most extreme exhibitions of irrational hate. And yet this white woman sitting beside him was ready to press on, join hands with his African American brothers and sisters in the struggle against Jim Crow while he, Mark Maynard, would not have the time or the will to join the rides.

"I can't right now. I'm looking for someone," he told her.

The AME church was about five or six miles from town but still in the valley and in the shadow of Lincolnville. Unlike the typical African American wooden churches in the south, it was built of solid brick with a thick impregnable teak door and stained glass windows barred with steel rods. At appointed times, it served as a place of refuge and renewal for Christians and non-Christians alike. So it was no wonder the Freedom Riders had chosen the AME church to retool and plot the next lap of their journey to Birmingham and to Mississippi, which, in the sixties, was known as the belly of the beast.

Like hardy hikers before a trek into the dangerous hinterlands of the Amazon jungle, the riders assembled to undergo further training and orientation. Pastor Williams, a mild-mannered and dignified African American with a soft velvety voice, was in charge. He bowed his head and led them in a long meandering prayer while the organ riffed in the background.

"Remember, my brothers and sisters, in our darkest hour there is a God above to be supplicated, to be asked for His protection in the wildest storms, for His deliverance from the wicked, from the iniquitous in this racist heartland of America in which we are about to enter as we continue our pilgrimage. We must show them there is no animosity in our hearts. We are all the same, black and white, the same humanity, children of the same God. We come in peace, freedom is our only mission. We will not meet violence with violence. We will rise above their hate and brace ourselves against their brutality. Our cause is just. Truth and justice will bind us and give us strength. Our purpose will not be swayed. Our minds will not be corrupted. We will speak to their collective conscience and appeal to their immanent sense of fairness. We will force them by our steadfast humility to see the evil of their ways and the goodness in our hearts. May God spread his wings over each and every one of us as we press forward tomorrow into the heart of the Deep South."

Then the mild-natured pastor raised his head and his face morphed into the face of an ogre out of the dark wilderness, baring his teeth, snarling, growling, glaring maniacally at the congregation. He stepped away from the lectern and strode down the aisle, hollering at the students, calling the blacks "niggers" and "coons" and the whites "nigger lovers", indiscriminately slapping their heads, punching their arms, pulling their hair, tugging them from their seats and tossing them bodily into the aisle while pretending to kick them in their heads, their faces, their chests and their groins. Mark was seemingly spared the humiliation on account of his injured head. Just when the riders thought the role playing was over, he returned to the altar, filled his mouth with supposedly holy water and started back down the aisle, his cheeks bulging and spewing water thinly like a geyser on the people, on their heads, in their faces, on their clothes as if he were some raving ranting racist. Two students failed to suspend their natural instincts, showing their indignation, flailing their arms in protest. They were instantly marked as failures and disqualified from the campaign in disgrace; the others who remained unperturbed were praised for their stoicism. Then the pastor returned to the altar and to his former congenial disposition, smiling and commending all those who had passed the test of passive resistance and nonviolent confrontation.

"Now, go forth, my brothers and sisters, and show the haters the power of love," he shouted to the crowd as they all applauded with celebratory high fives, smiles and glad-handing all around. They had graduated to the highest level of Ghandiism.

The training session turned into a rally with loud strident singing that continued until late in the evening when they broke for meals — hog feet, chitlins, ribs — donated by church members. It was dark when they boarded the church bus to return to the Cobbler's Inn anxious to rest and rejuvenate before the next leg of their trip into Birmingham. Their spirits were uplifted, there was much rejoicing and singing on the bus like campers on an outing in the country.

As the bus crested the hill and started the descent into the valley of Lincolnville, Mark perceived a difference in the lay of the land, the houses, the trees, an air of disquiet, of perturbation in the air. From a distance he saw black clouds hung low over the valley. As they got closer, people were milling around the spot where the Cobbler's Inn had been standing, except the motel had disappeared.

Before the bus could screech to a halt, he hopped off and elbowed his way through the crowd and came upon mounds of wet smoldering wood and twisted metal. The Cobbler's Inn had been burnt to the ground. Particles of burning ash were still floating in the night wind like clouds of fireflies. Wisps of black smoke were rising intermittently from the earth like tribal messages to the gods. The firemen had come and gone without leaving a verdict or an explanation for the fire. He looked all about frantically searching the crowd for the motel manager, going from man to man scrutinizing the faces of old men, pleading, "You seen Mr. Bates? Please, anybody seen him? Where is he?"

With tears of fear welling in his eyes, he turned to a wizened old man, standing around, leaning on his cane with both hands, staring at the destruction, occasionally shaking his head slowly from side to side. Without a word the man pointed his cane to the sidewalk a short distance away where a rumpled sheet lay over a mound that Mark intuited was the dead body of the motel manager. He imagined Mr. Bates had locked himself in as he always did at the end of the day and in the midst of the smoke and the flames was unable to find his door key to escape the inferno.

Remembering the old man's fears for the safety of the motel, Mark knew he had inadvertently led the skinheads the night before to the place where he was staying. Having crossed over to the white section of town, he had been spied emerging from the door of the hotel at night, and was easily thought to be consorting with one of their women. A mere cut on the head with a bottle was a penalty hardly befitting the crime. A more adequate punishment was the one meted out to the old man's son years ago. Someone had to pay and so the old man had paid with his life; and he, Mark, had gotten away with his. He walked over to the body on the sidewalk, knelt and peered under the sheet at the stiff charred body of the old man. He remembered his last words though he wasn't sure he meant it.

"Goin' close up this joint and meet you in New Yawk. Is that a deal?"

Suddenly he felt the unsettled contents of his stomach heaving to his throat. With his cheeks bulging, his hands pressed on his midriff, he raced to the alley next to the liquor store and vomited until his ribs hurt. For the first time in years, he wept openly.

Now looking around, he marveled at the stupefied faces of black men, staring as if in a trance at the destruction before them. The lack of agitation, of aggression, of hate, just a murmuring among them like the baying of wounded cattle. He wanted to go from man to man and singlehandedly urge them to get themselves together, round up a posse of their able-bodied and storm the town of racist skinheads, armed with any and all the weapons they could muster. He had a picture in mind of the gladiatorial Cherokee tribesmen of yore, unified, advancing and chanting in their Iroquoian tongue, their tomahawks in the air, their arrows flying, repelling the intruders, many dying as the intruders returned fire but also fleeing. Many of these men here would be killed but death would be no worse than the lives they were living in the hellhole of Lincolnville.

The man he had questioned had seen his tears and had sensed his distress. He walked over.

"You's a friend o' Vic Bates?"

"Yes."

"He was my friend too. Well, y'know ol' Bates didn't deserve to die like that. They say these two men on horseback in white robes and their faces covered like ghosts come over the hill and douse ol' Bates place with gasoline, and in no time at all the whole damn place up in flames. Po' Bates didn't have a chance."

"They always cause trouble in Lincolnville?" he asked the man.

"No. They usually let us be. Never cause us no trouble at all. 'Cause we keep to ourselves, y'see?"

The man turned his attention to the Freedom Riders. "You's one of them riders from up north?"

"No."

"Well, I don' mean no disrespect, mister, but since y'all come to Mon'gomery we seen all kindsa disturbance. Things usually quiet 'round here. Never seen no torchin' in Lincolnville. Never, first time. So tell me, how them Freedom Riders fixin' to change things 'round here in Alabama? They plannin' to fight City Hall?" He chuckled, his words sopping with sarcasm.

"No, they're all about change through nonviolence. They're not warriors," said Mark, defending the riders.

"Nonviolence? See all these people 'round here? They bin nonviolent all their lives. Wha' did they get f'r nonviolence? Look at ol' Bates lyin' on the ground over there stiff as a log. That summabitch didn't even own a water pistol. You understan' what I'm sayin'?" Unlike the rest of the docile crowd, he had grown increasingly angry.

He raised his cane and pointed it to Sambo's Liquor Store only slightly scorched by the fire next door and to Nu-Cut's Barber Shop on the other side, which was spared and surprisingly intact. "So why they had to pick on ol' Vic's place?" he asked, knitting his wrinkled brow. He stabbed the ground with his cane in frustration.

But it was only he, Mark, who knew the answer. It would live within him and add to his torment.

"Time to go!" hollered the bus driver. He took leave of the old man still standing, leaning on his cane and staring at the unexplained devastation at the hands of the Klan. He told the driver to drop him off at the Greyhound bus station; he was going home. By home he meant the place he had chosen to make his bed until the task he had set for himself was completed.

His new friend at the Y had invited him to come along on the freedom ride and join her in the fight against Jim Crow. "Sorry," he told her, "this is not *my* fight. Plus the doctrine of Gandhi and Martin Luther King is not in my bones. I wouldn't be any good anyway on the rides 'cause I'm full of anger and on a different mission, a mission to find the one who killed my father." He envisioned the same kind of man who had killed Mr. Bates.

Once on board, they all twisted in their seats for one last look at the desolation. In his own eyes, new tears settled. Their only possessions now were the clothes on their backs while on his shoulders lay the guilt of his own indiscretion. But he said to himself, he had done nothing wrong or immoral or evil. He had crossed a bogus line in the sand that forbade his befriending a white woman. And for that he felt no guilt. Still, the weight of the dead motel manager would weigh on his shoulders for years to come.

7 – The New Chapter

October 1976. Fifteen years had come and gone since his return from the Deep South. Two of his heroes had fought their respective battles, had fought the good fight, had stuck to their divergent ideologies, albeit for the same cause, the cause of freedom; and each had been slain in action. The voice of Malcolm X had been silenced eleven years ago and three years later Reverend Martin Luther King, Jr. was shot and killed, the former at the hands of his "brother", the latter by a white man, a racist. He had come to learn that evil in all its forms was the province of all men of all races and that racism was the most pernicious of all evils.

He remembers returning to New York the day after Mr. Bates was killed, and alighting from a Greyhound at the Port Authority terminal with the sensation of having been delivered in a time capsule, transported from a different era, from a different world, from another America. Dispirited and frustrated, his heart ached with the realization his search for the killer of his father had led to the death of another. And most tragically to one who had lost his only son.

That night in the privacy of his bedroom he pored over the stolen papers, which he had seen before but only fleetingly. The first to greet his eyes was a full-page photo of men clothed in white, their heads covered with cone-shaped masks, peering through holes like children at play. The picture was striated with horizontal and vertical lines where it had been folded many times over, reduced to pocket size. Without the masks, the men could easily have been seen as saintly priests posing for the Holy See. On the back, in elegant penmanship, their names had been listed in left to right order, first or last names only, he couldn't be sure. He came upon the name, Hamilton, a name that stood out from all the rest, the one she had fingered as his father's murderer, the one she said was initiated into the brotherhood on her father's farm. Mark found himself back where he started, for there was no mention of his whereabouts, just Hamilton, a common name, a generic name belonging to hundreds in this city of millions.

Half a dozen of Senator Schroeder's letterhead memos, crimped at the edges, caused his stomach to flutter, his eyes to gape wide as an owl's, for he was seeing the minutes of clandestine meetings scribbled on official stationery. One page in particular laid out his sinister master plan for others to follow of how best to launch a new chapter in the state of New York.

Scouring telephone directories and public records for Hamilton's identity would be nothing less than a fool's errand, so he decided the only course of action was to dedicate his column at *The Renaissance* to putting their secrets out in the public arena and thereby flushing them out of their hiding places along with this Hamilton person. He would share with Holyfield this trove of incriminating stuff and solicit his sage advice.

Holyfield's *Renaissance News* operated out of a storefront on Broadway and 119th Street, a busy street known for its speakeasies during Prohibition. He had learned it was once the home of a Polish newspaper whose publisher fell on hard times and abandoned the business, the equipment and all, leaving behind a couple of rotary

Miehle printing presses, an antiquated hot metal typesetting machine and a floor full of restorable printing paraphernalia that fell into the hands of Holyfield. Since then several foreclosure notices had been tacked to the door but somehow the establishment had survived.

The newspaper plant was next to a building which was formerly a thriving furniture store until Saul Rosenthal, the owner, according to rumor, opened his cash register one morning and received a bullet to the heart. The majority of white-owned businesses had fled Harlem and the few proprietors who remained hunkered down behind granite counters, peering through bulletproof Lucite partitions and transacting their business like rats through holes in the wall. Honest citizens looking to do business had first to be appraised, examined up and down through an outer glass-paneled door, before they could be buzzed into the store while a finger poised nervously over a hidden alarm. But who could blame these owners when they are bombarded by the networks and the newspapers with stories about the whole of Harlem going to hell?

He entered the cluttered editorial office and laid the documents on Holyfield's desk.

"We have to get the word out, Ken. They are right here in our backyard."

This old publisher had always known about the Ku Klux Klan. At first he was agog at the idea of using his weekly column, but seconds later, like Mark, he thought it unwise.

"Mark, I agree, this is some volatile shit you have here. We gotta get the word out but we gotta be wise. And here is the problem: only African Americans read African

American papers. Only blacks read *The Renaissance*. Take the *Jet Magazine* f'r instance. Only black people read the *Jet*. Who are all the folks who subscribe to *Ebony*? Not Mr. Charlie. Even the big-time publishers in Chicago know that. That's why they have to go national and corral all the black people they could find all over the diaspora. We gotta engage all of New York in the fight against these animals, not only us."

Holyfield, in his newspaper, demonstrated his mastery of the English language but reverted to the vernacular of the street in the company of the "brothers", often peppering the language with a profusion of profanities when some threat to his civil liberties provoked him to anger. He was a large man with a thunderous voice not known to beat around the edges of an argument.

"So, what are you saying then?" asked Mark.

"I'm saying, get this business about the KKK out in the public domain. Put this shit in a book and get some liberal honky publisher to market it so all of the reading public will know Jim Crow is alive and well right here in the northeast of America. That's what I'm saying!"'

That was easier said than done. All he had to do was ask Ralph Ellison. *His* book, *The Invisible Man* had been invisible for a long time before it caught the attention of the public and won the National Book Award. Did this newspaperman have any idea of the cost and the labyrinth of rules confronting the small-time writer before his book could make it through the gauntlet of a publishing house and out into the hands of the public? But he's right, it's a story that has to be told.

Holyfield was fast becoming agitated. He had a history of cardiac issues that landed him twice in the ER of Harlem Hospital in the past year. Notwithstanding his own reservations, it was best not to argue with this octogenarian publisher, so Mark indicated his assent with an intermittent nodding of his head. On second thought, there was some merit to Holyfield's proposition, for how else could light be shed on the scourge of the Klan and their plans to exploit the tenuous fabric of a multi-cultural New York!

"But Ken, what help would that be in finding the one who killed my father?"

"Mark, listen to me! Your father was killed by a Klansman, so let's put the names of all those bitches in the book. Sooner or later this Hamilton fella is sure to raise up his friggin' head."

"And then what? We can't prove it, Ken."

He remembered his mother's admonition: "Be careful, son. Don' take de law into yer own hands. If they don' find who kill yer father leave whoever it is in God's hands." But his mother's words were now straw cast to the wind. If it so happened that one day the suspect surfaced with ample evidence that he was the one, he could not be sure he would risk relying on the law to dispense justice. Neither would he leave him in the mercy of God's hands.

"That summabitch will be a marked man wherever he goes," said Holyfield. "He's bound to spend the rest of his life looking over his shoulders … if one of us don' get 'im in the end."

He had one more piece of sober advice to impart to his young columnist. "*The Renaissance* is not the place to tell our story. The Klan will burn this friggin' place down f'r damn sure." And these words stung because they brought to fore the indelible memory of the charred body of an old man and the smoldering rubble of a motel in Montgomery. After sixteen years he still had not forgiven himself. Neither would he forgive himself for bringing to Holyfield's long-standing newspaper the same fate that befell the Cobbler's Inn.

He said goodbye and took leave of the publisher sputtering and stewing in his execrations, a stream of invective pouring out of his mouth, cursing all the world's racists *in absentia*. But he also left him enthused, as an old warrior, with the idea of co-authoring a book that would in effect be waging war. He imagined him already delving into his history books, researching once again the provenance and evolution of a hateful group of World War I veterans, all the way from the cradle of the Klan in Nashville and, down through the ages. And now reaching into new territory in the suburbs of New York where the only way they could be dispersed — like roaches at the flick of a light switch — will be to expose them with his book to the light of day.

He will title the book *The New Chapter*, fittingly so, with the foreword written by Holyfield chronicling the era from the Emancipation Proclamation up to the present. While *he* will write about his hellish couple of days in the segregated South; about the fearless Freedom Riders risking life and limb for equality; about his narrow escape from the skinheads in Alabama and now scarred for the rest of his life for the transgression of being in the company of a white woman; about the firebombing of the Cobbler's Inn and the murder of Mr. Bates and his son, Luther, who was found hanging from a branch of a poplar back of the General Store in Lincolnville. He would drop the names of the dreaded brotherhood throughout the pages so they could not be redacted without sacrificing the integrity of the story when presented to a prospective publisher. He will name names, highlight and underscore the name Hamilton, but he will draw a line at naming the source of his evidence or mentioning the Schroeder name and endangering the life of the one who, with great self-sacrifice, had come to his aid.

He will interview the *Renaissance* men, from the compositor to the unskilled who sold the paper on the streets, for they all grew up in the South and had their own stories to tell. He will meet with the sharp-tongued Brother Sheldon, who would be bursting with his scriptural condemnations and damnations and insist they be included in the book. So will every other Harlemite with his own axe to grind.

That night he lay in bed putting his thoughts together before putting pen to paper. He eventually drifted off to sleep.

The telephone rang about two in the morning as it did several years ago. Again he grabbed the receiver on the second ring fearing an emergency call from his family in Barbados.

The caller was Paula Schroeder. They had spoken on the phone from time to time.

"How's your book coming along?"

"Still thinking it through."

"I'm leaving home, Mark."

"Why?"

"I'm an outcast in my hometown, that's why. Ever since the rides."

"But that's sixteen years ago, girl."

"I know, but ever since then I've been seeing hell. In college. In town. In church. In my own house from my parents. Even my own brother, Brad, says I dishonored the Schroeder name, turned against my own people. I'm a pariah, Mark, I walk down the street and people see "Freedom Rider" pinned on my back."

"Where'll you go?"

"I'm thinking San Francisco. Got a doctor friend who lives there. Wants me to go with him to the Congo in the spring with the Peace Corps. They've got a polio vaccination program going on in Central Africa. I'll be safe in his apartment. He's gay anyway."

"Whyn't you come to New York, Paula. You can stay with me 'til you get situated. Maybe you could lend me a hand with this project."

As soon as the invitation left his lips, his brain was clouded with misgivings. Would others accept her, ignore her, or worse look upon her with contempt, accusing her of crossing over without paying her dues to the cause despite the penance she had paid with the freedom rides? It occurred to him she might be no less ostracized in Harlem due to her family connections than she was in her own hometown, though should he be honest with himself, he had his own concerns about their divergent cultural upbringings. Even the trivial things might come between them. The rhythms of the islands were still deep in his bones, her heartbeat was to bluegrass and country music.

And the most perplexing thought of all: how would he explain to people that inviting her into his house was not the same as taking her to his bed? He was fully aware that even in the seventies America had not yet warmed to black and white couples. In the conservative South, intermixing and interbreeding were anathema, challenging the mores of the state; whereas in the North it was all about procreation, people masking their hypocrisy in concern for the offspring, the mythic effects on the young 'uns.

But, he thought, *"To hell with the gossipmongers and the divisive! She was the only one who had gone out of her way, even turned her back on her family, even put her life in danger to help him find his father's killer."* So with this indebtedness on his conscience, he said with elation in his voice: "Yes, pack your bags and call me from the bus station."

And, as it turns out, she was no less elated.

"No, I'll fly," she said.

8 – Pemberton Publishers

February 1977. Now today he is standing at the corner of Madison and 57th in NYC, at the center where America invents new ways to romance her consumer society. Madison Avenue, the advertising center of the nation. He is standing at the foot of an intimidating building of granite, steel and glass, one of a dozen skyscrapers lining both sides of the block. The bone-chilling winds are gusting down the avenue, brushing past him as though he were in a canyon with the wind slapping his face. He stands out from the crowd in this maze of cement where in the dead of winter no one stands still and few look up except for the occasional tourist gawking at Manhattan's vertical monstrosities.

But this one is graceful. It faces him square and erect, then leans away and climbs, each story diminishing in size like a layered cake until the topmost floor is a spire. A gigantic neon sign from one side to the next of the façade proclaims this building the home of Pemberton Publishers, one of the largest publishing houses on the East Coast.

He prepares his mind to enter, flushed with the eternal hope that lies in the breast of every writer. Before he changes his mind, he briskly climbs the half a dozen steps, pushes through the revolving door, crosses the marble floor and approaches the receptionist. He is an elderly black man with salt-and-pepper hair, formally attired, seated behind a pretentiously large and highly polished desk, flanked by two green ten-foot potted cacti that give him the appearance of being in the company of his own guards. The man perks up, his eyes open wide.

The plastic nameplate on his desk is incised with the word "Receptionist" but he is also a watchman, a guard, a detective. His role is to vet unlikely visitors like this one, a black man wandering in off the street and into his sphere of authority. The visitor is greeted with a stern "What can I do for you?" But then the suit and tie and the confidence in the visitor's bearing elicit a half-smile and a softer "May I help you, sir?"

"Yes, I have an appointment with Mr. Thatcher, head of Acquisitions." he replies.

"Your name, sir?"

"Mark Maynard. Please tell him that his ten o'clock appointment is here."

"Please have a seat, sir, while I call upstairs."

After sixteen long years Mark has completed a book, all five hundred pages of typewritten pages, generating a dozen synopses, excerpts and summaries, dispatching them to a dozen publishing houses all across the east coast, waiting anxiously for one or the other to take an interest in the subject. No one responded, not even with an acknowledgement of receipt. Then lately he received a letter from one Mr. Thomas Thatcher, the man who conceivably approves any work of literature that manages to make its way out of Pemberton Publishers. He had asked to see the complete manuscript whereupon Mark had complied. In his letter he had referred specifically to two or three paragraphs, asking for clarification but not questioning the veracity.

The notorious Ku Klux Klan through the 1960s is not the organization you remember. The fraternity has mutated into a different beast but their bite is no less venomous. They have hung up their white robes and no longer peer through holes in white hoods. They dress like you and me and in the light of day they are as genteel and urbane as any other on these northern streets. They no longer ride into town on horseback like their Imperial Grand Wizard was known to do. They sit next to you and me in the subways and smile in our faces. They attend our churches and pray to the same God. They infiltrate our political parties and influence our leaders.

But comes night and like werewolves they transform themselves into predators and mischief makers, burning crosses on suburban and rural properties that belong to people they fear, strewing their seeds of hate on the streets of this state wherever they be. There is a new chapter of the Klan about to be founded and I have their plans and the names of those who have been chosen by their leaders in the South to expand their web of terror right here in this state of New York. Read further and you will see their names including the name of one suspected to have killed the author's father.

Then came another letter in the mail with an invitation to come in and discuss the work. In his book he examines the social fabric in America, recaps the freedom rides and his sojourn in the South. In it he points a finger of rebuke at politicians who tolerate the Klan, is even obliquely critical of the media as a whole for not doing enough to champion the cause. Central to the work is a message to New Yorkers. It is couched as a dire warning to all who read his book. He boldly exposes the Klan's secret plans and damning the brotherhood of racists, naming names and, as the saying goes, "taking no prisoners". Finally he writes about his beloved father and that he had died unmistakably at the hands of haters for the crime of crossing the color line.

HIS FATHER'S FOOTSTEPS

The work had been sitting like rancid fruit in the pit of his stomach, and during intervals between his columns at *The Renaissance* he had found the urge to puke it all out. Still, for some time afterwards, he had had moments of remorse in which he wondered if he should ever had written such a damning account of the other America. Belatedly he wondered if it should ever have left his desk. With a fair amount of immodesty he wondered how many reckless fires his book might ignite in the criminal minds of some, just waiting for their own resentments to be articulated and sanctioned, though he cared not for a moment about offending the powerful and the heartless. Poring over the most volatile lines he had thought of tempering the explosiveness of his words.

Paula, a history major, who now lives with him in his father's brownstone, has assisted him in the endeavor by contributing the story of her upbringing in the segregated South. But she is not a party to his manner of bluntly excoriating politicians, from the highest office to the lowest. She had favored more subtle, more diplomatic prose. Never one to hold back, she had said to him one day after one of her editing sessions: "Listen Mark, don't flatter yourself, you're no James Baldwin, Ralph Ellison and certainly no Eldridge Cleaver in my opinion." And she was right. But there is no anti-imperialist or anti-American sentiment that pervades the work but empathy for his brothers below the Mason-Dixie line.

He admits he was once a political animal. All his friends know he had been a Freedom Rider sympathizer in the sixties, though he was never inclined to join the nonviolent campaign. He was not about to immolate himself on the altar of racial integration. Then during the restive college years, like every other pacifist, he had protested against Nixon and his escalation of the Vietnam War. But he had drawn a line at destroying campus property or joining rebellious youths locking themselves into faculty quarters and occupying their space until demands were met. He was never extreme in his protestations, whatever the causes. Perhaps now that he is going on thirty-six, the old civil rights heroics are reawakened like the stories aroused in the minds of war veterans.

The receptionist fumbles across his desk for his phone directory, dials an extension and then peels off a visitor's sticker which Mark slaps onto the lapel of his blazer.

"Forty-eighth floor, elevator on your left, someone will meet you there, sir."

He cannot help but think that this old receptionist has never seen the second floor, much less the forty-eighth, and sits all day in this dreary exorbitant vestibule showcasing the perception that equal opportunity shines on every floor. All week, last week and the week before, he has seen visitors come and go, and now who is this brother in his monkey suit? Who does he think he is?

The elevator door slides open and there to greet him is a petite bleached-blonde with a hand outstretched, beaming a smile that lights up the hallway. He is not sure if the smile is contrived to put him at ease but he returns the smile anyway. Strangely for a corporate setting like this, her manner of dress in floral shirt and hip-hugging jeans strikes him as less than appropriate until he remembers that in the publishing and artistic world the bohemian lifestyle is the norm.

"Welcome! I am Mr. Thatcher's secretary, we have been expecting you. Please follow me."

He follows her down a long carpeted corridor lined on both sides with offices behind whose doors might sit graphic designers, illustrators, proofers, readers, reviewers, copyright lawyers and the critics who hold the future of budding authors in the palms of their hands. Eventually they come to a spacious and ornately furnished room which he assumes is the inner sanctum of Pemberton Publishers. It juts out from the building like a turret so that through the gigantic bay windows his eyes are immediately drawn to a three-sided panorama of the city: Park Avenue, Fifth Avenue, Broadway, Times Square. Life-sized portraits of famous dead authors adorn the walls: Fitzgerald, Hemingway, Chekhov, Nabokov, Jane Austen. He is in awe. The secretary with the fake smile takes her place at the far corner of the room. Her desk is surrounded by a profusion of fake flowers, a fake fireplace with fake flames. They caution him against assumptions of anything said or promised within these walls. Seated at the head of an oblong glass-topped table is a heavyset man wearing red moire suspenders, his sleeves rolled up above his elbows. Evidently he is the one who sits in final judgment with his stamp of approval or his curse of rejection. He is distinguished by his glossy black toupee, which is clearly not properly fitted and makes no pretensions of being his natural hair. He introduces himself as Tom Thatcher but does not bother to introduce the stone-faced man sitting at his left in a grey-striped three-piece business suit and with his hands in his lap.

"Come in, Mr. Maynard, please join us. Can I call you Mark? May I get you some coffee or tea or anything?" There is a jaunty air about him, yet his eyes are wide, piercing through his spectacles, examining his guest from head to shoe.

Mark declines the refreshment and they both rise with the perfunctory handshakes. He takes a seat at the other end.

"Are you British, Mark? I was curious about your spelling."

"No, I'm from Barbados."

"Same thing. Little England." He knew his geopolitical history.

The manuscript in question, supposedly read, reviewed and dissected, sits at the top of a pile before the publisher. Earlier, he had all reasons to imagine it an already convicted felon awaiting their formal verdict before it hit the shredder; after all, he had not the faintest illusion it would be accepted for publication by this prestigious house, for in it he had leveled his literary guns at the whole publishing industry in America and some pages could be seen fairly or unfairly as a direct rebuke of the same people in whose presence he had now found himself. He had researched the hundred-year history of Pemberton Publishers and his suspicions were confirmed that no literary work by a black author, whether or not it touched on the struggle, had ever been graced with the Pemberton imprint. But he had been careful not to directly accuse this publishing titan, for he realized his own precarious position as a small fish in the business.

No wonder then, that he is stunned, totally caught off-guard when Mr. Thatcher looks up from the manuscript and smilingly says, "Mr. Maynard, we are going to buy your book." That the publisher now reverts to his last name indicates that a business transaction is about to take place. But a frown creases his brow as he stares questioningly at his guest.

"First you have to tone down your language and references to certain people. It's much too harsh, don't you think?"

"I'll have to explain, Mr. Thatcher. There is a new political and nefarious dynamic about to take place in this city."

"Very impressive words, Mr. Maynard, but then you're naming names, albeit first names, actual people f'r Christ sake, and all their transgressions. Is that a wise thing to do?"

"But every word is the truth, Mr. Thatcher, and every name is someone who is about to do great harm to this city."

"The truth may set you free but it could send a lot o' innocent people to jail. Including you for libel."

Mark paraphrases the scriptures. "Put not the truth under a bushel but on a candlestick so it giveth light unto the world."

The man ignores the scriptural reference. "Have you shopped this book around to other publishers?"

"Yes, but I chose Pemberton first," he answers half-truthfully hoping the flattery would leverage him a bit more favor in the bargaining. After all, they had not invited him to a meeting for coffee and chitchat."

"Any bites?"

"No."

"Well, then, you should know why. *You* might want to be sued for defamation of character but no publisher is gonna volunteer to accompany you to prison." The other man chuckles.

For several seconds Thatcher presses two fingers against his lips as if to plug them until his thoughts could be fully collected and his words properly positioned.

"Mr. Maynard, this gentleman and I have read your manuscript. We think it is well written from a literary standpoint. I'd be lying if I said it doesn't have some merit. But frankly we do not agree with the defamatory nature of the contents though Pemberton has never been shy about getting involved in volatile subjects. It would serve no purpose to publish allegations about people about which we have no proof. In fact it would be downright dangerous and would do great harm to the reputation we currently enjoy in this city".

"You are assuming, sir, that I have no proof."

"Well, show us the proof."

"I can't until my accusers challenge me on a charge of libel in a court of law. Until then I might be endangering those persons who have entrusted me with the proof."

"Well, there you go, Mr. Maynard, it's a classic case of Catch 22, isn't it?"

But the evidence that corroborates the allegations in his book would do great harm to the one he is obligated to protect. The original papers signed and approved by her Klansman father, should they be exposed to the light of day, would send shockwaves all the way from Maine to Calilfornia.

The publisher pauses and riffles through the manuscript, finds a page that has been deliberately dog-eared and points to a paragraph highlighted in yellow in preparation for the meeting.

"You have made some reprehensible statements about some elected officials, even in the White House."

He begins to read. "'Is it unreasonable to conclude that during his tenure, our President of the United States, Richard Milhous Nixon, did nothing to ease the misery of apartheid in Pretoria, deeming the children of Soweto thugs and reprobates while calling the children of America impatient? I ask you, my brothers and sisters, 'Who is the reprobate?' "

Mr. Maynard, you are an intelligent man, a writer versed in the English language as evidenced by your earlier works, a writer possessed with a vocabulary beyond the scope of the average reader. You know very well that a "reprobate" is a depraved and wicked person, rejected by God and beyond hope of salvation. Why then would you ascribe such a vile term to our 37th President? Oh yes, freedom of speech you say, but does this freedom of speech serve to help your own people or does it not foster resentment in the hearts of decent people who love this country and our esteemed President, people who would otherwise rally to your moral cause?" He stares at Mark over his spectacles and waits for an answer, but for a moment Mark's own words set him back on his heels.

"Yes, you have a point, Mr. Thatcher, that was a bit harsh, I agree. But when a man has your life in his hands and you're on the ground and you're hollering and he doesn't hear you and doesn't see you, then you need to reach up and grab his testicles to get his attention. Know what I'm saying?"

His secretary, seated at the far corner of the office, raises a hand to her face and stifles a laugh. The publisher shakes his head, rocks back in his chair and glares, first at Mark and then at his secretary. In spite of his bravado, Marks knows quite well that Thatcher holds the cards; one negative mention of his name at the Publishers' Annual Conference in June could bring down the curtain on his fledgling career.

"You of all people should appreciate the power of language," he continues, "it's the inflammatory nature of your writing that does your people great harm. The young and easily incitable will take their cues from these lines and not understand that you are being melodramatic in order to sell a book. And before long they will think every white face is the enemy and resort to the same violence on the street as depicted by your incendiary words. It is high time you and your fellow writers be responsible or you will continue to have blood on your hands." The head of the other man is nodding in accord as he continues his lecture.

"Moreover, why are you so impatient? Your people have come a long way. Never mind the South, which, to tell you the truth, was always backward, but when I was a boy in this city your people had to step off the pavement for me to pass. We joined with your people to change that unfortunate state of affairs and look where we are today. You, a black man — excuse me, an African American — can walk into this building on Madison Avenue in New York City, no questions asked. Do you not call this progress, Mr. Maynard?"

"But once I'm in the building, will you give me a job on the forty-eighth floor?"

"Well, dammit Mr. Maynard! Send me a person of color, bright, college-educated and with the right qualifications who can prove to me that he or she can do the job and I swear to God I'll hire that person tomorrow." His voice fills the whole of his cavernous office.

And those words from the publisher's mouth to his ears bring to mind none other than Nakeisha. She is an NYU graduate with an MA degree, the beneficiary of a full state scholarship. She is worth much more of a salary than the newspaper can afford and with no lack of ambition she is ready to move on. Her résumé must have landed on the desk of every employment office in Manhattan, yet she had never been invited in for an interview, for over the phone it appeared her name, Nakeisha Okonjo, in the corporate world downtown conjured up the sub-Saharan jungles.

While he is musing about such farfetched possibilities, Thatcher continues. "I am on your side, Mr. Maynard. And don't you go giving all the credit to Dr. King, Mr. Abernathy and Mr. Rustin. If it weren't for fair-minded people like me you would still be in the back of the bus. So you see, this is not a white versus black antagonistic world any longer, the good protagonists come in all colors in the fight for justice."

The publisher's face takes on an increasingly florid complexion, as molecules of brown spittle are seen shooting across the table. "But, that aside," he continues, "it is not the reason we sent you an invitation so we could meet face to face. It is that you make the preposterous claim that a southern-style KKK organization is setting up an outpost in our suburbs, and eventually will be infiltrating our local politics. Do you really believe this to be true, Mr. Maynard?"

"Well, with all respects, Mr. Thatcher, the much maligned Communists, Marxists and Socialists have been known to succeed in doing the same over the years."

"But if what you claim is true, don't you think the networks, print media, the civil rights people and all the conspirators would be onto the story?"

"Not necessarily. Maybe they're all asleep."

"Again, what evidence do you have that the media in this city do not possess? Show me your supporting data. We have a problem, a lack of corroboration."

Mark needs to move on from the controversy. He wants to know what will become of his book, what will it take to get the book printed, published and out on the streets. He has every reason to believe that once the publisher is finished with his disquisition he will make him an offer subject to one or two redactions. Why would he have sent him a letter and schedule a meeting to discuss the work when a standard rejection letter would have been simpler and less time-consuming? He thinks he knows the answer. *The New Chapter* is a powder keg that cannot be allowed out in the open. He is about to ask the question when the man gathers up the manuscript and slides it across the table to his guest.

"Mr. Maynard, we are not prepared to publish your book in its present form with all the aspersions, but we are willing to take it off your hands for a nominal sum just so it doesn't get out into the open and poison the atmosphere in this city. But you would have to cede to us all ownership rights plus accord us the right of first refusal of future books of this nature."

At this moment Mark can almost hear the hissing of air as it quickly leaks out of his inflated balloon. He cannot bear the thought that the fruits of his labor might be edited to death, or worse, committed to the publisher's shredder.

He dares to ask the question: "So does this mean the book is thumbs down?"

"Not unless you agree to perform some major surgery."

As a last resort, Mark decides to play one desperate ploy. He taps the inside pocket of his jacket and says, "I have the proof right here, Mr. Thatcher, names, signatures, faces and minutes of Klan meetings. They support every claim, every charge, take my word."

"Well, hand them over."

He is prepared to play hardball because he knows they want the book, not to publish it but to destroy it.

"Not until I have a publisher's proof in my hands, sir, printed and bound, ready for release. Sir, I am prepared to make some changes but not a whole lot. You see, I have an ulterior motive, to see that these men are exposed. It's personal and it's visceral. One of them killed my father."

"Sorry to hear that," he says dismissively. "But you haven't heard what we are prepared to offer for an expurgated version."

"What's to prevent me from agreeing to your offer and writing another book, naming the same persons, and espousing the exact same opinions in the exact same language?

"That would not be a principled thing to do. Would it?"

Mark refuses to point out the irony of contrasting principles for fear of pushing his luck and being thrown out of the office for sheer impertinence. He lets it linger in the air.

"For what it's worth," says the publisher coolly, "the offer is ten thousand dollars for full rights to the book payable indirectly by Pemberton Publishers and directly by the gentleman sitting here at my side."

A wall of silence falls between him and the two men. It is broken by the words uttered softly by the gentleman on his left, who had not yet joined the conversation and seemed eager to lend his sycophantic support to the publisher. He says, "It's a win-win arrangement, Mr. Maynard. You get a few bucks for your effort and *we* don't have any trouble."

"I didn't get your name?" says Mark.

He smiles benevolently, but strangely he doesn't give his name. Instead he reaches across the table to shake hands and in the effort the sleeve of his jacket rides up. A miniature swastika is tattooed on his wrist.

Clearly this book is a hot potato judging from the rejections. Moreover, if it were accepted, it is not a book that would command much of a return in royalties, though he never expected to make a killing, it was never his motive. He is reluctant to accept the offer of ten thousand bucks to quash the truth because the truth has a right to be in the hands of the people. But the offer is so unanticipated that he needs to get his bearings before he gives them a response, though he is inclined to tell them no.

In his entire life he has never had that amount of money in his hands. Once, in Barbados, he had won a contest for poetry on the local radio station and had been awarded the grand prize of a Cadbury chocolate bar.

In his short writing career he had never thought it financially prudent to involve an agent in his few negotiations which, to tell the truth, had yielded royalties so hard-fought that he would have been destitute today had an agent intervened in these matters and dipped into the eventual earnings for his twenty or thirty percent. He is intrigued when Mr. Thatcher says to him with total confidence in the offer: "Ten grand is a lot o' cash, Mr. Maynard. Take your time, chew on it, give us an answer soon."

He calls out to his secretary for a large manila mailer that bears on the flap the proud logo of Pemberton Publishers, an oversized red cursive P. The secretary tucks the manuscript inside and hands it to Mark with her patented smile. With the deftness of a magician he makes the motion of emptying the non-existent contents of his inside pocket into the envelope and gets up to leave.

"Ellen, whyn't you walk Mr. Maynard back to the elevator." He has been dismissed.

On the way back down the corridor he casually asks Ellen, "Who was the man sitting with your boss? I didn't get his name."

"He's a book merchant from somewhere down south. That's all I know. They are all very hush-hush."

He leaves the meeting without the slightest regret or compunction for having written the book. Stubborn by nature, he loathes having to change a single word for any price, for the truth cannot be bought. Exiting the building, he sees that a light snow has been falling and already there is a film of ice on the steps. Stepping gingerly down to the sidewalk, he cannot help but wonder if there might also be a thin film of treachery on the forty-eighth floor and in the minds of Mr. Thatcher and his cohort. Suspicion weighs heavily on his mind.

He steps off the curb and hails a yellow cab. The driver pulls over.

"Whereto, Mister?"

"Harlem, 127 West 135th".

"Sorry, buddy." He pulls away.

North of 72nd in the city is a war zone in the minds of downtown taxi drivers. He understands their paranoia when a black hand is in the air, for many a cab driver has lost his life heading to Harlem when his passenger prefers to take his life rather than pay his fare. So when the next cab comes along he yanks open the door and plants himself firmly in the back seat. Only then does he announce his destination through a hole in the bulletproof partition. In a way he commandeers the cab and tells the driver, "We're heading to Harlem, ol' chap". The man grunts his displeasure and reluctantly heads uptown.

9 – Harlem Streets

Already the streets of Harlem are carpeted white. The traffic has slowed to a merciless crawl. The meter clocks up another dollar to his tab. Darkness creeps in and the gas lamps along 125th Street are blinking in the falling snow, casting a yellowish glow on the almost deserted sidewalks. A few pedestrians are braving the cold, hands buried in coat pockets, collars upturned, bodies bent forward bracing against the wind. As the cab inches along he changes his mind and asks to be detoured to 119th Street to *The Renaissance.*

The newspaper bears on its masthead the name Mark Maynard, Columnist, but he hasn't penned a column recently, devoting all his time to putting the finishing touches to *The New Chapter.* All the workers are his friends, from Holyfield to the lowest man on the totem pole, Mr. Rogers, the old man who loads his pickup every Sunday morning and drops a paper on every doorstep in Harlem. With every good reason they are poised to launch a book promotion, a bombshell that will rock the city. Now that Thatcher has put a new spin on his plans he may have to put the book on hold. The promotion is off.

In some ways *The New Chapter* was Holyfield's baby too; he had written the preface, a masterpiece in everyone's opinion. It was an in-depth chronicle of the civil rights movement before and after the Emancipation. His contribution was professorial in tone in contrast to Mark's caustic writing style, which turned out to be one of Thatcher's bones of contention. But granted, he was not the sole offender; there were others on the staff who had contributed their own true-life experiences, those who had a right to be more embittered than he, those who still bore in their minds the scars of whippings and images of their forefathers swinging from live oaks, and who were still trying to trace ancestors torn from their mothers' breasts. He documented their stories to the last word and included faded tear-stained clippings from *The Atlanta Courier* and *The Mississippi Emissary* depicting the callous faces of lynch men standing together on scaffolding erected for only one purpose, men pleased with the outcome of the hunt, surrounding their catch bound and awaiting the inevitable; and women with babies in arms, hovering under the trees, pointing and grinning at the lurid spectacle of a dead body dangling high in the air at the end of a rope. In what other terms did Thatcher expect him to describe these unspeakable horrors? What other names did he want him to ascribe to these vile people? What less obscene words could be conjured up to convey the moral obscenity of slavery?

By the time the taxi pulls up to the front door of *The Renaissance*, the snow is pelting down dense as confetti and thick as cotton balls. He dispatches the cab, barges into Holyfield's office, removes his coat, flings it into a corner and slumps into a chair without a word.

"What's the matter with you, man?" asks Holyfield, gazing at Mark's hangdog face. "You didn't get any tonight?"

He gives him a thumbs-down. "The book is a no go."

"So what? Pemberton is not the only friggin' game in town. I know a hundred book peddlers. We can shop it around."

"I already did, Ken, you don't understand. Pemberton wants to buy it for a fee and quash it."

"What? So you are telling me you are thinkin' of takin' the money?"

"Ken, I'm not sure what I'm gonna do," he answers wearily.

Holyfield is an aging, portly, white-bearded black man, who is kept alive with the assistance of his second pacemaker. He is mild-mannered and huggable as a stuffed bear, but when confronted by the face of a bully, he transforms himself into an elephant run amok, petulantly stomping around his office until, exhausted by his own weight, he flops into a chair. Then he summons his secretary, Nakeisha, and dictates an excoriating letter to the offender, whether an individual, a corporation or an institution. In the next edition there would a blistering article in *The Renaissance* and every reader would know who did what to whom. He is a master propagandist for the cause of civil rights and the newspaper is his torch that lights the way for his people in Harlem.

Now he eases himself up from his double-cushioned armchair which breathes a sigh of relief as he removes his bulk. He grabs his umbrella which doubles as a walking cane, before setting out on his perambulation from one corner of the office to the next and back again, punctuating each sentence with a stroke of his "baton" in the air like a maestro.

He bellows: "Mark, we're not talking here about a goddamned cookbook f'r Christ sake. This book is about people's lives. This book is about the secrets of survival. This book is about the struggle to free us from the clutches of these maleficent bitches. This book is about Marian Anderson's journey from the cotton fields to the steps of the Lincoln Memorial. This book is about Michael Schwerner, Andrew Goodman and James Chaney. This book is about Martin Luther King, Jr., Rosa Parks, Medgar Evers, Malcolm X. This book is about the Birmingham bombing that killed four Negro girls in church. This book is about the Freedom Riders like your own 'what's her name' from Arkansas. This book is about ..." He pauses to catch his breath, coughing with a hand to his chest.

"Ken, take it easy," says Mark rising to take his arm. He leads him back to his desk and sits him down, and his armchair once again groans under his weight. He is an old warrior whose mind is ready to do battle while his weakened body will no longer cooperate. As a young man he fought for his rights on the streets of Tuscaloosa and knew the inside of the state prison like the interior of his own house in West Central Alabama. He joined the Great Migration to the North that changed the face of Harlem in the turn of the century. He swapped his sword for the mighty pen and devotes his life to shining light in dark places, waging war against injustice wherever he perceives it.

Mark pours him a glass of water from the office kitchenette and returns to the topic. "Ken, I think there is something fishy about a man offering to buy the rights to a book just to make sure it goes nowhere. Don't you think?"

"And a whopping ten grand. We created a friggin' bombshell, my friend. Let's make sure it doesn't explode in our hands."

Through the window in Holyfield's office he can see snow has given way to sleet and rain. Thick fog is also creeping into the night. Roadways will be slick. Travel will be hazardous. Taxicabs will abandon the streets. He will have to start heading home on foot. He is well aware of the rash of muggings and murders in the area. Holyfield has no worry; he lives at *The Renaissance*. Nakeisha and the rest of the crew have been long gone.

"Take my umbrella," Holyfield offers. "You can return it in the morning or whenever." He tells him that his umbrella poses as his shelter from rain and snow and, since his hip replacement, it is his crutch and walking cane. Then he whispers in his ear a secret that no one else knows: that it triples in its utility as his secret weapon. At the other end of the ivory-tipped handle is a retracted blade of the sharpest steel that, when triggered, will shoot out and snap back like a lizard's tongue.

"D'yuh want me to show yuh how it works?"

"Nah, I just need the umbrella."

He tells him that he bought it in Chinatown from a shifty-eyed Korean woman, who sold from under the counter a variety of unorthodox weaponry ranging from a pseudo-pen switchblade to a refillable cigarette lighter that jets out a paralyzing dose of pepper spray. And in a neighborhood where crime runs rampant, Holyfield, with his hip disability and the disadvantage that his obesity presents, needs an innovative tool to defend him on the street.

The distance from the doorstep to his home on 135th Street is sixteen short blocks; he has walked it before but always in the day. He steps out from the shadow of the building and plods along the lonely avenue in the sleet and rain. There is no sign of humanity on the way except for one or two piteous people in darkened doorways, curled up under burlap blankets and sheets of cardboard, homeless and too dispirited or demented to seek refuge in city shelters. Even the occasional pimp in the alleyways and his girls on the block have called it a night. He crosses the more heavily trafficked main street of 125th and is doused from head to foot with grime and muddy slush as a bus barrels by indifferently. Few cars go by, slowly, gingerly, no traction. He keeps going. A few more blocks and he will be home and changed into dry clothing.

Then he hears the slushy sound of footsteps in the snow. He looks back but there is no one around. He chalks it up to his imagination. He hears the sound again. This time behind him a shadow retreats behind a retaining wall. He crosses the road and the shadow does the same. He wonders if the fuzzy image was planted in his imagination by Holyfield's warning about these Harlem streets. He stops for a second, turns around and stands perfectly still, daring the shadow to reveal itself. Again there is no one. He trudges on through the snow telling himself it is all in his head, just a mirage born of fatigue. But when he turns onto 135th where he lives, a ghostly figure darts from behind a juniper hedge and confronts him head-on. A dark woolen hood and earflaps envelope the head and face; he wears an oversized grey sweater and unbelted jeans that hang loosely below his waist revealing blue-striped boxer underwear which is clearly meant to be seen. Mark is not about to run; he is strong and physically able to defend himself as long as the playing field is even. He instinctively assumes a pugilistic pose, planting his feet firmly, crouching, squaring his shoulders and tightening his fists.

"C'mon, you want me, fella?"

A passing car casts its headlights in their direction and reveals the creature. His face is black as coal, he is short and slight of build. There is a gum-chewing swaggering arrogance about him as he comes closer and closer clearly unafraid. Mark is convinced he can take him on without much of a struggle, he is a mere lad of fifteen or sixteen.

"Wha' d'yuh want from me, fella? You're making a big mistake, I'm warning you."

The boy grins and reveals two gold-capped incisors. A gold chain loops halfway down from his neck to his waist. He has a steely expression that is cold and impassive as death.

"Hold it right there, pal. Don't come any closer." But the boy continues advancing until Mark can see the veins in his eyes.

Alas, this creature is not alone; he has a partner who creeps up from behind and thrusts something hard and pointed in the curve of his back. He sees himself again on a darkened, deserted street in the South, his head about to be busted by young skinheads in Montgomery, except that now the offenders are black like him. Moreover, there is nowhere to run, no way to escape, with a knife in his back.

"Don't move an ass-ol' muscle!" says his assailant between his teeth, "unless you tired o' livin'."

From the sensation of his breathing at the back of his neck, they seem about the same height, as he gives off an odor that stinks of salty sweat. The urge to turn to see his face must be resisted since he has been warned not to move a muscle. The person methodically lifts his coat in the back, reaches into his pants pocket and extracts his wallet. With the feel of the boy's hand on his backside, he has the humiliating feeling of being violated. Nevertheless he stands riveted to the ground, the manila folder under his arm while he holds Holyfield's umbrella in the other hand.

"What's in the envelope, ol' man?" asks the one with the weapon, as he jabs harder. Mark feels the cold steel cut through his coat, his jacket and touches his skin. *He called me an old man*, thinks Mark, *a double insult from this punk.*

"Just some papers," he answers.

"Let's have it!"

"Why are you doin' this? I'm your brother, man."

"Brother, my ass! Hand it over if you wanna live! I ain't goin' ask you twice!"

"But why …"

Before the words leave his lips, he is struck with a fist in the solar plexus by the kid in front. The blow knocks every bit of oxygen from his lungs. He bends over and gasps for air and catches a kick to his chin that buckles his knees. He holds onto the Pemberton folder as if it contained the Royal Crown Jewels for no other reason than obstinacy and pride. A stubborn voice inside him is saying he shouldn't be surrendering to these street punks, that next they'll be demanding his coat and shirt and maybe even his trousers.

"Leave 'im to me, Ben, he's mine," says the one taunting him with another jab in the back.

The sad irony of it all is, he is about to give his life to the ones whose lives he has dedicated his book to save. At that moment he comes to realize that neither his pleas nor the surrender of his money and papers will appease them nor quench their bloodlust; he is not sure how much longer this confrontation will last until his own life becomes their prize. He hands over the folder that contains his manuscript. He passes it over his shoulder. What good is it to them anyway?

"Now empty yer jacket! What's in duh pocket?" he asks, punctuating the demand with another stab.

It was the pocket he had used for his pantomime earlier of holding secrets to deceive Thatcher and his companion. His pocket is empty but how can he say so without antagonizing his assailant? The boy is furious. He claws at his shoulders in an attempt to rip the jacket off. Tonight no color, black or white, will save him, he must save himself. He wishes now he had let Holyfield demonstrate the secret weapon hidden from view in the tubing of his umbrella. It is too late now, there is no time for experimentation. He runs his fingers along the crook of the ivory handle, feels a tiny notch, perhaps a switch, squeezes it and sees the steel blade spring from its sheath like a dragon's tongue. He whirls like a discus thrower and swings the umbrella in one wide circle. It misses Ben, the youth in front, who with remarkable agility leans back and out of the way, but the knife's trajectory catches the other boy in the neck. He curses and falls to his knees still clutching his loot; his knife falls to the ground. The other one grabs his fallen partner by the arm, helps him to his feet as the blood oozes from his neck and trickles between his fingers. They run towards the end of the street and disappear. A passing motorist slows; takes a good look at the scene, but moves on down the street with no sign of concern.

His heart is thumping but, more than scared, he is hurting on the inside; the faces of his young attackers are the same faces in his book railing day and night against the white man and his perpetuation of unfairness. Yet he, their brother, their ally in the struggle, walking innocently among them, bears the brunt of their wrath and feels the anguish of their vengeance as a shiv is thrust into his back. A gun in their possession could have blasted him away in one split second of irrational hate. Had they been white, would the hurt now be different?

He reaches his house, unlatches the gate and steps into a pool of slush before climbing the steps and foraging for his keys. Then there is another, more decorative gate of the hardest steel that needs to be unlocked before he tackles the deadbolts that secure a heavy one-inch-thick oak door. Then a steel rod that braces itself against the door from the inside needs to be slid away with a separate key.

Once upon a time, windows on the street were merely loop-latched and doors were managed with a simple twist of a key; now law-abiding citizens are imprisoned like caged cockatoos behind metal gates. He remembers how his street had once been gentrified by immigrants from the Caribbean and beleaguered blacks fleeing the South. In the halcyon days of The Harlem Renaissance, elms lined the sidewalks, beds behind the houses sprouted boxwood shrubs and ivy. Every house boasted a floral garden, however modest, and on snowy days the children walked up and down the street armed with their shovels to clear the steps of neighbors' houses for a quarter. Now those same kids have grown; some have gone off to college; some have been sucked into the maw of the military and gone off to fight wars against foes they have never heard of. Others have prevailed and become respectable citizens. The criminal system has siphoned off many while others remain trapped and have become muggers on the streets.

He stamps his shoes on the doormat, slips them off and enters the house. He places Holyfield's umbrella to stand in a corner with the same respect he would accord to a comrade who had saved his life. Paula is standing in the hallway holding a cup of tea; expectation is etched on her face. He pecks her on the cheek and silently brushes past on the way to the coat closet. She follows him.

"How did your meeting go?"

He turns to remove his soggy coat and hears her scream as her cup falls to the floor.

"Oh my God, you are bleeding, Mark! What happened?"

Surely blood is seeping through his shirt and dripping to the tiles. He has no idea he had been cut but now that she brings it to his attention he belatedly feels the sting of his assailant's knife. The pain had been cancelled out by a more acute, a more devastating hurt, the fact he was attacked by his own people. It is not a deep wound but something tells him that another thrust of the blade might have pierced his spine. His meeting with Pemberton and everything else must have now vanished from her thoughts.

He makes light of his narrow escape. "Just another walk on the streets of Harlem in the dark."

"Could've been your life," she says.

But in the aftermath a voice keeps repeating in his ear: *"Mark, they were after your papers, not your money and not your life"*. But he refuses to believe the "they" could be his own brothers. It just doesn't make sense.

10 – Breaking News

Up to that moment he had felt no stirrings of romantic feelings towards Paula, just a sense of gratitude for her sacrifices and self-endangerment in helping him to find the answers he'd been seeking for sixteen years. After Maria had gone to spend time with her aging parents, he and Paula had always slept in separate bedrooms in his father's spacious house without displaying the slightest notion of being other than friends, collaborating against a common enemy, reviewing and critiquing *The New Chapter*, dining and conversing together in quiet times and never in their close proximity touching or kissing or betraying the slightest hint of sexual attraction.

It was always Nakeisha with whom he shared a bed on those nights when their sexual cravings begged to be mutually sated. It was Nakeisha for whom he never questioned his feelings and when they made love there was never a sense of duty but a sense of oneness, for at the peak of their sexual excitation they became one and the same. Now that he has brought a woman into his house she lately rejects his advances. He thinks it unfair she has allowed a chill to come between them.

Between him and Maria Townsend, however, he had always detected an aura akin to a high-tension wire that, if once disturbed by either party, he would find himself drowning in a sea of guilt and remorse, and in the end his fate would be the same as his father's. Perhaps for this reason he was happy she had decided to be away for an extended period, taking care of her ailing parents, for he could not be sure he could always trust himself to abide by his own scruples and find himself wanting to relive the dissolute life of his father.

Now with his blood oozing from an incision in his back, he is the recipient of more than Paula's usual attention. She anxiously hurries him into the bathroom, strips off his bloody clothes and turns on the shower. Later, as he stands naked, she hovers over him with her tray of bandages and antibiotics and analgesics, and in her teary eyes is the fear that, were it not for luck and his stubborn will, she would have lost him.

She walks him over to his bed, tucks him in and lies beside him. There is no smooching or sweet-talking or romantic prelude; for the first time they are lying in the same bed and somehow the transition from being friends to having sex seems a natural and even an inexorable progression. He had never slept with a white woman before, so from the moment he enters her, his mind wavers between curiosity and the promiscuity of having strayed into illicit territory. Detected in the act in another time and in another place, he would have been risking a lynching and she thirty days' hard labor irrespective of the consensual nature. The searing pain in his back inhibits the reciprocal movement of his hips, so he lies practically still as she willingly takes charge and brings them both home to mutual satisfaction. Afterwards, they lie motionless. She exudes the heat of the afterglow with a faint, unfamiliar odor of sweat, not unpleasant but unfamiliar. And so they had "made love", though he wasn't sure it was love but a consummation, a celebratory bonding of two friends. Now that it is over he questions whether their relationship has been forever changed, for his carnal mind is no less contented than if they had been lovers. But whereas to him it was just one night, to her it might be an inaugural event.

He looks across the room at the photo of his father. There is an impish hint of approval on his handsome face. He gets up and looks in the mirror on the dresser and sees his father, his eyes, his nose, his mouth, no less real than if he were on the other side of an empty frame. He looks back at the bed. He is seeing Maria instead of Paula reaching out to him with both hands, beckoning him back to bed, and in that instant he is filled with shame, the son emulating the father, reliving his life to perfection, following in his footsteps to the grave.

By morning the rejection of his book, the specter of street thugs and the deadly sensation of a knife in his back have all but drifted to the back of his mind. And when the early sun seeps through the curtains, he remains under the covers listening to the thud and scrape of snow plows and the screaming of tires fighting to free themselves from the ice.

He gets up and tugs open the venetian blinds. It's a bright new picturesque day in Harlem. The street is lined with cars, tightly parked and asleep under tons of snow, as though in hibernation while city plows work around them as best they can, purposely shoveling more snow onto their roofs. Houses are capped with snow like giant cupcakes with cream cheese frosting. The deciduous pussy willow just outside the window is weighted with ice, her branches now and then snapping and crackling and falling to the earth. Children are up and down the street, indifferent to the cold, rolling in the snow drifts, building snowmen, tossing snowballs in the air. He thinks about last night and how terrifying was the same street outside his door. He is seeing himself spread-eagled on a patch of reddened snow, a knife protruding from his back and the same children hovering over his dead body. Now the same street is a picture of gaiety and serenity.

He climbs back into bed and clicks on the television across the room, props himself up and prepares to watch the news, the usual fare of murders, muggings and miscellaneous crimes. Then the next story grabs his attention. The CBS newsman is reporting from Woodville, a sleepy hamlet in the Long Island suburbs. He is surrounded by a crowd of curious excited neighbors and is pointing to a wooden cross, the symbol of the Christian faith. Four feet tall and crudely built with slow-burning firewood, it was planted in the middle of a snow-covered lawn. It is inches away from the front steps of someone's home and is the focus of everyone's attention. The camera zooms in and reveals that the cross is singed and what was snow around the base is now a pool of water. The field reporter knocks on the door and a delicate black woman emerges, timidly at first like someone who had been in solitary confinement and is glad to see a friendly face. She is wrapped in her night gown, bed slippers on her feet, her hair wildly tousled. Evidently she had been rudely awakened. He queries the woman, as he holds the microphone between them. Squinting into the bright lights of the camera, she speaks softly with an island accent. Her words are firm, deliberate, her voice controlled, her emotions restrained.

"My husband and I had our closing yesterday. We're tired from all the packing and moving. Trying to get some sleep. We heard a dog bark, got up, looked out, and this is what we see, a cross on fire on our property welcoming us to the neighborhood."

The house is a hundred-year-old Tudor-styled house flanked by houses of similar style. The sameness of their architectural features all the way down the block and across the street conveys the appearance of one big close-knit family. Even the snow-flecked hedges from house to house are practically linked together, the illusion of neighborliness.

"Where'd you move from?" the reporter asks.

"From Brooklyn. Been renting in the projects in Bed Stuy. Saving for years for this dream house. But now ..."

The interview is interrupted when a man, presumably her husband, a huge barrel-chested man in pajama shirt and short pants bursts out of the house like a madman. He is holding a hunting rifle in the crook of his arm. He raises it in the air and shoots off a round. The neighbors rush back from the lawn and scatter in all directions like roaches. He grabs the microphone and starts to speak and the station's expletive bleeping mechanism is immediately put to the test.

"No mutha(bleep)ing person is goin' drive me an' my wife out o' this (bleep)ing house. All you mutha(bleep)ers want to bring your (bleep)ing Jim Crow (bleep)ing laws to Woodville." Raising his Remington shotgun again in the air, he shouts out to no one in particular: "Next time you mutha(bleep)ers come I'll be waiting for yuhs. I got something for your (bleep)ing

~ 140 ~

(bleep)." He steps forward, grabs the partially burnt crucifix, snaps it into pieces with his bare hands and tosses them into the street.

The reporter's face has turned the color of a beet. He says to the lady softly, "Excuse me, I didn't get your names."

She shouts out for the neighbors within the range of her voice to get the message. "We are the Brathwaites from Brooklyn and we are here to stay." With that the two turn their backs and reenter their new home.

The scene comes to an end, the station breaks for a commercial and Mark is still staring at the tube seeing the reporter and his crew packing up their gear and moving on. The Woodville neighbors are back in their beds and fast asleep while the Brathwaites will stay up all night listening, waiting, watching for the next sign. Next day the story in the news will likely be about a crazed man brandishing a gun. Was it a licensed gun? Did he endanger the neighbors? Did he fire the weapon? And the burning cross will be an inane mischievous prank. But Mark is not a naïf, he knows better. A burning cross, the mark of the Klan.

Then he switches to WFCA, the channel that carries the local news, and the newscaster prepares to welcome her viewers to another glorious day in the land of the free. While they were all slumbering peacefully, the news people had done their duty and recorded every misfortune under the cover of night to befall these brave denizens. She knows well that they have long been numbed, wearied, indifferent to human disasters and will pay her little attention, yet she insists on doling out her morning dosage of bad tidings. She dons her mask of horrified dismay and begins to read.

"It was reported that last night, sometime around eleven, a young gentleman identified as the grandson of Conroy Solomon, well-known New York City Councilman and close friend of Mayor Beacon, was wheeled into the emergency room of Harlem Hospital, having lost an inordinate amount of blood and suffering from what the doctors said was a life-threatening laceration of the neck. The gentleman's name is Elroy Solomon. If anyone knows how this young man came to be assaulted, please come forward and talk to the police."

Mark sits up erect. He knows vaguely of the councilman though they have never met. He is said to be a stalwart supporter of civic matters in the community.

"According to Mr. Solomon's companion, Benjamin Hanks, he was approached and assaulted on 135th Street as the two made their home from the cinema. The knife-wielding assailant has not been identified but is said to be of light-brown complexion, of average height and disguised as a man of business impressively attired in suit and tie. While this young man clings to life the Metropolitan Police is asking your help in tracking down this individual who may be dangerous and who needs to be taken off the streets before he does harm to another unsuspecting pedestrian. Our best wishes go out to Councilor Solomon and his family."

She turns the page and, without missing a beat, segues into another bloody scene. Mark and Paula look at each other.

"Yeah, that's me," he says, "the Nightcrawler of Harlem, walking the streets at night, looking to harm and kill my own people. I need to be taken off the streets." But she is visibly not amused, blood drains from her face.

He must find a way to tell his side of the story but he distrusts the police; he learned his lesson many years ago in their bungling of the investigation surrounding his father's untimely death. Moreover the mugging is fast becoming a national story and he has been portrayed as the villain in an astute reversal of the roles, the victim and the assailants.

He muses: *Should he forget the past and surrender himself to the integrity of the law?* He feels a moral compulsion to clear up the matter with the police but seeks a second opinion.

"Paula, what do you think I should do? Go down to the precinct and tell them the truth?"

"Don't be crazy, Mark. It's your word against two."

"But hey, one look at me and they'll see I don't fit the profile of a street thug. A man in a suit and tie walking home from a business meeting."

"Mark, listen! You were a black man in a suit. A black man in a suit is still a black man. You can't take a chance. You almost killed the blood relative of someone important in this community. They need to pin it on someone … anyone."

11 – Harlem Hospital

He decides to go down to Harlem Hospital to look his assailant in the face. He will take his chances and attempt to clear his name with the next of kin. He holds no rancor in his heart for the boy. He and Benjamin Hanks had been duped by a cowardly and opportunistic enemy. Pitting blacks against blacks is one of the oldest tactics in their playbook. Ben, his partner in crime, did the right thing getting him to the hospital posthaste. He, Mark, could well have been the one rolled into the emergency ward on a gurney or today be stiff as a plank in the cold drawer of a morgue.

He forgives the lie that he was the assailant, for what else could they say? However, it was preposterous that anyone could think him capable of a street crime, much less harming a brother, whom he had defended assiduously in his writings and on whose behalf he had paid a debt and was wearing a battle scar to prove it. He dons a lumber jacket, sweat shirt and jeans, and sets off to meet the injured Elroy.

Harlem Hospital on Lexington Avenue sits aloof from a cluster of starkly decrepit buildings but there has never been a question of its service to the community with the same dedication to the poorest as to the richest. It had been credited with saving the life of the revered Reverend Martin Luther King, Jr. after he had been stabbed by a deranged woman on a Harlem street. Now the same institution has in its hands the life of a street punk. What a paradox in the rule book of the profession!

As he approaches the building, men, women and children are gathering in a motley crowd on the hospital grounds. A neon Emergency sign looms above their heads. Ambulances are coming and going. A muted buzzing among them echoes a common concern. He taps the shoulder of a man standing alone. He wears a knitted hat that resembles an air sock that drapes from the top of his head to below the nape of his neck; in it he stores his dreadlocks.

"Excuse me. What happened?"

"You en hear? Young man strugglin' fer he life up on de t'ird floor. De grandson o' Councilor Conroy. I don' know de boy but de councilman does do a lot o' good fer de people o' dis community. I had to come down to show my sympat'y."

"How about his parents?"

"De mother is Shonelle Solomon, de card reader. Look she standin' over there yonder."

"How about the boy's father?"

He laughs. "De boy father could be anyone o' we."

He thinks it would be good for his own soul if he ventured over to Mr. Solomon, introduced himself and offered his sympathy. But the gentleman is encircled by a hundred fawning, tearful constituents reaching out to him in a circle so densely packed he is lost in their midst. Even if he elbowed his way to within arm's length, there would be no chance to whisper a confession in the man's ear. A peek through a gap in the crowd reveals the Councilman. He is a hump-shouldered elderly man, with a dignified manner of acknowledging the adulation of the people. A pipe hangs elegantly from his lips.

Hundreds of people are huddled in sympathy at the foot of the hospital, seemingly more on behalf of a beloved government official than in caring for Elroy. Suddenly he feels a hollow space forming in the pit of his stomach. What wrath would descend on his innocent head right here on the steps of Harlem Hospital if the people only knew he was the one who had almost severed the neck of the gentleman's grandson.

The woman identified by the Jamaican as the mother is mostly ignored by the people. She stands alone and apart from the crowd. He approaches her with a comforting word.

"Ma'am, I'm sorry about your son. I wish him well." Far from distraught, as one might have expected, her eyes deep-set in a strikingly beautiful face, are dry, her expression remarkably calm.

She turns to him and says softly with a fatalistic tone of resignation in her voice. "I knew this would goin' happen, I knew it. I seen it straight up in the cards. The signs were right there for me to see this was goin' to happen to my son. Elroy is a good boy, he wouldn't hurt a fly. Whoever did this to him, I pray to God he rot in hell." The words in his ears are like a witch's curse.

He is not about to disabuse the card reader of the notion that her son was an angel and it is clear to him there is no room in her heart for either truth or redemption. His only interest now is in the whereabouts of the manuscript, for therein lies the trail that will lead him to the ones who hired her son to do their dirty bidding. It is logical to assume she was the one who relieved her injured son of his ill-gotten loot. It is a delicate time to broach the subject but somehow, sometime, he will need her help to follow the trail.

12 – The Councilman's Daughter

Holyfield is ensconced in his armchair, his head cocked back, his eyes closed, his mouth wide open. His chest rises and falls almost imperceptibly but sufficiently to prove the old man is resting and has not suddenly succumbed to his final cardiac arrest. The paper has gone to press; his work is done.

Mark strolls over to his own office, an eleven-foot-square cubicle with one chair, a desk and an Olivetti typewriter. Immediately his eyes are drawn to a package elegantly gift-wrapped, bound with red ribbon and bearing his name on the side in large cursive writing. It sits on his desk. He searches his memory for any reason he should be the recipient of a gift and none comes to mind. He grabs a letter opener, rips open the package and is jolted back by the sight of the contents. Staring him in his face are the pages of his stolen manuscript. The book is shredded to pieces and smeared with dry blood. Enclosed is a leaflet blazoned with the fearsome KKK insignia that has terrorized many a black man and woman. It depicts their infamous white cross against a red background with a drop of blood in the center. He is repulsed at the sight of it all but quickly recovers his composure. He holds the envelope disdainfully between thumb and finger and drops it into the wastepaper basket. The rest he also discards.

He decides to mention it to no one, surely not to his intemperate friend, Holyfield, fearing one of his precipitous outbursts that could well be his last. Once again his stomach is aflutter. He is determined now more than ever. Seeing his mutilated book smeared with blood reminds him that the hounds are still on his trail. They think he will run to Thatcher, his tail between his legs, and surrender his book, his principles, the truth, while in the dark the parasitic rats hatch their pernicious plans for New York.

By morning he will restore all five hundred pages from his electronic files. And they know it. It was just their cowardly and morbid attempt at intimidation.

As night falls, he weighs his options. He is tossing and turning in bed, mentally fatigued. She sleeps beside him contented and still as a rock. Eventually he drifts off, and in the morning he performs his duty. Then afterwards, as usual, she reaches for a cigarette and goes off to the bathroom to begin the morning's ablutions. He reaches for the TV remote. The tube flares to another hour of depressing news. The newscaster puts on her dour face and prepares to deliver.

"We have breaking news. The grandson of well-known Councilor Conroy Solomon has died overnight in the Harlem Hospital."

Her opening line strikes him like a brick. He props himself up on his elbows.

"Teenager Elroy Solomon was attacked with a knife by a well-dressed man as he made his way home from the movies with a friend, reported his companion, Mr. Hanks. Our sympathy goes out to the Councilman and his family.

Now the weather ..."

Her lips continue moving but he hears no sound. He rolls out of bed and stares at the floor. The telephone rings. Maybe someone he knows is calling to say, "Watch the news", but he does not answer. What does it all mean now that the boy is dead? He, who has never lifted a finger to hurt another human being, has taken a life, albeit in defense of his own.

A police siren wails from afar, grows louder and louder, then fades in the distance and melds into the cacophony of morning traffic. He has done nothing wrong, he is convinced of his innocence; it was his either life or the boy's, and he is glad he prevailed. He would like nothing more than to tell his side of the story, of being stalked in the dark, of the knife in his back, the cuff to the stomach, the surrender of his money, the threat to his life and his reflexive action, not to kill but to defend.

How can he tell them what really happened and unburden himself when the only witness, the one they called Mr. Benjamin Hanks, is not on his side, and with good reason to lie? And the one to die is the kin of a revered politician, one with such stature as to qualify for breaking news preempting the all important weather forecast. Old man Solomon had said on the news that someone must pay. In fact the one who should pay has already paid with his life for attacking an innocent person making his way home on that dark night of snow, rain and sleet. But the truth must stay hidden to protect the reputation of the Solomon name, though the family should have had the foresight to discipline and raise the errant Elroy to be a law abiding citizen. So now he will say nothing; his conscience is clear.

HIS FATHER'S FOOTSTEPS

◆ ◆ ◆

Two days later, the body of Elroy Solomon is reposing next to the altar of The Church of Divine Intervention in precisely the same spot where sixteen years earlier the body of Daniel Maynard had lain. This eerie coincidence is not lost on Mark but it is not for him to judge the dead; they await their final judgment in the beyond.

It is standing room only, as dozens of Elroy's peers swell the congregation in this small but elegant chapel at the corner of 116th and 7th. There is no doubt in Mark's mind, as he sits in the back of the church with Paula at his side, that most of the adults have come to pay their respects, not to the dead but to the living in the person of the councilman seated in the front row. Strangely, the boy's mother, Shonelle Solomon is nowhere in sight. What depth of disregard for her own blood could cause a mother to stay away from the funeral of her own son? By the same token one might expect the father to crawl out of the shadows for humanity's sake but neither parent is present.

Mark is present neither to mourn nor extend his condolences; he is here to meet Benjamin Hanks. The boy is nowhere to be seen.

Brother Sheldon puts on his funereal face and steps to the lectern. He intones an extemporaneous eulogy picking the words out of the air, for in Mark's ears they are nothing more than a steady stream of blabber as the pastor proceeds to exalt the deceased as an angel about to ascend to Heaven, one whose life on earth had been cut short. Now Mark is having a flashback to that night in the dark when the boy stabbed him in the back as he uttered the foulest language, calling him names under his malodorous breath, taunting him like the Devil himself, saying to his partner, "Leave 'im to me, he's mine." Now bouncing off these holy walls and all the way up to the clerestory are a continuous ripple of undeserved Amens and a burst of moans that border on the ridiculous.

"This young man, this beautiful creature, has been plucked from our community in the prime of his youth just as he was about to flower and flourish and contribute to society in the true tradition of the Solomon heritage, a heritage that has given us …"

At the mention of the Solomon name, the applause cuts through the eulogy and only accentuates the absurdity of these pretentious words out of the clergyman's mouth to Mark's ears.

Brother Sheldon waits for silence, then acknowledges the presence of Mayor Beacon seated next to Councilor Solomon. Furthermore he proceeds to convey a message of sympathy from the Governor of New York and it is obvious that this outpouring of condolences and encomiums had little to do with the deceased but was on account of everyone's love for his grandfather.

On the spur of the moment Mark decides to join the viewing line to see his assailant's face for the first time. Paula declines. The young are the first in line. Their faces are sad and drawn, boys and girls dressed in black hooded sweaters, saggy jeans and unlaced sneakers, the raiment of the street. He reaches the coffin and looks into the face of Elroy Solomon. He is indeed an angel; he wears the most cherubic smile, as if he had confessed with his last breath and had been absolved of his latest crime. He reaches in, places his hand on the boy's brow and says, "I too forgive you, brother."

At that moment in his peripheral vision his gesture of forgiveness has been observed by a young boy. It is Benjamin Hanks. He finds it hard to believe that the boy with an ingenuous air about him is Ben. He looks even younger than he did that night. His gold chain still loops ostentatiously halfway down to his waist. His clothes are the same grey oversized sweater and baggy jeans, except that his underwear is no longer on display.

"Hi Ben!" The boy doesn't answer and turns his face.

"Remember me?"

"Listen, mister. I ain't got no business with you. I come to see my friend."

"We need to talk, Ben."

"Leave me alone, man."

"I just want to ask you about that night, you and me and Elroy."

"What night? I don' know what you talkin' 'bout, man. Never seen you befo', awright?"

Ben glances at his friend in the coffin, turns and walks briskly down the aisle with Mark in pursuit. He reaches almost to the exit and is about to escape when, standing in his way with her arms outstretched, swanlike across the aisle, almost to the ends of the pews, is Paula. She grabs one arm, Mark the other, and all three exit the church, arm in arm, and no one seems to notice that the boy's arm is locked so he cannot escape.

Soon they are huddling at the side of the church on a marble bench in a small graveyard surrounded by old mildewed headstones, oak trees and dead flowers. They are seated next to a freshly dug hole beneath two planks of wood. Alongside is a pair of snow shovels stuck in a neat pile of clayey dirt.

"This could've been yours, Ben," Mark says, as he points to the empty grave awaiting his friend.

The boy shrugs.

"I didn't come here to get even, Ben. So you can relax." He releases his grip.

The boy has seemingly lost his desire to flee since there is no tension or vengeful feelings between them. But he knows they came to the church to see him.

"Wha' do you want from me, mister?"

"I need your help, Ben. The people who paid you for the book is *your* enemy and mine. They are against all black people wherever they live. They are called the Ku Klux Klan."

"Look, mister, I ain't tellin' you no lie, it was Elroy who took duh money, not me."

"Who was it that paid him for the papers?"

"I don' know, some guy."

"Do you know his name?"

"No."

"Do you know where he lives?"

"No. Only Elroy know duh guy and where he's at. And Elroy ain't talkin' no mo'. "

"How come you got involved?"

"Elroy come to me and say he know how we can make some quick bread and that some guy he meet at duh carwash duh same day on 123rd where he work at offer him five hundred bucks that he would split between me and him, that all we have to do is take some papers off some guy. They say duh guy live on 135th Street."

"How'd you know I was the guy?"

"He say duh guy had a scar face."

"Did the people with the payoff want me dead?"

"He say it was up to me and Elroy, that he just want duh papers, that duh papers was a will duh guy steal from him and he want them back. So Elroy say if he double duh money he would get duh papers back but only f'r a t'ousand, not a dime less and in advance."

"So did he get paid in advance?"

"Yes, but only half, he say we would get duh rest when he get duh papers."

"So where is the money?"

"I don' know, man. Ask Elroy mother. She is duh one that take his t'ings home from duh hospital includin' duh papers in a bag."

Mark is further perplexed. If the boy is speaking the truth the trail somehow needs to be traced from the Solomon's household to the one who recruited Elroy as his hitman, and since, according to Ben, Shonelle Solomon had the book in her possession she must have turned it over to someone else. And *that* someone is his tormentor.

"Know his mother?" he asks Ben.

"She and Elroy didn't get along," Ben says. "Bitch almost kill 'im one day with a poker stick. They had to call duh pigs."

"He was your good friend, wasn't he?"

"Duh best, man, duh best." He looks away as his eyes moisten.

"Know where she lives?"

"Lincoln Heights on Sevent' and 124."

"By the way, y'know, you and me, we're both in trouble with the law. They want me for murder and when I talk they're gonna want you for a felony. If we tell the truth to the police we can both go free. They can't touch Elroy."

The boy shrugs his shoulders. "They'll put me away f'r good. Too much baggage. Y'see, I got a record. Killed a man in the pool hall two years ago. He owed me money. But it was self-defense, y'see? I was a minor so I caught a break in Corrections."

"Why are you telling me this?"

"So you know I would help you out but I can't. See?"

Mark feels a soft feeling welling up inside of him for the boy.

"Since you didn't get paid off, you got any money?" he asks him.

"Not really."

Mark empties his pockets and hands the boy a twenty and in return expects a modicum of contrition. Instead he gets the eerie feeling he has just paid part of his own bounty.

The boy says "Thanks, dude" and gets up and walks away.

Mark calls out to him. "Come see me sometime. You know where I live."

He turns to Paula. "Let's go find Miss Solomon. Express our condolences to the bereaved."

"Do I detect a trifle bit of sarcasm?" She asks. "After all, she didn't bother to even attend the funeral of her own son. Can you believe that?"

"Well, that's not my concern. I just need to know who got their hands on the book. If she was the one who took possession of her son's things at the hospital, then she might have passed it on. Whoever had it next decided to shred it and deface it with blood and drop it off at the office in an attempt to intimidate me."

They walk the eight blocks to Lincoln Heights, which is in reality the lower-income city projects but wears the false patina of luxury apartments by virtue of the euphemistic "Heights". From a distance he sees a cluster of gray toy-like boxes pocked with tiny holes for windows but as he draws closer there are signs of human habitation, over-hanging terraces, clothes and rugs hung on the railings, and even signs of modernity, the profusion of antennae and television dishes on the roofs. Down below, between the buildings, are immovable concrete benches for the old folk and, for the young, basketball hoops and graffiti-smeared walls given over to the talented, the artful and the dispirited. He sees Lincoln Heights as an encampment of the poor, the forgotten and the hopeless flung together in this cluster of nondescript boxes. For these people there is no help forthcoming, for, according to the media, the City is on the brink of bankruptcy and he finds it incomprehensible that in this rich, fat country of this United States, one state can go broke.

He checks the directory at the communal mail kiosk and sees that Shonelle Solomon resides at number 13. Along a winding walkway littered with Styrofoam cups, paper plates and empty fast-food packets, they come to the basement apartment at the far end. Not surprisingly the number 13 is missing. The entrance is below street level and descending the steps to the door has the feel of entering a mine shaft. He knocks on the door but there's no answer. He waits a while and knocks again. Maybe she's asleep or not at home. He scribbles his name and telephone number on the funeral program. "Maybe she'll call, maybe she won't," he says matter-of-factly. He squeezes the paper between the door and the frame and is about to leave when, to their surprise, the door swings open. He yells from the doorway, "Hello, is anyone at home?" Again, there is no answer. Treading cautiously, they enter and are instantly struck by an overwhelming stink, the stench of putrefaction like the smell that emanates from a pile of compost. She appears nauseated and runs back out the door where, bending over, she proceeds to retch convulsively on the steps. Pinching his nose, he gropes his way from the interior to the kitchen, then to a bedroom where the door has been left ajar. Shonelle is lying across the bed completely naked and perpendicular to the headboard, her legs hanging to the floor. Her legs are splayed grotesquely as if she had been violated. Her eyes stare quizzically at the intruder, fear and astonishment anchored to her face. The drawers of her dresser had been yanked out from their recesses and her personal things had been rummaged through and strewn all around the floor. The intruder was in search of something. At her head is an empty plastic bag bearing the name Harlem Hospital, the kind of receptacle that totes patients' personal belongings. He recognizes the paper placed over her genitalia as a show of disrespect and lack of compassion for the dead woman. It is another of those propaganda flyers that had been delivered to his office. It bears the infamous KKK insignia. He folds it in half and pockets it for no reason in particular. A nylon stocking is tied tightly around her neck and a thin trail of dry blood leads from her mouth to the bed to the floor. It is clear that whoever killed this woman had used her blood to smear the pages of his book, before leaving their official mark of hatred.

He reaches for the telephone on her night table. Still braving the smell of death, he is about to dial 911 before he sees the line has been ripped from the wall. With his handkerchief he methodically erases his fingerprints from the receiver and walks out the door. He finds his friend still heaving from the odor of putrescent flesh, but more likely from revulsion at the whole sordid affair.

"Jesus Christ, Mark! What kind of men are these? We are the ones that know their goddamned secrets. Not her!"

She is sobbing uncontrollably. He retrieves his note from the door and hustles her away from the steps and the smell and the crime. Deep down he is certain, beyond the shadow of a doubt, that he'll be next.

13 – The Intrusion

All he ever wanted since the day he came to America was to find the one who killed his father, and that the killer, man or woman, was made to pay a price that was deserved and just in the eyes of a civilized society. Then if justice did not prevail to quench his torment, he would take it upon himself to unload his vengeance on the head of the guilty. Once his father's death was avenged he would pack his valise and return to his home in Barbados, rejoin his family, try to pick up the pieces of his shattered life and start again. He would lament leaving behind all things beautiful and virtuous about America. In many ways he had grown to love her; in other ways not, but would not be sparing in his gratitude for all her good. But when the time came he would turn his back on the ugly, leaving her wicked in the hands of the Creator.

He had used the only talent he possessed in an attempt to reveal and trap the killer. Now the book he has written has become a lightning rod attracting unto itself the vilest of creatures and the most heinous of crimes. Through the years he has witnessed man's inhumanity towards humanity but the latest display has left him numb and sick to his stomach. In one depressing moment he wonders if he should abandon the mission and let the killer go undetected. Would it bring an end to the blood and the carnage that follow in his trail? Then he remembers his promise to himself, to his family and to his father: he would not give up the chase.

Ermajean in her letters says his brother still mourns his father, that he absentmindedly checks the mailbox now and then. Thirty-something years old, a decade later, and he still cannot let go.

"Ma says you should come home and leave the wicked in God's hands. 'Revenge is mine to pay, saith the Lord,' she murmurs in her nightly prayers."

Mark and Paula walk away from Number 13 Lincoln Heights, horrified and saddened, thinking of the savagery they have just witnessed, a new and incomprehensible dimension in the playbook of the Klan. In stunned silence they hurry down 125th Street. She sobs relentlessly. He hands her his kerchief to stem her flood of tears. He slips into a phone booth, drops a quarter in the slot and dials 911. "There's a dead woman at 13 Lincoln Heights," he says and hangs up without giving his name.

They walk to the corner where he picks up a copy of *The Amsterdam Daily*. A cursory glance through the pages of the tabloid shows the police are no closer to profiling the killer of the Solomon boy.

"Why would they?" she asks through her tears.

"Well, a couple o' cars did drive by that night, slowed and moved off again. Wonder if anybody stepped forward, called the police, said he saw this guy with a scarred face swinging a knife."

He takes some comfort in knowing he and Ben are in a virtual standoff: if the boy fingers him to the police as the one who killed his friend, he only incriminates himself when he speaks in his own defense against the mark of a knife incision as indisputable evidence. But then he looks back and muses, should he have gone to the police before the tables were turned, before he became the "villain"? It was his fear of the law that had kept him silent and out of the light. He had learned from Sergeant Kaufmann the law would not be always on his side. Paula too, in her skepticism, had told him the law could not be trusted. He remembers her words that night: "You were a black man in a suit. A black man in a suit is still a black man."

All the while he keeps seeing the face of dead Shonelle Solomon, an innocent soul caught up in a roulette of murder and spite, one who had the misfortune of having come in contact with his book and, having seen the intruder's face, had to be punished and then exterminated. He ponders the circle of death in which he finds himself; still he believes the secret files would eventually lead him to the one. But he keeps saying to himself over and over: *People are dying, Mark, people are being killed all on account of your book.*

Nevertheless he cannot waver from his course; he must find a way to have it printed, bound between hard covers and out in the open for the benefit of the public. To publish the work by himself is sadly out of the question, for he lacks the money or resources. No publisher, big or small, wants to touch it. Pemberton is the only exception but their terms are restrictive: they want to gut the pages, remove all references to the enemy, leaving his book weak, effete and ineffectual.

Then the man had the gall to say to him with a straight face: "Mr. Maynard, we are willing to take it off your hands for a nominal sum just so it doesn't get out into the open ..."

Was he in cahoots with the Klan or was he a member himself? Mark is wondering but the thought does not reach the level of suspicion, for he cannot imagine a reputable publisher like Pemberton wallowing in a cesspool of such disreputable men. But then who was the man sitting anonymously at the meeting and indirectly offering a handsome sum for the book? Was he posing as a book merchant? Was his name Hamilton? What, if any, was Thatcher's cut if the offer had been accepted there and then? Who had recruited Elroy at the car wash to do his dirty deed? He could see the boy's eyes light up at the prospect of a payday of a thousand dollars. On the way home he ransacks his brain for possible answers to these questions but none stands out as a credible lead.

They are now at their doorstep at 127 West 135th and Mark forages in his coat pocket for the keys to open first the outer metal gate, then behind it a solid door made of oak that would withstand the most violent storm. A chill enters his body. He freezes. The steel bars have been ripped from their hinges. The metal has been mangled, snipped at the joints, and strewn on the steps. A jagged hole appears in the wood where the deadbolts had been clamped to the doorframe. He pushes the door. It swings open. The interior is in darkness. The house has been broken into. Someone is inside or maybe someone has entered and left. They sidle into the hallway, slowly, stealthily, backs against the wall. He turns on the light in the foyer. The only sound is the screaming of an electric kettle. She runs to the kitchen and pulls the cord from the wall. There is no one there but hot white steam fills the air from floor to ceiling. He heads to the living room expecting to see everything they own of value has been taken. But no, the fixtures: the wood-encased floor model TV, the vintage radio, the prized stereo equipment, the Ethan Allen furniture; they are all there in place and intact. Then he goes to his study and is stricken with such unspeakable horror he falls to his knees and clasps a hand to his chest. His computer has been smashed to smithereens lying on the floor in a barely recognizable tangle of plastic casings, glass, knobs, buttons, keys, cables. His magnetic tapes that stored all his files were ripped from their reels, unwound and lying in a spaghetti-like jumble, strewn across the room along with the contents of his drawers: papers, pens, staples, stamps, ink canisters ... His study is in chaos, his chair upended and tossed to the wall. His metallic file cabinet has been emptied and lying on its side. His telephone sits on a corner of his desk, silently like a hotline to Hell.

"The book, Mark! The book!" she hollers.

He stands now, his hands on his hips, his heart racing, fuming, staring incredulously at the spot where his computer with all his hard labor had been sitting.

He mumbles through his teeth, "No, they no longer care about the book, they came looking for the secret papers. Bastards!"

He flips the chair upright and slumps into it gratified that all is not lost, that the cache of secrets they are seeking is still in his possession, stashed away for safe keeping. He had stuck the papers under his father's bed between the mattress and the box support, a symbolic hiding place. Still he knows the destruction of his equipment was an act of intimidation, a warning not to proceed.

The phone rings but he ignores it. She picks it up and says "hello!" She hands him the phone. The voice at the other end says, "We didn't get what we wanted. But if you recreate that book, you're a dead nigga. You're just lucky you got a guardian angel."

He doesn't recognize the strong deep-throated voice; it's not the voice of the mysterious man who shook his hand at Thatcher's meeting; that voice was high-pitched, unctuous and tremulous like the rattle of a snake.

"He said I got a guardian angel," he says to Paula. "Is that you?" And they both know the answer, for she is in the protection of her Klansman father and Marks happens to be in the penumbra of her protection for the time being. He doesn't want him killed just yet; he doesn't want to devastate his beloved daughter and run the risk of losing her forever.

There is no point in informing the police; burglaries and break-ins are common events in the neighborhood and are rarely reported. On the rare occasions they do turn up to investigate, they ask one or two perfunctory questions, jot on their notepads copious notes about what was taken and the value thereof and nothing ever comes of their investigations.

Questioning the neighbors about whether they might have heard strange noises would have been an exercise in futility, though the process of dismantling a steel gate and blasting a hole in an oaken door must have sent shockwaves across the street and all the way down the block. No one ever claims to have seen or heard anything, so the unfortunate homeowner will do what everyone does in the aftermath of an intrusion: send for a locksmith, replace all the barriers and pray. That's the way it is in this marginalized fringe of the big city.

Paula flicks on the television for whatever distraction would lure him out of his despondency. They learn that all across America winter is inflicting its misery. For the first time snow falls in the state of Florida. Heavy blizzards wallop New England all winter and claim a hundred lives in the process. Meanwhile San Francisco is rocked by the most horrific earthquake in years. And the New York media cast their sights far and wide, to the farthest corners of America to report on these phenomena while on their doorstep an insidious enemy is stealthily creeping into their own backyard like forest snakes, infecting whole communities with their venom.

14 – Ella's Diner

After the day's gruesome discovery in Lincoln Heights and the tragic disaster under his own roof, his nerves yearn for a break to save his mind from the brink of insanity. As the long afternoon hours drag from midday to dusk, he resigns himself to sitting quietly, reading the *Amsterdam News*.

Buried in the back of the tabloid on page 23, next to the Sports Section, is a story that grabs his attention. It is an article under a picture of a woman named Lillian Brathwaite. It says she lived in Woodville in the borough of Long Island and had been a resident of public housing in Brooklyn until recently. She is standing on the street frantically watching the flames as they lick and lunge at the remaining walls of her new home. The report says she was on her way home from the Long Island Railroad station when she saw the smoke spiraling and when she neared the house the firemen were dousing the ashes just for the sake of it. She said her husband didn't make it. "He worked at night, he was a strong sleeper". She spoke these words to the same reporter who had covered the incident of the burning cross the Klan had planted on her lawn months before. Her husband, fearlessly brandishing a shotgun that day, had said he wasn't going to be forced out of his house no matter what ... and he wasn't. No mention was made in the newspaper of who or what had caused the fire, no witnesses, no suspicions, no comments from neighbors, except everyone said it was the fault of the Brathwaites; they should have known better; they had dared to move into forbidden territory in the first place, provoking the good citizens of Woodville and bringing notoriety to their bucolic suburban village. There is no doubt in his mind that the Klan had torched the house of the black family.

Two o'clock in the morning finds him still awake in his chair and fully dressed. His troubled mind, alternating all night from one decision to another, has now formulated a plan of action. He has decided not to wait for the Klan to come to him; he decides to go out and meet them head-on. First he will retrace his steps, go back to Pemberton and confront Thatcher and his man. What does the publisher know about the organization? Who were the people prepared to quash the publication of his book for a fee? Who would better know than Thatcher himself?

At the break of dawn he tiptoes into the bedroom.

"I'm going," he whispers.

"Where're you going?"

"Goin' to meet the man," he says.

She needs no further explanation. In the parlance of the day "the man" is the enemy. She had often heard Mark on the telephone repeatedly placing calls to Pemberton, asking to speak to Thatcher and had seen disappointment etched on his face when he was told the man was not available.

The hands of the clock point vertically to six. It is much too early and dark for a trip to the city. Undaunted by warnings never again to walk the streets of Harlem in the dark, he strolls down to the coffee shop at the corner of 125th and 7th to meet his friend, and his dad's best friend, Carmichael He plans to drill him for everything he knows about the killing and to solicit his suspicions, whatever they might be.

One by one the street lamps give way to morning light. The night has had its time and begins to withdraw, casting its shadows between tall buildings where the homeless and the hopeless still hunker down under their makeshift blankets. On the sidewalk three or four white-bearded old men crouch over an oil drum stoked with a pyre of burning wood, rubbing their hands and passing from one to the other a flask likely of cheap wine. But this aura of despair quickly vanishes with the rise of the sun when the street comes alive, the traffic surges, the sidewalks hum, the bodega owners turn up to unlock and swing open their metal gates. Harlem welcomes a new day.

Ella's 24-hour diner is a typical New York diner, a basic Quonset-type structure of corrugated steel that caters to truck drivers, night crawlers, early risers and men with hangovers hankering for a cure. It was named after Ella Fitzgerald of jazz fame, the darling of the people. Inside is a long laminate counter complemented with a dozen red-cushioned stools, a pinball machine and a few cedar tables in private booths against the walls. A Wurlitzer jukebox in the far corner is played by remote control. But this early in the day no one comes to the diner for music or games; they are there for the camaraderie, the conversation and the coffee. This is the place to which Carmichael had invited him a long time ago to mingle with the blue collars and the white collars of Harlem.

Today he plans to stay clear of *The Renaissance*, for how can he muster the nerve to tell Holyfield that all their work including backup had been destroyed and see him gasp for air and clasp a hand to his chest. He had known him to suffer spells of severe heart pains for lesser traumas than this. The book was near and dear to his heart.

As for him, he is guilty of not having lifted a finger in recent days to tackle his Sunday columns, for no topic comes readily to mind. He can only hope that Holyfield will take into account his distracted mind, for he cannot bring himself to think of anything else but the Klan while the name Hamilton pervades his every thought, his every dream. He could serialize *The New Chapter* in a whole month of columns but the story needs to be told beyond the parochial concerns of the community. It needs to be read and to seep into the consciousness of every urbanite and suburbanite in New York before it is too late and the tentacles of the Klan are dug in far and wide and thereafter become ineradicable.

Carmichael is seated in a booth at a table set for four, punching a calculator and jotting notes on a pad. He stops at Ella's every morning to be caffeinated before he heads downtown to his job at Bank of America. Today he wears a dark suit, white shirt, maroon tie and sparkling gold cufflinks, the sartorial splendor of an ambitious up-and-comer, a chip off the aspiring masses determined to find that magical key to success.

He puts away his work.

"Hi Mark!"

The waitress waddles over with her pot of fresh coffee.

"Coffee, young man?"

"Yes, thanks."

He immediately gets to the point of his meeting with Carmichael.

"You were his best friend in America, so any idea who killed him?"

"Bruno Giuseppe," he answers, without lifting his head.

"Are you sure?"

"Man, what other proof you lookin' f'r? Your father almost land de man in prison."

"But at least my dad didn't squeal on him, did he?"

"Yeah, but Bruno always said he was the snitch that let de cat out de bag in de first place. I think it was Bruno who set 'im up f'r de kill."

"The police don't think it was he. Y'know, the white sheet and all."

"De police scared o' de Mafia, man, scared as shite. But I am tellin' you that Bruno Giuseppe is de one. Just don't quote me."

The exchange is interrupted when a friend of Carmichael walks in and joins their company. He introduces himself to Mark as Ali Rahman, professional saxophone player and student of the famous John Coltrane. He plays alto sax all night at the Cotton Club on 142th and, after his gig, ends up at Ella's for coffee. He removes his skull cap, sits and closes his eyes; they appear heavy with sleep. He orders a coffee and before long his chin is resting on his chest.

Carmichael hastens to change the subject of their interrupted conversation.

"Heard you wrote another book, Mark," he says playfully. "Heard it from the guys down at *De Renaissance"*.

"Yup".

"What's it about?"

"It's more or less a recap of the sixties, Jim Crow and the freedom rides, you know, those days in the Deep South."

"Good Lord, Mark! Dat was sixteen years ago."

"Well, y'know, in the words of Miss Angelou, 'There is no agony like bearing an untold story inside of you'. Plus it's a story that has to be told over and over again."

Carmichael lowers his voice to a whisper. "Let it go, man! It is not *your* story. You're a West Indian like me. Besides, de past is de past. Look at me, blacker than midnight, a vice president at a bank on Wall Street, doin' well, drivin' a Caddy, a Bajan livin' de American dream. Man, you no better than those damn Confederates, still up in arms, still fightin' de civil war. You gotta wipe that chip off your shoulder, my brother, it don' belong to you. If you want to live in de past, write about de Union Jack and de Mother Country. That past belong to you and me, brother."

Swinging his arms in the air like an animated maestro, he sings: "'Rule Britannia! Britannia rules the waves, Britons never, never, never shall be slaves.' Remember that song?"

And surely, Mark remembers those days in Barbados under the British, when Lord Compton, the school inspector from Great Britain paid a visit to St. Lucy's Parish School, when all the children had been coached in the lyrics of the catchy song, and when he refused to sing the chorus because it was the rallying cry of former enslavers, as soon as the lord left the grounds, he had to bend over a desk to receive ten blistering lashes on his backside. He had committed a sin akin to heresy.

They both laughed.

Now hearing Carmichael speak he is reminded that when he arrived in America, he too was aloof, fitted with blinders, seeing America's racism only in the periphery of his vision, seeing himself more English than the English, a step above his American brothers. Now he wears a scar on his head that tells him he was wrong, that tells him the real truth of who he is, of how he is perceived.

The bleary-eyed saxophonist has heard every word from Carmichael's lips in spite of his whispering. For years his ears have been attuned to the soft murmuring of the jazz organ, always listening for that bridge when the organ takes over and for the other side when it is handed back to the horn section.

He snarls at Carmichael across the table. "You's a West Indian? You don't look Indian to me, Carmichael. You's a Chinook, Cheyenne or Comanche? And why you livin' in Harlem anyway? Why you not in Brooklyn with yer own from the Caribbean?" He stresses the last syllables of the word "CaribBE-AN" mockingly.

"I can live anywhere I choose, Ali," the Bajan shouts back, surprised and not a little embarrassed he had been overheard.

"No you can't," Ali retorts. "Try rentin' in Riverdale or buyin' in Bedford in the burbs. You livin' with us 'cause we *let* you live with us. And now you sayin' you don't share the same history? Let me tell you this, Carmichael, when whitey is looking at you, whitey is seein' me. You ain't no better in America."

The West Indian held his tongue, not having a fitting answer and not wanting to set on fire the ill-tempered Ali Rahman, who simmered for a while then went back to sleep.

And Mark could not help but ponder these two men, so much the same and so different, two seeds from the same pod but sown in different fields not of their own choosing. It was Carmichael who had chosen not to look back to where he had begun but only to the place where he had been deposited, and he clung to that Caribbean heritage of his because it was easier to bear. They were both comfortable in their skin but Ali, the jazz player, perhaps preferred to look past America where he had lived his whole life, for his identity was moored in the Dark Continent. He used his sax every night to ease the burden of his own history, as he closed his eyes and lifted his horn in homage to all those great artistes of the past who had learned to subsume their pain in the subtlety of jazz.

The jolly-faced waitress waddles over to replenish their coffee and changes the subject.

"Did you guys hear about Shonelle Solomon?"

She injects an air of gloom and death into the atmosphere.

But Carmichael is not about to let her steal his thunder as the newsmaker of the day. "Oh yes, they find she last night stabbed to death on de street."

Once again he jolts Ali Rahman from his slumber. "No, no, no! The woman was raped and strangled in her bed. Coulda been her boyfriend or a jealous lover, who the hell knows?" Ali, the night owl at the table, has credibility on his side.

"Wasn't her boy killed on 135th Street de other night by a man wid a sword?" asks Carmichael. "Some witness drove by and reported he saw the whole t'ing and that de killer wuz a light-skin fella."

"Yeah, that's right," confirms Ali. "Ol' man Solomon fixin' to put up a thousand dollar reward for an arrest. Right away a fella walks into the station the other day and gives them a rundown, a damn good picture of the killer right down to his shoe laces."

Mark glances down unconsciously at his shoes.

Ali points facetiously at the one with the lightest complexion at the table. "Sure it wasn't you, Mark? Walkin' around Harlem at night stabbin' people?" They toss their heads back and laugh heartily, stamping their feet and slapping the table, blown away by the exquisite timing and keen sense of humor. Mark pretends to join in the hilarity.

But he had come to the coffee shop that morning to learn what they had heard and seen of strangers in the neighborhood, of white men they had never seen before, of license plates up and down the streets of Harlem bearing the emblems of southern states, of the Klan and their propaganda leaflets, of burning crosses on suburban lawns, of the torching of a home on Long Island that threatened the homogeneity of a suburban community. But they had known nothing and had heard nothing of these things. They were of no help to him. He hadn't learned a thing. In blissful ignorance his two friends sat there wolfing down their eggs and bacon and waffles and grits as he listened to their incessant chatter and hand slapping. They had no idea the Ku Klux Klan was right there at their doorsteps.

Then at nine o'clock sharp, his two friends disperse, each man to his respective calling, Carmichael to his job in the city and Ali Rahman, who after his fifth cup of Columbian coffee is ready to head home and go to bed.

Mark is left alone at the table staring at the empty dishes, the dirty cups and the smoldering ashtrays. The busboy comes over and takes everything away and he still sits there oblivious of his surroundings, staring into space, hearing that gruff, fiendish voice at the end of the phone line, "Nigga, we're coming f'r you next", seeing the decomposing body of Shonelle Solomon, brutally violated and throttled to death, and the face of her wayward son lying in a casket; all because of a book he had written that held the secrets and names of evil men, a book intended to warn the people of impending terrors, a book to bring to light the one who had the blood of his father on his hands. Where will this trail of blood lead in the end?

The waitress hovers above his shoulder with a fresh pot.

"More coffee?"

He thinks about it for a second. "Yeah, why not!"

"Why you so glum today, may I ask?"

Without hesitating, he says to her, "I'm worried about my people. Last night the Klan did their dirty work right here in Harlem … Shonelle Solomon."

She replenishes his cup. Standing there with her other hand akimbo, she says with a look of matriarchal authority: "Listen to me, son, ain't no Ku Klux Klan in this city, baby. Here we may have our Puerto Rican gangs, Russian gangs, the Mafia and the Panthers. But the KKK we left them summabitches long time ago in the South."

He is not about to argue. To convince her he would have to tell her everything he knows. He finishes his coffee, leaves his tip on the table, gets up and walks away.

15 – A New Deal

The morning turns solemn and drizzly as he makes his way to the city-bound train for his second encounter with the cantankerous Mr. Thatcher. His anger is rising again like an irrepressible fever. At the center of his ire is the destruction of his equipment with all his work. It was like a sucker punch to his ego when his back was turned. The anger yields to an irrational fear that threatens to consume him. He casts a furtive glance over his shoulder now and then, as on the night of the mugging, and now like an escapee from the law. At his back, every white man within arm's length is his pursuer and the rare one on 125th Street is an assassin. Paula has sought to assure him he is tangentially under her protection, by virtue of being a friend of a prominent Klansman's daughter, but he knows their hatred of the black race has neither bounds nor reason.

He blames the paranoia on his insomnia but it is more than that: he is plainly vulnerable to the over-zealous police eager to close their books on a high-profile case. Then he remembers the prescient words of Ali Rahman: "The police have a like description of Elroy's killer." He could well become their person of interest.

He enters the station, buys a fifty-cent token and enters a car filled with a heterogeneous crowd of commuters heading to work. Their faces reflect the ethnic mix of the city: white, black, brown, yellow, and every complexion in between; immigrants come from east, west, north and south of the planet. This mosaic of colors in this vast and crowded city is reputedly cursed and despised by the Klan.

He is reminded that New Yorkers are avid readers. The elderly lady seated on his right is engrossed in her bible, fingering her string of prayer beads; on his other side a gangly youth is into his Stephen King horror novel *The Shining*, while every other commuter's head is buried in the *News* or some other paper, all oblivious to the bucking and lurching, their shoulders swaying from side to side as the train trundles on from station to station on the way to Grand Central.

In his mind's eye he is seeing instead *The New Chapter* in the hands of each reader. He sees their eyes agape with horror, their lips quivering as they read of a wave of terror they never imagined would make its way out of the Deep South to sweep their fair city. He imagines their faces contorted with disgust; some are grim and ready to confront the enemy, while others shake their heads from side to side in a remorseful gesture of "how could it be?" But alas, the book with its shocking revelations is no longer in his possession. To rewrite it would be a herculean task and, even so, no publisher wants to be involved in the project for fear of evoking accusations of slander and being sued in this, the most litigious city in the world. In any case, by the time the new version is completed it would be too late; their communities would be poisoned with hate.

The devout lady with the prayer beads gets off at the next station. A black soldier in Army fatigues with a duffle bag slung over his shoulder takes her place dropping the bag at his feet. He had always looked upon African

American soldiers going off to war as gullible victims of unrequited love. Nevertheless, he respected them for their love of country the way he felt about the spurned lover who never gives up.

The soldier, who might have been a scrawny kid a year or so ago has been "retooled" for battle and is now a strapping lad with bulging muscles, V-shaped in the chest and broad at the shoulders.

"Where're you heading, soldier?" he asks.

"Port Authority for the bus to New Orleans, sir. That's my home, sir." The word "home" illuminates his face while "sir" has been programmed into his brain.

"Looking forward to seeing your folks, I bet."

"Yes sir. I missed my dad's funeral. Got stuck in Cambodia, sir."

"You a draftee or volunteer?"

"I was drafted for the Army, sir."

He wonders if the soldier knew that the magnanimous President Carter, earlier that year, had pardoned anyone who dodged the draft and fled the country. The soldier, had he ducked out to Canada, might have been at his father's bedside when he exhaled his last breath. Who knows?

A commuter gets up, abandons his newspaper on the seat and exits at the next station. He picks it up and leafs through it for any news of Shonelle Solomon. Eventually he sees an article stuck in the middle of the paper telling the story of a woman strangled and raped in Lincoln Heights. The paper quotes her next-door neighbor, who is unequivocal in her statement to the police.

HIS FATHER'S FOOTSTEPS

The killer was a well dressed brother man. I would say, oh, 'bout five eleven more or less. Big scar on the side of the head. A real hitman. Officer, I was standin' on my terrace on the seventh floor across the road when I see the son-of-a-gun leavin' Miss Solomon's apartment with a white woman. They took off down 124ᵗʰ in a hurry just like Bonnie and Clyde but I sees them plain as day. Yes, I did. I could recognize those criminals anywhere.

He rips the page from the newspaper and pockets it.

He leaves the train at the Madison Avenue station and walks two blocks to Pemberton Publishing. Today is Friday but there is no sign of a city winding down; every day is a whirlwind of a day in Manhattan. It is no longer dismal and drizzly; it is a beautiful spring morning unlike the time he first set foot on the steps of this gigantic building. It was cold and windy that day and he was shaking in his shoes, from the cold but also from the uncertainty of what might become of his meeting with the publisher.

He is on a different mission today, not to sell a book but to find the ones who had offered to buy it in the first place. Therein lies the identity of his persecutors and in a little while he will again be in the presence of the one who should know. He needs answers and he needs them today. He is tired of being in their crosshairs; he wants to move on.

He climbs the steps, pushes through the revolving door and walks boldly up to the receptionist beaming a broad, radiant smile, hoping for instant recognition as the brother who visited just the other day. Since that day how many colored faces would have approached his desk to

---

compromise his recollection of the name Mark Maynard and his recognition of a young man of letters who had come to see Mr. Thatcher? Perhaps the old man will see no harm in waiving the requisite appointment since he has already been vetted. Perhaps he will just be handed the obligatory visitor's sticker and sent on his way to the forty-eighth floor.

"Good morning, sir! Remember me, eh? Back to see Mr. Thatcher."

His eyes are cold as they were on the first day. He is stiff, toffee-nosed as an English butler straight out of Masterpiece Theatre.

"Do you have an appointment, sir?"

"Not exactly, but Tom knows me, it's okay."

"Well, I'm afraid you will need an appointment, sir. They don't like people calling without an appointment."

"I understand. Perhaps you could let 'im know that Mark Maynard is in the lobby and stopped by to see 'im. Could you?"

"I can't do that either. Sir, the rules are, nobody gets by me without an appointment. I have been with this company for the last twenty-four years. At my age where am I gonna go now for givin' a brother a break?"

There is no point in humoring this old man; he is too calcified in the commandments of the company to make one little exception for a brother. There is an open elevator not ten yards away that could whisk him up to the forty-eighth floor in less than a minute. Before it closes he makes a dash for the elevator while the receptionist jumps up and, surprisingly for an old man, races him to the door with his arms flailing. He punches the door shut and as the elevator is rising, the man is seen mouthing the words, "Sir, I can't let you …" as he disappears downward from view.

He strolls down the hallway, casually in order not to attract attention, but is aware, nevertheless, that by now security must be on his tail. He bursts into Thatcher's office. He is seated at his desk, seemingly dictating to his secretary. He looks up, swivels in his chair, lowers his head and peers over his spectacles. His face betrays neither alarm nor irritation at the intrusion. He smiles and says calmly, "I've been expecting you, Mr. Maynard".

"Well, I've been trying to reach you," replies Mark.

"You mean about the offer?"

"Yes, I need to know who made the offer."

"Well, are you ready to do business, Mr. Maynard? There is a check waiting for you in my desk along with a contract for your signature. The contract clearly states that we will be the sole owner of the publishing rights for your book and have first right of refusal for any literary work of Mark Maynard's for the next ten years. And may I remind you that in our retention is a staff of the most qualified and relentless lawyers in this city."

Thatcher clearly doesn't know the book no longer exists, or is pretending not to know.

"I still need to know who is bankrolling the offer."

"I can't say but names are academic anyway. What does it matter as long as you get the money? I have to live up to my promise to keep the name in confidence. After all, I'm a man of honor."

"Is it Hamilton?" Mark throws out the name like a fisherman's net.

"Don't know who you're talking about." He either doesn't know a Hamilton or he doesn't bite.

Just then there is a rush of air as the door to the office is flung open and two security men burst in. They are visibly out of breath and braced to make an arrest. Thatcher immediately raises a hand in the air to indicate to the men that the uninvited visitor poses no danger. They turn and walk away with hunched shoulders, seemingly disappointed they had not been able to lay hands on the intruder.

Mark reaches into his back pocket and fishes out two pieces of paper. One is the newspaper page about the rape and killing of Shonelle Solomon and the other is the crumbled KKK leaflet her killer had placed on her naked body that day. He places them both on Thatcher's desk face-up and right under his eyes. He searches his face for the faintest expression of familiarity with the story. The man is visibly shaken by what he reads, pushes back from his desk, reads the story again, stares at the leaflet and shakes his head as if in disbelief, pausing as if to reconsider his vow of silence.

"I'll tell you what," he says, regaining his composure, "let me see the manuscript again. I'll take another look at the names you say belong to the Klan." He reaches forward for the book.

"I no longer have a book. And I'm afraid all my files and backup tapes were destroyed."

He removes his glasses. His brow is furrowed, he seems genuinely irritated, confused. "Then why the hell did you come to do business f'r Christ sake when you don't have a book?"

"Well, there is a slight change in the deal, Mr. Thatcher. I am prepared to release all the evidence that your buyer wants to suppress. All of their secrets. Every piece of the data that supported the book. But I will deliver it only to the buyer at an agreed-to public location and for a price of fifty thousand dollars."

"Fifty thousand bucks, eh?"

There is a moment of silence in which Thatcher looks over to his secretary as if to implicate her as a witness.

"And one more thing, sir. The evidence is in joint possession of myself and one other person. If I should die by natural or unnatural causes before the transaction takes place, every bit of the evidence will find its way into the public domain."

Dead silence. The air is thick with threat and tension. Thatcher's lips seem to be quivering, struggling for a fitting retort. Instead he settles for an answer both compliant and dead serious.

"I will convey your new terms, Mr. Maynard, but first I will tell you two things. If you can connect the dots between this rape and murder to the man who wanted your book, I'll do everything in my power to bring him to justice. But if you are disrupting a legitimate business deal and wrongfully accusing a professional book buyer who approached this company with the sole intention to keep scurrilous lies out of the public domain, then your feet will be held to the fire for the rest of your career. That's all I'm gonna say".

He turns to his secretary, who has been paying close attention. "Ellen, escort Mr. Maynard to the elevator."

Mark reaches forward to shake his hand goodbye but he has already swiveled his chair and turned his attention to other matters. She leads him down the narrow corridor, swaying her hips, with an occasional backward glance, wearing her characteristic smile. For the first time he finds her pleasant demeanor quite genuine. She casts a furtive glance, right and left, as they walk by each office door, and without breaking her stride she whispers in his ear, "I skimmed over a few pages of your book … very interesting. Sorry about your father."

"Thank you!"

He enters the elevator, the door is closing and he is about to descend when for the first time he sees the smile fall from her face.

"I know who ordered that woman killed," he hears her say. He fumbles to reopen the door.

The elevator starts its descent so she raises her voice and yells, "I know who killed her. Watch yer step, mister! Call me on Monday! I'll tell you what's about to go down."

"Is it Hamilton?"

But his voice is trapped within the four walls of the express elevator as it drops through the shaft on the way down to the first floor.

She has long disappeared from view.

16 – Another Casualty

The weekend rolls by slowly, painfully, as the secretary's warning reverberates from an echo chamber deep in his brain: "Watch your step, mister! You may be next". As he waits to make that pivotal phone call on Monday at the strike of nine, he imagines then she'll be settled at her desk, alone and able to speak freely. He prays she will tell him everything she has learned at the feet of her boss. If she indeed knows who killed Miss Solomon, there would be no question she holds the clues to whoever also wanted him dead.

He remembers the last words from her boss's lips and now is inclined to see him in a different light, one of neutrality. His expression as he learned about Shonelle Solomon was one of utter abhorrence. But he seems to have been duped, hoodwinked into what appears a bloodless business deal that has everything to do with procuring a book of scandals. Publishers are traditionally on the lookout for deep-pocketed book merchants. Who knows if the man who came calling on Pemberton Publishers portrayed himself as one?

But that day, it was not the time or the place to be leaking confidences; she could easily have been overheard in the hallway. When he stepped out of the elevator on the first floor he knew it was unlikely he would ever again be allowed into the building. One look at the hard-nosed receptionist's face as he walked by the lobby told him he was barred for life, for when he smiled at the old man apologetically he returned a scathing scowl. He was no longer a brother.

His only recourse now is to reach her on the phone. But he must be prudent, he doesn't want to jeopardize her job; it is clearly an enviable position being the secretary of the company's head honcho.

◆ ◆ ◆

Monday morning comes around. He sits by the phone. At nine he dials Pemberton Publishers, the number he had been given at their first meeting. First, he must thank her profusely, then assure her that whatever she offers him, a name, an address, a source, a motive will be held in the strictest confidence; that she has nothing to fear; that he will not leave a trail to endanger her or her standing in the company.

He reaches their switchboard. "Good morning, may I speak to Mr. Thatcher's secretary?"

A long pause ensues as if the lady operator is undecided as to whether she should interrogate the caller for the benefit of the one being called, or adhere to another rule of strict company protocol.

"May I ask who's calling?"

"I'm a relative of Ellen's from out of town," he lies.

"Your name, sir?" she insists.

"Um, well, I just dropped in from out of town and wanted to surprise her. You see, we haven't spoken or seen each other for a while."

Another pause lasts for several seconds. What if Thatcher comes on the phone, what should he say?

"Sir, Ellen Murphy is no longer with us," he hears.

He is stunned by these words. The likelihood she had been fired from her job without notice fills him with stages of sympathy, disappointment and outrage. She was his last hope to confirm his darkest suspicions.

"Ma'am, do you know where she went … um, I mean her address … her phone number at home?" His words ramble in desperation.

"Sir, I told you I'm sorry to say she's no longer with us." There is a tone of finality in her voice. The phone clicks off.

"She's no longer with us", the euphemistic words to describe the dead. The receiver drops from his hand to the floor. The noise alerts Paula in the next room. She comes running. She finds him collapsed in a chair, his face in his hands.

"What happened?"

"I have another casualty on my conscience. They said Thatcher's secretary is no longer."

"That could mean anything, Mark. Maybe she moved on."

But paranoia has his mind in a stranglehold. It allows him to believe nothing less than that Ellen Murphy was wiped out for saying too much, that she had been overheard spilling secrets and promising to tell him more.

Paula is right. The words could mean anything. But his tortured mind refuses to be convinced.

17 – A Fair Bargain

Guilt, fear, anger. These emotions weigh upon him and sink him into a slough of depression that lasts the whole day. Then an idea, playful at first then bright with possibility, rescues his mind. Thatcher, who swore he is open-minded about race, needs a secretary. Now is the time to prove that he is. Could there be a job opportunity for his Nigerian friend? Could there be an investigative role for her to play right under Thatcher's nose? He rushes to the telephone and dials her number. He tells himself he has to play his cards judiciously.

"Nakeisha, I need your help." There has long been a chill between them. His face reflects her reluctance but he persists.

"There is no one else I can call on. Please! I'll explain. Meet me at the Lexington Lounge at seven. We'll talk about it."

She relents. He smiles. It's a plan.

But in order for the plan to go forward, Paula must also be in accord; she is well aware of their former love affair, he and Nakeisha.

His African friend plays the role of a gadfly where she is concerned; she tells him he deserves a woman of color. She sees Paula as his passport, an enabler for access to white circles, proof to the world he is free of taboos and outdated prejudices, to show he is socially enlightened.

He believes her mind is still locked in a prison not of her own making while he sees a light looming in America that she cannot yet see. She has no idea of the road on which he and this woman had embarked, he to fight against those who had wronged his father, and this woman to make amends in some small way for her family's sins.

Still, he is conflicted. She compels him to question the meaning of love. Does he love Paula? Or are they just friends inextricably bound by mutual causes? From his subconscious springs an undeniable truth: it is Nakeisha with whom he shares the same skin, the same antecedents, indeed the same forefathers.

"You got yerself a white woman," she taunts him. "Now you should go where white people live."

And hearing these words he cannot help but think of his father and his sexual and romantic predilections. He too wonders about his own.

Some days in the office she puts a smile on his face with her good-natured teasing. He is sure she knows what she's doing when she brushes against him in that tight space between chairs, or bends over his desk so he can spy down her cleavage, or sits consciously cross-legged across the room in a meeting when her leather skirt deliberately rides up for him to lay his eyes on that triangle of underwear, when he would feel his blood rush and the tingling of a zillion synaptic cells. After all, he is only human and she knows she radiates a different kind of heat. "African heat," she calls it. Perhaps in her mind she is satisfied that there are no other worlds for him to conquer. But, alas, she doesn't understand the reason he is with Paula.

He turns to her. "What if my friend Nakeisha finagles her way into Thatcher's office and becomes his new secretary?"

"Nakeisha? Is that possible?"

"I don't know but it's intriguing. It's a long shot but if it works, she gets a great job and I get myself a mole in the wood pile."

"Sounds like a plan," she says. "Give her a call."

"I already did."

The Lexington Lounge is between 124th and 125th in the heart of Harlem. The iconic bar and jazz joint on Lexington Avenue boasts the likes of James Baldwin, Langston Hughes, Sarah Vaughn, Duke Ellington, among the pantheon of former patrons whose autographed faces adorn the walls. He was told it had risen to fame as a dinner club catering to white patrons only. Every night, back in the old days, the rich folk drove up from Germantown and the silk-stocking east side of Manhattan. They spilled out from their chauffeured limousines and swarmed into the Lounge to listen to black folk's music in the years when entertainers were buffoons in burnt corkface, sneaking in through the back door, shuffling onto the stage in baggy pants and humiliating themselves for the amusement of white folk.

Now black and white enter hand in hand, all resplendent in the most elegant of evening wear. They intermingle without hard feelings either shown or harbored by those who were once barred. Under the lights they twirl and jitterbug in one continuous iridescent swirl and the Lexington Lounge swells to one harmonious hive of humanity.

In less than an hour, Nakeisha is perched on a stool at the mahogany bar sipping her first glass of Cabernet, waiting for her ex-lover to enter and cross the checkered black-and-white floor for their first tryst in years. She wears his favorite hip-hugging, black-sequined dress, the one she wore on Wednesday nights when they sat in the balcony at the famed Apollo Theatre. She is made up quite a bit more than he is used to seeing her at work, where she prefers to be casual, sometimes in one of her old NYU tee shirts and bleached-out jeans fashionably torn at the knees. Tonight, her head, her neck, her hands are bedazzled with jewels she seldom wears. She throws off just the right hint of Chanel No. 5, his favorite.

No doubt the memories come flooding back from a time long past when they first met at his father's funeral. He was a sad and bitter man then. Night after night she had done all she could to ease the pain and anger roiling inside him. But to help him find the one who killed his father, she had no clue; she didn't even know the late Mr. Maynard. Then he found someone who professed to have the answer, and after that person came to town their future dimmed and sputtered to an end.

Now lately he needs her help, the help that no one else around him can offer. He needs a woman of color, a woman of his own race. Shame!

It is early and the usual jazz crowd has not yet descended on the club; some muted recorded music lends a soft romantic air to the space occupied by less than a dozen early birds. Before long the music of Billie Holiday, Miles Davis and Lester Young will be bouncing off the walls, as their imitators, talented in their own right, take to the stage.

Now here he comes striding towards her at the strike of seven. Here he is with that self-assured gait of his. But as he greets her, there is no kiss on the lips, no lust in his eyes, no hug that envelopes her in his arms as it once did. Instead his demeanor is all business.

"Keish, there is an excellent opportunity waiting for you in the city." He blurts it out, the trump card he could have played much later in the evening after an hour or so of nostalgic banter.

In this moment he might have well had doused her with a pail of iced water. But she quickly composes herself and conceals all expectations, for her pride will not allow her to concede disappointment and furthermore kindle within herself a fire of resentment, which would be unfair since he had not willfully led her on. Instead he had brought her a gift, good news, the promise of a full-time job downtown in the city, the kind of job that would pay her twice as much as she earns as part-time proofreader-*cum*-secretary at a lowly community newspaper.

He orders a vodka, straight up, water on the side. He doesn't want whiskey which would leave a sourness on his breath when he gets home. The smell of whiskey would be like lipstick on his shirt, both innocent but evoking all kinds of imaginings not on the script. He is not much of a drinker but he needs a relaxer to put his cards on the table. The suggestion he has in mind is only a hunch, but if it works it could help them both.

"Still looking for a job, some decent pay?" he asks her.

"Well, yeah but …."

"What do you know about Pemberton Publishers?"

"Not much, they publish books, I guess. That's all I know."

"Well, they're more than that. They're one of the biggest and the richest on the East Coast."

"So?"

"Well, I happen to know they need a secretary, Keish, a black secretary, and I know you would be perfect for the job." Since he could only assume the job was still available he saw no harm in bolstering the assumption with a minor prevarication.

"So that means I need a whole new wardrobe, dark suits, buttoned-down shirts, high heels, conservative wear?"

"No, you would be fine. In the publishing world people dress as they like, but you have to hurry before it's taken. Just ask for Mr. Thomas Thatcher. Call him in the morning, here's the telephone number." He scribbles the number on a napkin and slides it over.

He jokes: "And f'r Christ sake, Keish, use your best Caucasian accent on the phone. That'll impress 'em, make 'em think you're from England or the Caribbean, an Oxford-trained Negress.

"And flaunt your credentials, college degree, state scholarship and great references."

"What references? I have no references."

"Don't you worry. I'll have Holyfield get you a few from some of his white friends. And he doesn't mind you deserting the paper, you'll be one less on his payroll."

"What makes you think they'll hire me?"

"I spoke with Mr. Thatcher. He says he's open-minded about race and whom he hires, so we'll see. You tried every business downtown all year and came up empty. Give it a shot."

"Listen, Mark, don't ask me to change my name because it ain't gonna happen."

It is true, her résumé must have landed on the desk of every employment office in Manhattan, yet she had never been invited in for an interview, for it appeared her name in the corporate world conjured up the sub-Saharan jungles. And, if truth be told, her mode of dress would not have helped. Well-meaning friends suggested she change her name and tone down her wardrobe but she would not be persuaded; it was against her nature. Carmichael had gotten a job in a downtown bank and for the interview he had said goodbye to his luxuriant Afro and adopted the accent of an English lord. But not Nakeisha, oh no! Here she blends seamlessly into the landscape of Harlem, whereas in some downtown Manhattan office she would be the topic of conversation at the water cooler with her exotic regalia of African jewelry, her Ethiopian bangles, her multi-layered Masai necklace, her beaded dreadlocks that hang past her braless breasts, breasts daringly peeking out from her top, arousing all kinds of concupiscent thoughts in the minds of young and old men. In some bank on conservative Park Avenue or Fifth Avenue she would be disruptive just by being who she is, but here in Harlem she is seen as an African princess.

He thinks if Thatcher is interested in the elevation of black people, as he said he is, then she will present an opportunity for him to prove it. Keisha becomes the gambit to flush him out while learning all there is to know about the people behind rejection of his book and the reason they are trying so hard to keep it off the streets.

Alas she suspects an angle, some stratagem in which he needs her help, for the next words out of her mouth are: "So what's the catch?"

He guzzles the remainder of his vodka and orders another round, wetting his throat and preparing his mind to launch into the long-winded story of how *The New Chapter* came to be; how and why it had been rejected by Pemberton; the coercion, the bribe, the suspicions, the lies; how it had been stolen only to reappear on his desk as a blood-spattered and shredded batch of loose pages; how they had burgled his house and destroyed his computer, his backup tapes and all; how they had threatened his life on the phone; how they had … He kept going until he had lost her attention, for all through the recapitulation of events she kept staring lustfully at his lips and occasionally moistening her own with a sweep of her tongue. In the end he had discreetly skirted the death of Shonelle Solomon and, God forbid, the suspected sentence of death meted out to the publisher's secretary. Such revelations would have frightened Nakeisha away from agreeing to be his mole. Once she gets the job she will likely be privy to secrets her predecessor was willing to reveal before she was snatched away from his view when the elevator closed. Keisha could pinpoint the connivers and even save his life, for who knows if the threats against his life are being hatched right there in Thatcher's office? One thing he *does* know: she'll be forewarned to be on her toes and not careless as the late Ellen Murphy had been.

In the wee hours of the morning the Lexington Lounge was never the place for serious conversation; the loud big band music would always intrude. It was the place where jazz aficionados came to celebrate their idols, dance and stomp their feet to the rhythms of a bygone era. Hours had slipped by and multiple drinks had been consumed before he felt the crush of the crowd and realized that every seat and barstool had been taken. When the syncopated frenzy of Count Basie's *One O'clock Jump* reached his ears, he looked at his watch and indeed it was ten past one. He had wanted to stay only as long as was necessary to brief Nakeisha, convince her to apply for the job and solicit her help, but the night and the music and the ambience had stolen his sense of time. Nevertheless every bit of tension had been released from his mind and body.

He felt that she, on the other hand, was ready to accede to his every bidding the minute he entered the club, but now there was no longer the illusion their meeting was solely about the plan. Now it was late and they should be going. He settles their tab and, easing himself down from the barstool, he feels his feet a trifle unsteady; the checker board floor is tilting one way then the next. She holds onto his arm but she is no less tipsy and together they shamble along to the exit to hail one of the gypsy cabs queued up at the curb.

"135th and 7th first stop," he tells the driver, since Nakeisha lives a bit farther, then he leans back and closes his eyes. When the taxi comes to a stop, he realizes he had been dozing and the address outside is not his own but that of Nakeisha's fourth floor apartment.

"Whyn't you come up for a cup o' coffee, freshen up before you go on home," she tells him.

He knows quite well that coffee is not what she has in mind, and under other circumstances he might have declined, but he needs her help more than she needs his. He would therefore hold her hand and climb the four flights to her apartment and eventually to her waterbed, as he had done many times before. And although that was a long time ago, he still remembers well the layout of her boudoir, pictures on the wall of bejeweled African kings and queens, her dresser laden with a battery of powders, creams, lotions and unlabeled vials of secret potions. On one side, glued to the wall, is the same horizontal, elongated mirror that back then reflected their naked bodies and nightly performances.

HIS FATHER'S FOOTSTEPS

But tonight his time is short, he has to hurry home. So she needs no pillow talk, no preamble, no pretensions or flaunting of the intellect. Tonight there will be no flickering of scented candles in the dark, just a dimming of the lights; no soft seductive music from the stereo. No affectation of sweet talk will rekindle their affair, for they both know where his heart lies. But neither will she feel the guilt of poaching another woman's lover, for though he is not hers he belongs to her world. And in his case, whatever guilt rises to the surface, he can say to himself he is simply striking a bargain.

He lies in bed and watches her kick off her shoes, prop one leg at a time on a chair, raise her skirt and roll down a stocking, then another. Then she unbuttons her blouse, flings it off her shoulders, reaches back, unclips her bra, then leans forward and jiggles her breasts playfully. She laughs. Still on her feet, she wriggles out of her skirt, then her slip, and let both fall at her feet, then steps out of the tangle of clothing and throws herself on her waterbed. Naked, they bounce and sway like two kids on a trampoline. Then they cut to the chase with the briefest of foreplays to awaken the juices, then to reenact the same passionate sex to which they had been accustomed for years without having to think or invent or pretend. Except that now he is more pliant than assertive. And with every thrust, bite, scratch and dig into his captive body, she punishes him with such vindictive passion that he feels himself lashed by angry waves as her bed tosses and gurgles, all for having deserted her for another woman all these years. He knows it. Then having made her point, she reins herself back to an easy canter to hold back the inevitable explosion, all the while whispering in his ears tantalizing reminders of how their world used to be. Finally she loses control of the reins and they both rush to the finish. It is over and a wave of contentment flows over them both. Like a rock she falls asleep while he forces himself to stay awake with an unnatural stare at the ceiling listening to her deep rhythmic breathing.

After a while he gathers up his clothes she had flung on the floor and dresses noiselessly. He tiptoes to the door, his shoes in his hand. Then he hears her voice, soft and slurred with sleep.

"Mark, I can't do it."

"Huh?"

"I can't do it, I'm sorry."

"What d'you mean?"

"I can't … I mean I won't leave *The Renaissance*. I changed my mind. I can't do it. Please don't ask me."

"But you said you wanted …"

"I know I said I wanted to move on, but y'see, that other America is not f'r me. I'm happy just where I'm at, doin' what I'm doin', helpin' the cause, workin' f'r my people. Y'see, money ain't everything."

"Goodbye then" he says.

"And thanks for a beautiful evening," she murmurs. She rolls to her side and goes back to sleep.

It's four in the morning. No doubt, Paula is in bed. In that certain space when the mind drifts in and out of shallow sleep, she must be haunted by second thoughts of having agreed to his stepping out to see his friend. Ambivalence and vulnerability must now invade her reasoning. She knows his weakness, his penchant for the company of a beautiful woman. She has met Nakeisha; there's none more beautiful. It was an ingenious plan nevertheless, enlisting his former lover to be his sleuth. But while it might have been rewarding for him, it was risky for herself, trusting her man on a date with a woman from his past, one who might still be in love with him though pride would not give her consent to say it.

No doubt, Paula is reaching across the bed even though she knows he's not there. Soon she will hear the sounds of a car door slammed shut and the acceleration of the taxicab as it pulls away from the curb. She will hear the scratching of the key in the door lock, a squeaking of the hinges, then the sound of his unsteady footsteps padding down the hallway to the shower where he will proceed to wash away all the delicious sweat, the guilt, and the sweet bewitching fragrance still in his nostrils, in his clothes, in his hair.

Now he climbs into bed and slides under the covers next to this woman, who lies perfectly still with her eyes closed, perhaps pretending to be asleep to preclude awkward, unneeded explanations, for she already knows where he has been, and with whom, and why he has done what he had to do. But they do not touch. He knows that in the morning she will love him no less, for it was only one night, and they have travelled too many days and nights to stumble on a single night of infidelity.

18 – The Confession

The dawn of the next day failed to alleviate the shame of last evening when he had tried to induce Nakeisha to do his bidding, albeit in her interest. Instead he had fallen for her seduction and though he had left her apartment sexually fulfilled, both his body and his ego had taken a beating. He was no wiser and no closer to the plot that he suspected was hatched in Mr. Thatcher's office.

He had gone to his newspaper job to put on paper whatever socially redeeming value he could make of any story of the day that could be the topic of his weekly column. He found none. Every word, every phrase, every sentence he could think of drifted away and out of his thoughts, so that when he handed his copy to Ken Holyfield, nothing he had written was particularly cogent or had made any sense.

He returned home and sat alone in his empty study. As in a game of chess, he shuffled and reshuffled in his mind all the players in a story of murder and deception where his father had been the king checkmated to death. Yet the one who dealt the blow refused to reveal himself. Or herself.

He picked up his pen to write another letter to the Honorable Mayor of New York City. It would be the last of maybe two dozen letters he had written over the years. He had lost count.

HIS FATHER'S FOOTSTEPS

Dear Mr. Mayor,

I have written several letters over the years beseeching your office to impress upon your District Attorney to reopen the case of the killing of Daniel Maynard, shot and killed on July 22nd 1958 in the borough of Richmond Borough outside the Hard Nuts Café. I have yet to receive an acknowledgement from your office, and until I do, I, Mark Maynard, the son of the man who was slain and whose murder has been allowed to slip through the chinks of your bureaucracy will persist in writing to you until my writing hand atrophies or my eyes fail me, whichever affliction comes first.

Respectfully and Persistently,
Mark Maynard

♦ ♦ ♦

It is late summer 1977. The city is in the grip of another hot, sweltering heat wave, like on that night, that fateful night, when three bullets were fired into the dark, into his father's head and no one heard and no one saw and no one stepped forward, except a discredited drunk who had been lying in a wine-induced stupor outside the club and was thought to be in search of his five minutes of fame.

Today, July 14th, he looks back to yesterday, a most dreadful day when the streets were all black, evil-looking. He remembers awakening to voices from the street below yelling in the dark. *Blackout! Blackout!* The entire landscape, as far as the eye could see, was plunged into total darkness. The power grid that streamed life to the boroughs had sputtered and died. In Lincoln Heights people bounded out of the ghetto like rodeo bulls, crashing out of their pens. Women and men, old and young, all poor, all repressed, all desperate in a city going broke, stampeded the streets, ransacking stores, burning, looting, helping themselves to goods they could never afford in their entire lifetimes.

On 125th Street, businesses rushed to board up their windows and doors. The police were overwhelmed; another pedestrian was stabbed to death on his street outside his door. The killing did not rise to the level of breaking news: his next of kin was an unknown.

Today, as the city cries and smolders in the aftermath, the Mayor from his fortress at City Hall pleads for calm. This year is an election year and he feels the heat. This criminal atmosphere becomes a reason for politicians to march towards the elections under the banner of law and order. The opposition will seize on the mayhem, the Mayor's lack of control, his shameful inability to create miracles, to create light where there was darkness; they will lay them all at his feet.

Mark is imagining the Mayor's predicament through the prism of his own frustration. He is a fine Jewish gentleman, short of personality, short of stature but with an avuncular charm that endears him to the people of Harlem. But he has another problem beside his own homegrown criminals that could cost him his reelection. Who is this Mark Maynard, he likely wonders, who writes to him from a Harlem address three and four times a month, begging him to look into some murder case in Staten Island that happened a decade and a half ago when it wasn't even Staten Island but Richmond Borough and the man in the house was Robert Wagner? So why is he calling on me now about a crime that happened on Wagner's clock way back then. So much needs to be put right before the elections, like dealing with the perception fostered by his political enemies that he, the Mayor of the greatest city in the world, is soft on crime. Then some West Indian guy, who lives in Harlem, writes and repeats the same preposterous warning that a rogue band of racist criminals exported from the Deep South, recruited outside his jurisdiction and domiciled in the suburbs might very well be organizing to rampage through his city, and even march down Fifth Avenue on St. Patrick's Day, or invade his city the day the electorate head to the polls. For the sheer improbability of it all, can he risk ignoring another letter? He knows he has the Jewish vote in his pocket but he needs the black vote from up yonder in Harlem. That vote could make all the difference. His main political nemesis is hated by blacks.

Another sobering consideration is, should he fail to go after the Klan with their Aryan dogma and swastika banners he will draw the ire of his own Jewish people.

Though the latest letter from this Mark Maynard will go unheeded, maybe if his administration could bring to closure the baffling Solomon case, he will earn the faith and respect of the African American community as their crime fighter in chief.

No wonder, then, that the NYPD is stepping up their patrols all across Harlem, questioning any and all suspects fitting the vaguest profile of the man who killed the councilman's grandson. No wonder, next day, this Friday morning, they come knocking on his door. He opens it a crack, the new door hung in the frame just a week ago and reinforced with the most impregnable deadbolt locks he could find. Standing on his doormat are two officers of the law flipping open their silvery badges. One is an overweight linebacker type with a ponderous stomach that overhangs and partially conceals his gun belt. His face, round and jowly, is a picture of boredom, nevertheless he forces a smile. The other officer is a young angular African American, likely a rookie in training. It is politic for patrolmen on the streets of Harlem to travel in pairs, one white and one black, for no other reason than for the perception of equal opportunity or for the illusion that everyone is equal under the law.

"The burglary happened weeks ago," he says to the officers. "You must've heard about it through the grapevine because I didn't bother to file a report."

The linebacker is confused. He stays put in the doorway. "Sorry to bother y'all. I'm Officer Whitehead and my partner here is Officer Chapman. No, actually, we're canvassin' the area, enquirin' about the guy that slashed the throat of the Solomon boy. Heard about it? It was all over the news. An eyewitness drivin' by said it happened here on the block couple yards away. They got us down at the station house knockin' on doors, turnin' over every rock to catch this fella. When the Mayor and the Gov'na get involved in these itty bitty killings, the Police Commissioner goes ape shit. You know how it is when the family of the deceased got political connections."

The other officer jumps in. "I heard the guy was a scumbag anyway, a regular piece o' shit ... excuse me, lady!" He glances at the lady. She is sitting on the lower step of the stairway concealing her emotions.

Mark is openmouthed, his hand still on the doorknob, not sure if he should surrender, stonewall the officers or invite them in for coffee. Fear momentarily grips his tongue, then relief relaxes his whole body and he is able to return the officer's smile.

"Well, I'm your man, you've come to the right place," he confesses. "Take me in."

Officer Whitehead tosses his head back and laughs appreciatively. It is a jolly laugh with a heaving of the shoulders and a jiggling of dewlaps, applauding a timely and unexpected spark of humor. He must have apprehended a few killers in his career and the profile before him is the farthest he could conceive of the vicious sword-wielding killer in his report. No murderous thoughts could ever come forth from the mind of this benign person standing before him. His offhand remark could only be in jest.

He must show he too has a sense of humor. "Yeah, you're Jack the Ripper and I'm Santa Claus." A laugh rumbles up from deep in his belly, shakes his whole frame and explodes in a series of clattering waves. *"Haaarrrgh! Haaarrrgh! Haaarrrgh! Haaarrrgh!* Look, we're only here to ask if you seen or heard anything suspicious. Know what I mean? This way we can report a nay or yea f'r this address and move on. Frankly it's only a waste o' time if you ask me. Who the hell is gonna confess?"

Before he could find the words to impress upon the officers that he indeed was the one, they had already checked off his address, said their goodbyes and were clambering down the steps. He could hear them still laughing as they retreated down to the street. He stands there speechless while Paula is visibly amused, for she had heard his confession, witnessed his offer to turn himself in, and the officers just would not buy it.

Though he had not been able to convince the officers, he knows their superiors down at the stationhouse would be convinced that the roving assassin had finally confessed, for the stature of Councilor Conroy and the powers of the Governor and the Mayor have placed the lawmen under intense pressure. They would like nothing more than to deliver his head to the councilman on a silver platter. But in that moment of confessing to the officers he had felt the lifting of a burden, the disencumbering of the secret he had held much too long. Now between the fear of resting on the fairness of the law and the fear of the Klan, he is willing to face the authorities and take his chances. He needs to get this Solomon case off his back.

But should he walk into the clutches of the law without a lawyer or a witness? Could his word and good name exonerate him? Would Holyfield's illegal weapon hurt his case? He faces a moral dilemma, for while he harbors in secrecy the property of the Klan, he holds his own identity secret from the law. How long can he live with this moral contradiction within himself?

On the spur of the moment he makes a dash to his closet, rummages through his clothes and dons the same suit he wore the night of the mugging. The jacket is still ripped in the back where a deadly knife had made its mark. Then he retrieves from their hiding place the stolen documents, tucks them under his shirt and heads towards the door.

"Going to pay a visit to Mr. Solomon," he tells her.

"Good luck with that," she says with reservation in her voice.

19 – Sugar Hill

In the northernmost reaches of Harlem, in historic Hamilton Heights, lies a district they call Sugar Hill, named after the "sweet life" enjoyed by the elite who once lived there — luminaries such as William E. B. Dubois, Paul Robeson, Duke Ellington, and now the venerable Conroy Solomon. In stark contrast to the massive row houses with their rich architectural features is the unpretentious single family home of the councilman on Amsterdam Avenue overlooking the Hudson River. The house sits behind a ten-foot wall and a massive iron-spiked wrought iron gate. He was told it used to be Paul Robeson's house and was heavily fortified owing to his number of political enemies, before the singer and actor fled and took refuge in Paris.

He spies the old man through the gate. He is sitting on his porch in a rocking chair, smoking his pipe, in velvet smoking jacket and satin pajamas. His German Shepherd sits at his feet. As Mark approaches, he sees the contented look of one who has paid his dues to society, and the image contradicts that of an old man who, in a matter of a week, has lost his daughter and his grandson.

The dog jumps up and with a blood-curdling growl rushes to the gate, hell-bent on tearing the visitor to shreds. His huge front paws grab the crossbar. White foam is bubbling from his teeth like soap suds. His bark is like clatters of thunder.

"Rufus! Stop!"

HIS FATHER'S FOOTSTEPS

Rufus obeys his master's command, calls off his attack. The gate is electronically swung open like two welcoming arms. He notices the gate is activated from a switch on one of the balusters on the railing of the porch. The dog accompanies Mark up the walkway and expresses his apology by insisting on sniffing his shoes, his hands and his crotch.

Now to confront the old man with his confession. What would it be like to tell him that he was the one who killed his grandson, albeit in defense of his own life, and was indirectly the reason his daughter was dead, and that because of him his whole progeny was wasted since he had come to learn the old man had no other descendants? Should some credit be in order for his stepping forward to confess? Would his confession do anything to mitigate the old man's loss? Or was it too late? Did he lose credibility by holding back, fearing the law, fearing its lack of integrity, fearing the man he is about to beg forgiveness? He had come prepared to show the hole in his jacket and the wound in his back, not yet fully healed, all of which would buttress his defense as the real victim.

The councilman welcomes him with a smile. "I was just thinking I never see my neighbors walking by. It is so quiet around here. Once in a while a Jehovah's Witness or a salesman comes by with his snake oil. Other than that I could sit here all day and not see a single soul. I know you are not selling anything, my good man, 'cause you come empty handed. You come with news. Good news, I hope. You live in Sugar Hill?"

"No sir."

He climbs the three wooden steps to the landing and reaches out his hand. There's no beating around. "Sir, my name is Mark Maynard. I am here to …"

"I remember your face. The scar. Yes, now I remember. You were one of the folks outside Harlem Hospital. I was surrounded that day, hemmed in on all sides by folks offering sympathy. Couldn't get close but I saw you with my daughter. Yes, you were very kind to come down to the hospital to see us and …"

"Yes sir. Well, I am here to …"

"Take a load off your feet. Sit over there."

He motions to the only other chair in the veranda, a rocker that appears just as rickety as the homeowner himself. But Mark is anxious to get a load off his chest, to blurt it out, fully expecting the old man to issue forth another command to his dog. He can see himself almost being torn from limb to limb before he reaches the wrought iron gate. He had come to confess and now the words are trapped in his head.

The old man continues to rock and flap his gums. "Y'know when my daughter was born, to tell you the truth, I was a little disappointed though I didn't say this to my wife. Oh no! But in my heart I really wanted a boy. Y'see, a son would carry on the name. Not too many black Solomons in this country. When people first heard the name they thought I was Jewish and when their heard me speak on the radio they figured me for a black Jew. I went to Columbia Law on a scholarship and eventually got into politics and got a seat on the board of councilors for the city of New York. Don't know how much the name had to do with that either."

He seems a lonely man living apart from the riff raff and the less privileged, now in a place where everyone keeps to himself and minds his own business; he seems to be longing for company who would sit and listen without interrupting as he opens up with whatever random thoughts come to his old brain.

"... and then my daughter, Shonelle, had a son and I was on cloud nine because at last the little guy would soon grow up and spawn a few more Solomons before I close my eyes for the last time knowing that the name would live on, not just in the Jewish family, which has its share of Solomons, but in my beloved black community as well. And then this awful thing happened and that was the end of the line ..."

"Mr. Solomon, I am the one who killed your grandson, but ..."

"I know," he answers and continues to rock as blithely as before.

"You know? But how ...?" He is caught off-guard, stunned by the councilman's reply with such insouciance the chair continues to rock without faltering.

"Your name is Mark Maynard and you live in a brownstone on 135th Street with a white woman from down south. Heard all about you from the youngster, Ben Hanks. So what took you so long to come clean? Ben gave me the rundown. Told me you were innocent, that he and Elroy were guilty and my grandson brought it on himself.

He had a change of heart after he lost his friend. He says you got a raw deal but he couldn't go to the police with all his baggage to help you. I am seeing that he gets a break with the law and arrange for some rehab for the kid. He's had a rough upbringing just like Elroy."

Mark is still appalled at the old man's ingenious playacting. A load falls from his shoulders.

"Guess I too was afraid of the law," he explains.

"Young man, I've been involved in helping to shape the laws in this city for years. There is no reason to be afraid of the law if you have the truth on your side."

"How about your daughter?" he dares to ask. "Do you know who killed her too?"

"The Klan, who else? We put two and two together. The reason was to get their hands on your book that was passed from Elroy to his mother. To conceal their identity she had to be either blinded or killed. I learned about your book from my friend, Brother Sheldon. Glenmore cannot keep a secret if you beg 'im."

He proceeds to tell the councilman the whole story as it unfolded, of his trip to the South, his possession of the Klan's secret plans, the stonewalling of his book by a certain publisher. And finally and most touchingly he reveals himself as the son of the man who was executed outside a Staten Island club in 1958 when Staten Island was Richmond Borough, an episode with which the councilman seems vaguely familiar.

"Never caught the killer, did they?"

"No. The police dropped the case. The investigator in charge, one Sergeant Kaufmann, didn't give a hoot about a potential witness who said she came on the scene in the moments after they shot him. I was told the case went cold."

The councilman suddenly turns his head and yells over his shoulder. "Maxine!" A woman, comparatively young, her hair in curlers, emerges and shuffles to the door in her slippers and housecoat. He introduces her as his wife.

"Call Albany and get me Hugh on the phone, please. Tell him it's a matter of the utmost urgency."

He turns to Mark. "The Governor of New York is a personal friend of mine."

He continues to converse about the slow pace and laxity of the police until his wife returns with a handset which he places to his ear bringing his rocker to a standstill. Though Mark is not privy to the exchange, he gathers the gist of it at the ending as the councilman responds — "yes, 1958 ... name, Maynard ... execution style ... no real witness ... lousy investigation ... young boy lost his father ... yes, yes, yes ... please do that ... yes, let me know ... soon as possible ... thanks, Hugh." And his face, at first dark and insistent, turns to a soft mellow glow as he and the Governor seem to be on the same page.

He closes the phone, turns to Mark, leans forward and whispers with a boyish glint in his eyes. "My friend, the Governor, says he'll call Abe tonight at his home at Gracie Mansion. He's another friend and he owes me. He'll take care of that chief investigator, whatever his name is. It pays to have friends in high places. They're gonna restart the investigation into who killed your father. And we'll go after the KKK too. Tell me what you know about them setting up shop in this part of the country."

This is music in the ears of the one who, for much too long, had been David confronting the unassailable Goliath with little more than a slingshot, a 500-page book. They had threatened him, tried to bribe him and then scoffed at his feeble attempts with a book to stop their advance.

From beneath his shirt he produces the evidence that is the bane of the Ku Klux Klan and lays it in the councilman's lap.

"Sir, I am putting in your hands every piece of information that has been hiding in my father's bedroom for years between the mattress and the box spring. Every scrap of paper handed to me back in Montgomery, all the proof the law will ever need to go after these vermin hiding out in the suburbs secreting their poison, spreading their hate, disturbing the peace."

"Hold your horses, my eloquent friend. Our laws accord them the right to assemble and organize peacefully. We need first to nail them with a crime."

Tamping the tobacco in his pipe, he scrutinizes every slip of paper, all about their plans to plant their seeds of malevolence wherever they find a mending of fences between people of different races; about names out to launch a new chapter, which was the title of Mark's book. He will come across the name Hamilton, the putative Klansman who, according to Paula, was the one who targeted his father. Then he will understand Mark's eagerness to go after them with everything's he got.

And what a relief it is to finally put these secret files into the hands of someone who is in a position to bring them before the powers that be, from the Governor of New York to local political officials to make them aware of what could be a disastrous outcome if the Klan were allowed to continue setting up their outposts in the outskirts where the equanimity between races is tenuous at best.

Mrs. Solomon appears once again, this time holding forward a tray laden with teapot, cups and a smorgasbord of toasted cookies. She doesn't speak but cradles the tray like a peace offering. Her smile suggests a show of hospitality as well as a gesture of forgiveness. He joins them for coffee and between munches he tells them about his family back home and his pledge to find his father's killer, "come hell or high water," before he packs up and heads back to his beloved Barbados. He feels an incipient friendship blooming between him and the Solomons, a friendship that he had feared could never be. The old man seems not to hold in his heart the slightest thread of retribution for the man who had indirectly caused the death of his family.

He gets up to leave. The councilman places a gentle hand on his shoulder with a puzzled expression that normally precedes a question.

"I'm curious. In his confession Ben told me that after all he did to you, you still gave him money. What was all that about?"

"It's called 'paying forward', sir, 'paying forward'."

With that, he takes leave of the councilman, rocking contentedly, smoking his pipe, no sign of ill will, still perusing the incriminating papers. Smoke curls up from his pipe like a prayer of thanks to the gods that this madness is finally coming to an end.

The dog, wagging his tail, accompanies him down the walkway. The security gate swings open and he makes his way back from peaceful, high-class Sugar Hill to the crowded and crime-ridden core of Harlem.

20 – The Other Woman

Next day, following his visit with the Solomons, things seem to be going his way. Early in the morning he gets a phone call from Sergeant James at the Staten Island precinct. The officer is ebullient.

"Guess what! We have a lead on the elusive Angela Santana. We know where she lives."

At last there seems to be a change in fortunes.

"How about Sergeant Kaufmann? Is he ready now to bring her in?"

"Kaufmann is off the case. I'm now the one in charge. Don't know what happened but Kaufmann is out on patrol duty."

But, of course, it was foreseeable that the Mayor at the behest of the Governor and at the request of the influential councilman would topple the police chief from his arrogant throne, so now the investigation could be pulled from the pile in which it had been buried for years and given a whole new revival. In the hierarchical bureaucracy of New York one phone call had sufficed where all his letters had failed.

"Want to go pay the lady a visit?" asks the sergeant. "I'll pick you up at three before the traffic peaks."

This gives him enough time to revisit the councilman and thank him profusely for his hand in this change of events. He hails a cab and heads to Sugar Hill.

As he reaches the Solomons' gate, their dog is not there to greet him with his instinctual sniffing at his lower extremities as he did the day before. Neither is the councilman sitting out on his porch to let him in as he did yesterday. He thinks it best not to disturb the family at this hour. Since he doesn't have their telephone number, he is about to jot a thank-you note and leave it in the mailbox imbedded in the wall. Then he looks up and sees Mrs. Solomon in her housecoat, clambering down the steps, running to meet him, breathless, panting, hair still in curlers, obviously distressed, hands flailing, tears in her eyes. She flings open the gate with her handheld remote and greets him with a jumble of broken English and halting phrases.

"Mr. Maynard, they — they drive by late last night — after you — you was gone and — and they try to open the gate. The bastards shot 'im. Then they — they drive away. Can you — you believe these criminals — these vandals?"

He says to himself, *"My God! Not another one. Not Mr. Solomon. Please God, don't let it be this good man!* And without hearing another word he blames himself for having involved the old man, for having introduced him into this circle of death, and in that instant his thoughts flash back to Mr. Bates, the motel owner, whose death still weighs heavily on his mind. He clasps his hands in silent prayer, his heart thumping.

Then he hears her next spluttering words and everything falls into perspective.

"Mr. Maynard, he — he didn't die right — right away. We had to put — put 'im down, my poor Rufus, my poor baby!"

HIS FATHER'S FOOTSTEPS

He opens his eyes and looks towards the heavens. It is not good news about the dog but it is not the worst it could have been. As his heart regains its normal rhythm he must show Mrs. Solomon he is not indifferent to her sorrow; he holds her close.

He had come to thank her husband for his intercession with the Governor. Now he knows he had unwittingly drawn the Klan to his doorstep. They were following his every move. Mrs. Solomon doesn't know it was not money they were after. They knew that the damaging papers had changed hands. An old man and his wife would have been easy pickings but they hadn't figured on a ferocious canine waiting on the other side of the wall.

She is a trifle calmer now and no longer stutters. "I'll tell 'im you was here when he wake up. He had a rough night. After he hear Rufus barkin' and the shootin', he pick up his rifle that he ain't fired in years, that he keep under the bed and let off a few shots of his own and see the rascals take off but he keep shootin' in the dark before we call the police. I think they after Mr. Solomon's money. They believe everybody in Sugar Hill rich like his neighbor, Cab Calloway."

She reaches in the pocket of her housecoat and hands him a piece of paper. It's another infamous propaganda leaflet.

"They left this in our mailbox."

"Show it to your husband and tell 'im to mail it the Governor." He is sure his friend Hugh in Albany will arrange for around-the-clock protection.

"We're gonna miss ol' Rufus," she sobs.

"So will I," he offers in a feeble attempt to commiserate with the grieving Maxine Solomon. Little does she know the dog had given his life to save the last of the Solomon family.

He is back home, sitting on his stoop, his chin in his hands, counting the minutes, waiting for the sergeant. Finally, he is seen clipping the curb, rounding the corner at 135th in a flurry of flashing red lights and screaming sirens, barreling through, freezing the traffic with his official authority, shunting every oncoming car to the side of the road.

"We're heading to 408-161st. South Bronx. We'll see what she knows. Let's go."

He climbs in. "Are you gonna bring her in?"

"Cool it, Mark. Because she was with your father that night doesn't mean she killed him. We gotta have some substantive evidence to accuse the lady of being involved. We can ask her a few questions politely and hope she cooperates. It's too early to talk about a subpoena. In this country a person is innocent until proven guilty in a court of law and if she is guilty it could be another ten years before we can prove it, depending on the skill of a defense attorney."

"Man, she must've had a reason to lie about retrieving a coat and scarf on a hot steamy night when the mercury was hovering around ninety degrees. Right?"

"She said she was retrieving it, not wearing it."

HIS FATHER'S FOOTSTEPS

Mark has his own opinions. *Did Kaufman not see the implausibility before they removed her name from the records as a possible suspect, accomplice or even a motive? Instead she was ruled out as a witness and protected from the newshounds.*

He says to the sergeant, "If she didn't pull the trigger she sure as hell had him set up. That's why she didn't follow 'im outside the café. We gotta find out who she hired for the job. Know what I mean?"

"Well, okay, let's say she set 'im up? But why? We need a motive."

"How'd you find out where she lives?"

"Stopped by the café. The bartender told me."

"He told me he didn't know her."

"Well, you're not a cop. We know how to interrogate."

With lights whirring, flashing and sirens screaming, they fly up the Major Deegan Expressway as if on the tail of a serial killer before he nails his next victim. In minutes they turn onto 161st, a street that boasts more than the average complement of Latinos. Storefronts with signs all in Spanish and narrow bodegas line both sides of the street. Record shops are blasting out a medley of salsa music proclaiming this section of the Bronx the heartland of expatriated Puerto Rico.

"There it is, number 408!" He points with the exhilaration of a seafarer who finally sights land, for he realizes that finding Miss Santana may be his one and only link to the truth.

HIS FATHER'S FOOTSTEPS

They double park and climb the steps of the tiny saltbox nestled among other houses of modest size, houses clearly well maintained in this neighborhood of proud Hispanic immigrants.

The doorbell brings a pleasant four-note jingle to their ears and in seconds the raven-haired Angela Santana comes to the door hesitantly, questioningly. She seems to recognize his face but is taken aback by the presence of the law as she releases the chain that restrains the door.

She looks much different from the time he had first seen her at his father's wake. Unlike Maria's, her face seems to have lost its luster; there is no longer that youthful sparkle in her eyes; her hair has been cut pageboy style as if in an effort to reverse the years. Her hips and the wrinkles around the outer corners of her eyes bear witness to her years, but her smile, her movements and her sensual posture exude a charm he finds endearing.

And looking at her now, he thinks about his father and wonders if the years would have been equally unforgiving. But his mind would not allow him to recalibrate the image of his father as the aging gray-haired septuagenarian he would have been today, so he deludes himself into seeing him as he was, a young debonair Dan Maynard.

"Hello, you remember me? We met at my dad's funeral reception."

"Oh yes, of course. Dan Maynard's son. It's been a long time."

HIS FATHER'S FOOTSTEPS

"And this is Sergeant James. Just want to ask a few questions about my dad on that night … if you don't mind, since you were the last person to see him alive."

She glances down to the street as neighbors are already drawn to the ominous sight of a patrol car, the NYPD insignia emblazoned on the side. They gather around, exchanging their conspiratorial whispers, casting their suspicious eyes to her door. She wears hot colors, bright red shoes, matching shorts and sky-blue halter top, which reminds him of the inappropriate attire she had chosen the evening of his father's funeral. Now, much older, she seems no less ostentatious.

"Please come in," she says quickly. "My neighbors are a nosy bunch. I'm sure they think I committed some kind o' crime. But I know why you're here. Can I get you a drink? Coffee? Soda? I don't have anything strong."

The offer was likely intended to buy some time, settle her nerves and assemble her thoughts, steeling herself to field the volley of questions the visitors were about to lob at her. It is clear she was not expecting company judging from the disorder that surrounds them: pillows, books, magazines, pictures, record albums, strewn everywhere on the floor, on the sofa, on the coffee table.

"Let's sit in my office."

She leads them into her office and there is a man sprawled on a leather sofa, reading a book and smoking a cigar. He stands as they enter, removes his baseball cap revealing a head that is bald as an egg. Suddenly he appears seven feet or more. He is Germanic in appearance, though he could be of Russian or Nordic extraction.

HIS FATHER'S FOOTSTEPS

"This is my husband, Glenn Corbin, and we're throwing him out of my office. We kept our last names in case you're wondering." There are smiles, pleasantries and handshakes all around.

Her husband obligingly leaves the room, granting them privacy, leaving a trail of noxious fumes. She gets up and locks the door.

Her office is more like a wigmaker's warehouse than an office. There must be dozens of wigs everywhere, piled high on shelves, hanging from coat racks, on the heads of naked mannequins and pinned to disjointed skulls. The colors are dazzling: of blondes, brunettes, redheads, the auburn-haired and the interweaving of multicolored strands. The variety is mind-boggling: of afros, bangs, extensions, kinky tops, pony tails, even silky soft toupees for baldheaded men. And displayed on the walls are pictures of more wigs and their respective origins and prices.

"I sell wigs to the vain and to women in hiding," she says, seeing the curiosity in their faces.

She strolls over to a black dummy in the corner and removes a luxuriant clump of human dreadlocks. "This was the wig I wore the night Dan was killed. Now what else do you want to know from me about that night?"

A chill wind blows through her office window, the one that overlooks Yankee Stadium, and suddenly everyone seems to be shivering as she sits coolly awaiting a question.

Sergeant James breaks the ice with the incisive question that at some point needs to be asked. "Mrs. Santana, do you know who killed Mr. Maynard?"

"No, I don't," she answers bluntly.

A new item of interest presents itself now that it is known she's married and Mark pounces on this new information which may, or may not, cast a new light on the investigation.

"How long have you two been married?"

"We got married right out of high school, Amarillo High in Texas. I'm originally from Mexico next door to El Paso, you see. That's where I met my husband. We were married when I met your dad, if that's what you're asking. But Glenn and I were separated at the time. People grow old and they grow wiser and you can't live in the past."

"Would you tell us how you came to know him? I mean my dad."

"We met in Barbados. Me and a couple o' girls were there on spring break from Sarah Lawrence College. I was living in Yonkers at the time. He was visiting the hotel where we were staying. I believe it was the Sam Lord's Castle but don't quote me, it's been over fifteen years, my memory is not the same. We were sitting in the lounge with nothing to do when he came over, introduced himself, bought us a friendly drink, told us a few jokes, quite a nice fella."

"Was Maria Townsend one of the girls?" asked Mark.

Her nostrils flared perceptibly at the mention of Maria. She nervously tucked an imaginary strand or two behind her ears and answered, "Yes".

"Who was the other girl?"

"Marcia Landsberry. Black. Pretty American-born of Barbadian descent. Her first trip to Barbados. She was engaged to her gym instructor in White Plains. But it was *me* your dad took a liking to, not Maria. It was just as well she wasn't around."

"So what happened next? I don't mean to be personal," says Mark.

She seemed flustered. "Wha' do you mean? Do you want to know if we went to my room and he jumped in the saddle?"

"I am not that kind o' woman, maybe Maria *is* but I'm *not*. Neither was your father that kind of man," she adds, gazing directly at his son.

The sergeant intervened. "We need to know everything that transpired between you and him from the time you met 'til he was killed while you were retrieving your coat at the Hard Nuts Café." His last words were laced with sarcasm.

"Was it the first time you and he went to the Café?"

"No, maybe a dozen times, I don't know exactly."

"But you said it was your first time," says Mark.

"That was meant for Maria's ears."

"Listen, I was having an affair, alright? Things were not going well with me and Glenn at the time. He was becoming too possessive for my liking. I needed to breathe.

HIS FATHER'S FOOTSTEPS

I had to get away, which was the reason I joined the others on that little vacation. When I got back to the States I worked it out so your dad could apply for his Green Card. He said he wanted to come to America. Yes, Mark, it was me who sponsored your father. I was the one who brought him to America, not Maria."

"And all the time you were married to Glenn."

It was a question phrased as a sardonic statement of fact that seemed to strike a nerve as she bit her lower lip and tears brimmed in her eyes.

"You wouldn't understand. I'm going to tell you a story." She digs into her handbag, finds her cigarettes, pops one between her lips, lights it and sits back with the smoke billowing between them. "In July 1945 my mother, my father and me — may they rest in peace — left the stink hole of Ciudad Juarez heading to El Paso with nothing but the clothes on our backs and a shopping bag with water and two dozen empanadas. In sight of America, my father was shot dead at the border by a patrol guard. My mom died a month later in a holding cell. I escaped and made my way to San Antonio and four years later I became an American citizen. I am telling you this to explain why I sponsored your dad. Nobody gave us a hand to come to this land of opportunity. Instead they wiped out my parents and made me an orphan to fend for myself. So I was happy to give a hand to your dad. Your father was a special human being."

It was a sad story and seemed a genuine explanation given the tears, but it had contradicted the perceptions he had gotten from Maria. Still he found it hard to believe that she had become in such a short space of time his father's benefactor. He knew it was more than an altruistic heart that had compelled her to reach out to him, bring him to America and spend night after night with him in a darkened corner of a café in Staten Island. And all that time she was married to Glenn.

"Did you love my father?"

She arched an eyebrow. "What do you think?" Her answer implied the obvious.

Common sense would inform that the Hard Nuts Café was not a place to take a lady on an occasional tryst. The café was more of a watering hole for hard-backed men or lonesome souls in search of solitude and hard liquor to drown their sorrows at the end of another day's toil.

"So why did you two choose to go all the way to Staten Island to sit in a bar and have a drink?" the sergeant asks.

"Because it was out of the way. Far from the gossipmongers and the busybodies in Brooklyn where he and I worked."

"You said you were collecting your coat and scarf from the coatroom at the time he was shot. A coat in the middle of summer? Was there really a coat?"

"It's my blood, officer. My blood was uncommonly thin when I was younger."

"And why didn't you run to your friend's side instead of fleeing?"

"I guess I didn't want to be in the news. My husband would have killed me. I might have been having an affair but I still wanted my marriage to work. Dan went out the door ahead of me to fetch my car. When I heard the shots I pushed my head out the door and fled."

The interrogation was going nowhere. She had been curt but seemingly forthright. Her answers, her demeanor and her admissions of human weaknesses all seemed perfectly plausible. Mark had one final question that would shed light about her and Maria and the extent of their mutual disdain.

"Were you supposed to be her maid of honor?"

"He was never going to marry Maria. Let's leave it at that."

There is a knock. She gets up and opens the door. Her husband enters balancing a tray laden with glasses, ice bucket, canned sodas and dry crackers.

"Thought y'all would be thirsty."

He leans forward from his considerable height to lay the refreshments on the low table between them and, as his sleeve rides up, a tiny swastika appears tattooed on his right wrist. Mark is gripped with sudden panic and something cold and scary leaps up from his stomach to his mouth. He finds himself gasping for air. It takes him back to his first meeting with Thatcher at Pemberton Publishers. The other man who preferred to be incognito wore the same mark on his identical wrist.

Before Glenn could leave the room, he looks him straight in the eye and asks, "Do you know a man named Hamilton?"

He shakes his head. "No". A frown wrinkles his forehead.

Everyone seems dumbfounded at the strange question that came out of nowhere. Except Angela Santana, who smiles and doesn't bat an eyelid but takes another drag on her Virginia Slim. What secrets lie behind her inscrutable smile and unflappable cool? He wonders.

21 – Sexual Predilections

Next day he recaps the visit with Mrs. Santana. He had found nothing to link her to the killing of his father. On the way back he told Sergeant James all about the publisher's meeting, his book, and the stranger who had a perverse interest in the incriminating contents. Then he remarked on the eerie coincidence of the tattoo he had noted on the man's wrist and that of Glenn Corbin.

"I'll get the fellas down at Central Station to run a report on a Glenn Corbin from Texas. It's a long shot but if we find any kind o' dossier clinging to this guy we'll follow up."

As they made their way southward, down the bleak streets of South Bronx, barreling through every stop light, horn squawking, siren screaming, onto the Major Deegan Highway and across the 3rd Avenue Bridge, Sergeant James launched into a stinging indictment of his father.

"Look, Mark, the problem with your fair-skinned, curly-haired father is, when he came to this country he wasn't sure if he was black or white. But everyone else knew he was a black man. Didn't matter how he talked, how he walked, how handsome he was, who his friends were, if he was rich or poor, none of that mattered. The first thing you have to learn in America is to know who you are. And then if people think you are someone else, it don' matter 'cause you already know who. See what I mean?

HIS FATHER'S FOOTSTEPS

"Your father crossed over and there is nothin' wrong with crossin' over but when you cross over you have to watch your back. It is not just jealousy, man; it is downright fear, a mortal fear that a dude like your father could do f'r their women something they can't. I'd feel the same way if a white dude was hittin' on my wife and getting by. It's all about protectin' the herd.

"F'r twenty years I've been married to my Maybelline and not once was I curious about doin' it with another woman. Not curious enough to go snoopin' around another man's chicken coop f'r him to think I was fixin' to mount one of his pullets, and then f'r him to go lookin' f'r a gun. If your father couldn't keep his pants on, he should've stayed home with his family. And you wouldn't be here today chasin' some loony who couldn't keep tabs on his woman."

He had not heard anyone talk about his father that way since he died, attributing his death to his own misjudgment. Whatever his lack of judgment he did not deserve to die, surely not to die on his knees with three bullet holes in his head for his nightly assignations with a married woman. But that was in the fifties; things were different then. Or were they?

"Is 'interracial' still a dirty word?" he asked the sergeant.

He replied, "When they find the man who shot your father, you can ask him."

Now he thinks about his own life and the naiveté of his intimacy with the white woman in his father's house. He's not sure he loves her. Still they saunter blithely down the streets of New York holding hands, rubbing it in the faces of those who stare, returning the smiles of others, never once thinking they had strayed from their respective herds, according to the officer, and were thus blasphemously flouting some rule of conduct, the same infraction that had led to his father's demise.

He remembers well Brother Sheldon's words of caution at his father's funeral: "It don' matter, son. It's the perception, see? They don' like to see black and white too close like that together. Get away from her as fast as you can, or sure as hell you goin' be next."

The minister's words never gave him pause. Glenmore Sheldon, who had a big mouth, was known for his wild pronouncements.

On the way back, the officer decided on a detour down Amsterdam Avenue and onto 125th, the main street in Harlem always bustling with humanity: shoppers, vendors, hustlers, loiterers and young men standing on the sides ogling the women. It was Saturday afternoon and the women were out sampling the wares all along the sidewalks as far as the eye could see: ladies' shoes, handbags, dresses, jewelry, perfumes, lingerie ... He pulled over to the curb, parked and pointed up and down the street.

"Take a look at these fine sistas," he exclaimed. "Black as sable, some chocolaty, mocha, light brown like sugar, dark brown like burnt coffee, every shade in God's creation of the chosen. An' if you want lighter, go down Spanish Harlem, down in the nineties, you'll find the smoothest yellow skins, light skins, almost white but not quite, down in El Barrio. Sistas comin' out o' university with their Masters and Doctorates, ain't lookin' f'r no deadbeat dude to step out in the bright lights of New York. They're lookin' f'r a brother like your father was, handsome, stable and well-mannered. An' they won't have needed his money, they got their own. So why did your father get all tangled up with a woman that was not his own?"

He pointed to a conspicuous corner next to a bus stop. "This is where I met my Maybelline, walking home one day from Columbia U, an' parking my behind right there at the corner, checking out the herd, smiling and doffing my cap smartly as the ladies walked by, all kinds, some skinny, some slim, some fat, some ungainly, but all beautiful in my eyes, until I see this fine specimen, black as coal just like me. She smiled back, walked right up to me an' says, 'Hey baby!' an' I says, 'Daddy been standin' here waitin' f'r you, baby.' And the rest is history … twenty years an' still goin' strong."

In that moment Mark could not help but wonder if some genetic strain handed down from his father, and hence lacking in Sergeant James, had led him to think indiscriminately about women. He had insisted to his own conscience that, black or white, women were just women, and that under the skin the heart was all that mattered.

He is seeing himself back home in Bridgetown, in his college years, loitering around after school, lasciviously eyeing the native women, smooth-black, brown-skinned, fair-skinned, Creole, Bajan-white, and faces of indeterminate complexion, mingling with the pale-faced and sunburnt tourists and thinking them all beautiful in his sight and God's.

Now the sergeant forces him to think of his own "domestic arrangement", as he calls it, lying next to Paula in his father's bed, and their nightly lovemaking, which has now become more or less perfunctory, more a matter of duty than of desire. There is no longer that stirring in his loins when they touch as had been the case in the beginning when their screwing was a novelty, a few fleeting moments of curiosity.

Conversely, he thinks of how it had been with Nakeisha for so long, passionate, volcanic, before she repulsed him for having invited Paula into his house, and into his bed. But he remains steadfast in his commitment to the one whom he considers his partner in this journey in America, to one who has committed herself to his mission, to one who has sacrificed much in her life on his account. It is a relationship more worthy to him than either love or sex. But Nakeisha cannot bring herself to believe he must follow in his father's footsteps to find the one who killed him.

After leaving the company of the officer, he waited patiently for Maria to phone in order to query her about the contradictions between her version and that of her former rival.

"Angela is a lying bitch," she seethed. "Don't believe a thing she said. And check out her husband. Any bet they were both in it together to get rid of your father. She couldn't have him and so no one else would."

HIS FATHER'S FOOTSTEPS

It was clear they had become the bitterest of enemies, each one placing the blood of his father in the other's hands.

"Yes, the witch sponsored your father to come to America so he would be accountable to her and to no one else."

But Maria had not mentioned heretofore that her college friend had been already married or that his father had come under the auspices of Angela Santana. Now which of the two was the lying and secretive one?

"And how's your folks?" She had told him that George and Eva Townsend were well into their eighties. "Dad's had a hip replaced and Mom is losing her memory. I'm their only child so I have to stay. I keep telling them they should've had more babies when they could."

Neither was his mother doing well; when he got home that day there was a letter from Ermajean in the mailbox.

Ma wants to know when you are coming home, she wrote. *She sits in a wheelchair and we go walking in the evening. She likes to go by River Bay where the river meets the sea. She says it makes her feel you are not that far away, just on the other side of the horizon. She no longer goes to church. She is too vain to be seen being wheeled down the aisle like an invalid for communion, so Father Abrams brings her the sacrament every Sunday evening.*

She talks about your dad all the time and says she forgives him. I have become her fulltime caretaker. Your brother is not the same. Earl is so full of anger. Write soon.

Your loving sister, Ermajean

HIS FATHER'S FOOTSTEPS

He could see her now, tall, regal, plain but good-looking and totally without artifice like most Bajan girls he knew. She was never one to write long, rambling letters but now every nuanced word and every brief sentence conveyed the message that things were not going well at home. His mother's health was declining and she had become his mother's helper. She must have put her whole social life and education aside to take care of his mother. His brother apparently was too consumed with anger to fill the role of a supportive son compensating for his father's absence.

Between the lines was the plea that he should come home and give up the chase. How could he? He had come so far. And though the killer was still at large he had smelled his blood and could see his tracks like paw prints in a jungle that would eventually lead him to a hideous monster. He assured himself his mother would be well cared for in the grateful hands of the orphan she had brought into the family and nurtured as her own.

The Ermajean he remembers from a distant past was the only daughter of the elderly Cadogans, his mother's best friends, who had lived diagonally on the other side of the road in Crab Hill. They died, one after the other, in a wave of dengue hemorrhagic fevers that struck the island. Ermajean then moved in with Ma and became the daughter she never had.

She was two years younger than he, and Ma insisted she was her boys' new sister. But even as he tried in those pubescent years he could not bring himself to cast the new addition to the household as a relative. Neither could she.

And so they began innocently and surreptitiously meeting in the corn patch behind the paling to explore their sexual identities, and for some time after she was adopted, she continued to be the object of his libidinous attention.

Now that they have both grown and become two level-headed adults, whatever he and Ermajean shared in those precocious years has been buried forever under layers of more definable loves and would have been erased entirely from his memory except for the mark of their having ditched their virginities in one night of exploratory sex, on a moonless night, in a cane field in St. Peter. From what he could remember, he was eleven or twelve, and at that early age, blessed or cursed with an uncommon voracity for sex. It was distasteful now, looking back, owing to the incestuous nature of their behavior. Over the years they came to recognize each other as brother and sister, and the sexual attraction languished and finally died in mutual disinterest. Today they regard each other with wholesome affection, as he thinks it should have been from the start.

He sits at his desk, grabs a pen and ransacks his brain for the right words to appease his mother. Nothing short of a blatant lie will put her mind at ease and assure her he'll be soon on his way.

My dear Ermajean, thanks for taking care of Ma. I expect to be home very soon. Please tell her they know who he is. They are about to arrest Dad's murderer. As soon as he is in police custody I will be on the next plane out of here.

Will be seeing you all very soon.

Love, Mark

HIS FATHER'S FOOTSTEPS

But his conscience rebels; he has never lied to his mother and the letter is a flagrant lie, for he has reached a dead end with nowhere to go. He crumples the paper in his fist and tosses it into the waste basket by his desk. He is at a loss. He doesn't have the answer that would put her mind or his own at ease.

22 – The Dead and the Dying

Sunday had come and gone, that holiest of days back home when his mother would be gone the whole day and he and his brother would be left in his father's charge for whatever chore or game or lesson his father would choose to occupy their restless minds. He lay in bed fully clothed and recapped the events of the past few hours. It had been an eventful day with a tumultuous ending.

At Trinity Cemetery where he paid his weekly visits to his father's grave, he had sat on the ledge of the unlit mausoleum and talked to him in the dark in the manner of a psychic communing with the dead. He silently reiterated the same promise to his father that he had made a hundred times before, and once again a voice emanated from the sodden musty earth of the enclosed mausoleum telling him he was on the right path to find his killer, but to be wary of those around him whom he had trusted in his own lifetime. On his way to the graveyard, he had plucked a sprig of wild peonies, wrapped them with a couple wisps of fern and fashioned them into an impromptu wreath which he laid on the floor of the tomb. Then across his chest he made a halfhearted sign of the cross "in the name of the Father" and felt the presence of his father rising from the earth like the breath of early morning dew. In his mind his father's face appeared before him, not as the mummified visage he had looked upon with abject horror in the morgue, but he had been restored to the irresistibly handsome Daniel Maynard who would be remembered by all.

He still wondered why on earth Maria had been so extravagant in her choice of a marble and granite house for his mortal remains. As far as he knows, she had not been back since the interment. The flowers she had brought to the burial ground were now dead and matted into the earth. She had never looked back. Had he had the wherewithal at the time he would have shipped the body back to Barbados in a wooden casket, for he was a simple man, from a simple family, from a simple working-class community. It must have been her way of differentiating her love from the love of others like Angela Santana. Still he couldn't help but see it as a mockery of his station in life, not as someone of noble stature, but as a car salesman. Whatever the case, he would continue every Sunday morning to visit this airless chamber to talk to his father. These weekly visits infused him with a renewed energy to pursue the one who had taken his life.

An hour later, he was at his doorstep. For some inexplicable reason, Paula was standing on the landing outside the front door awaiting his arrival. An expression of anxiety and curiosity was painted on her face.

"There is someone here to see you," she said.

"Who?"

"A woman. She wouldn't give her name."

For one moment his feet were stuck on the doormat as his mind struggled to guess the identity of the visitor. Foe or friend, he could not be sure. Surely she couldn't be Nakeisha or, least of all, Angela. And Maria would have called ahead.

"Where is she?"

"In your study sitting at your desk." Trepidation quivered in her voice.

He went to his study, closed the door and there she was, sitting erect, her back turned, a black knitted shawl draped over her head and hanging past her shoulders. At the sound of his footsteps she turned, faced him directly and removed her sunglasses. His recognition of the woman jolted him back with such alarm his back crashed into the door. He shook his head and rubbed his eyes, for he was seeing none other than Ellen Murphy, the former secretary of Thomas Thatcher. Or was she an apparition?

She threw back her shawl and flashed the patented smile he remembered only too well from his visits to Pemberton Publishers.

"I'm for real, Mr. Maynard, I'm not a ghost."

"I thought you were …"

"Killed?" She finished his sentence and grinned. "Maybe I came back from the dead to finish my warning when you disappeared in the elevator.

"So you were fired," he said half-questioningly. "I tried to reach you."

"No, I wasn't fired. It was my boss who told me to run and I've been running ever since. It was he who warned me that I had been overheard in the hallway. He was told that someone was out to get me. He was the one who told me my life was in danger. That he couldn't protect me."

"So why would Mr. Thatcher warn you when he was a co-conspirator all along?"

"Tom Thatcher was never your enemy, Mr. Maynard. After you met with him that day he wised up to the ones who were trying to suppress your book. The man who was sitting with him at the first meeting is not a book merchant as he revealed himself to my boss. He is a knight of the Ku Klux Klan stationed here in New York. His name is Albert Graham and he was the one who gave the command to steal your manuscript, kill that Solomon lady and destroy everything that might have been sitting here on this same desk. They were looking for papers that belonged to them but never found them. The person who overheard me is an editor on the floor. He had befriended Mr. Graham."

The name, Albert, rang a distant bell. Paula had told him that an Albert was the other North Easterner at the initiation meeting of the Klansmen at her father's house many years ago.

So what about the one named Hamilton? A mystery still surrounds the other man, the one Paula insists was the one he should be after.

This torrent of information was too much and too rapid for Mark to absorb while on his feet. He dropped to the floor, pulled up his knees and rested his chin in his palms. Heretofore he had assumed that Ellen Murphy had been killed on his account just as others had been exterminated like Vic Bates and Shonelle Solomon and who knows who else?

One thing he knew for sure, the secretary of the one he had assumed was collaborating with the enemy had been privy to secrets only she could have known sitting at Thatcher's right hand. She was in charge of his correspondence, overheard his conversations and knew of his associations. Still it was hard to believe that a man so adamantly opposed to his book could suddenly change his mind and see through the veil of deception that had been placed before his eyes by the imposter named Albert Graham.

"After you left he had a change of heart. You opened his eyes, Mr. Maynard. He kept staring at the clipping you left on his desk, the story of the rape and murder of the woman in Lincoln Heights. I saw the horror in his eyes. For the first time he found your story credible. He asked the alleged book merchant on the phone if he knew anything about it and he told him something about having sent someone to recover stolen property."

Mark remembered vividly the well-dressed gentleman with the benign face and the genteel manner who sat next to the publisher and said nothing throughout the meeting until the end when he reached forward with a few laconic words to shake his hand but not offering his name. He had seemingly inveigled his way into the confidences of a powerful head of one of the largest publishing houses on the east coast on the pretext of buying the rights to a book that besmirched his friends.

"Mr. Maynard, it was only a business decision on the part of Mr. Thatcher. They were offering you ten grand for the book but they were giving Pemberton ten times more to buy you out."

She reached into her handbag and fished out an envelope from which she carefully removed the nonnegotiable copy of a check. She handed it over.

He scrutinized the markings, the amount of ten thousand dollars payable to Mark Maynard from a bank with an address in Hot Springs, Arkansas and bearing the signature of Gilmore Schroeder. In his hands it felt soiled, the cursive letters and numbers scribed with human blood. She replaced her shawl, covering her half-bleached hair and tying the shawl under her chin.

"What can I do for you," he asked lamely. It was a hollow request; he knew he could do nothing to protect her.

"You can make me a drink," she said. "Double scotch, or whatever else you have … on the rocks."

He went to the kitchen and returned with two glasses of bourbon, one for himself. But when he reentered the room she had already left. Obviously she wasn't serious about the drink. She had returned to the streets where she remained in the crosshairs of the enemy. Neither one could help the other after she had tried to help him and had fallen victim herself. She had listened to whispers around the office and found clues to the identity of the "book merchant". She had read between the lines of conversations swirling around her. She had formed her suspicions while her female intuition told her who was behind the killing of the Solomon woman. She owed nothing to the visitor, Mr. Maynard, but it was her sense of doing what was right, a sense of moral rectitude. She had read his manuscript, had related to his cause and empathized with the loss of his father. But the few words she uttered in the hallway had been overheard and she had paid with the loss of her job and with the sentence of death now hanging over both their heads like the sword of Damocles. His sentence might be deferred for a while, as long as the daughter of a powerful Klansman was his bedmate and had become his shield while this fair-minded woman, Ellen Murphy, was forced to run, and keep running to stay ahead of their reaches.

It's been several hours since she left. Paula, who had been standing unobtrusively in a corner listening to Ellen Murphy's startling revelations, might well have wondered why the name Hamilton never came up. He was never mentioned by the visitor. Yet she, Paula, was the one who had insisted all along he was the real culprit who had killed Dan Maynard. Now that Ellen was gone, she would do her part in putting an end to this trail of the bloodhounds.

She steps forward, her face hard and bristling with anger. She grabs the telephone and dials a number that has been incised in her brain.

"I'm calling my father," she says and presses the speaker button so Mark can listen in.

"Hello." A voice rasps through the receiver. It's a woman's voice, harsh and gravelly, the consequence of age or years of nicotine ingestion.

"Mom, its Paula." She recognizes the voice instantly.

A moment of silence between them. A pause is needed to restore the lines of communication that have been ruptured through disuse.

"Paula chile, are you ready to come home?" her mother whines.

"I'm home, Mom."

"Where're you, chile?"

"Where I've always been, in New York."

"Time you come to your senses, dearie. You's a southern gal and will always be, just like yer Ma."

"Can I speak to my father?"

There's a dry chuckle at the other end. "Your father is not here, he's lying in a bed in a hospice downtown. Been there f'r weeks. Dyin' from sump'n or the other. They say it's Karma. He's a fighter, the ol' codger is wrestling with the Grim Reaper and one of 'em goin' win. The question is not which one but when." It is clear she is using her sarcastic wit to deny whatever feelings she harbors now that he is dying.

But her daughter for the moment is not impressed. She tells her mother, "He'll die with blood on his hands on his way to Hell."

"That's for the good Lord above to decide, ain't it?" her mother answers.

"I need f'r him to call off his dogs in New York. His men are threatening me and my friend. He's standing right here."

"You mean your colored boyfriend that's been breakin' your father's heart, that's been embarrassin' your family all these years, blowin' his chance to be guv'na, sendin' your father to an early grave? You did this to your father that still loves his only daughter, that's been protecting you and him from people who would see you both dead? Ain't you ashamed? Well, sweetheart, you'll have to talk to him yerself. He won't listen to me. Whyn't you go see him? He's at Pembroke Memorial downtown. Maybe he'll forgive you and you can forgive him and all will be forgiven. But you'd better hurry, he don't have much time left."

She hangs up the phone on her bigoted mother, who evidently had been sloshed, given the slurring and the occasional incoherent mumbling on the line. He pictured this hostile racist woman with the receiver in one hand and a bottle in the other. Boozing might well drown her sorrow but would do little to obliterate the past and all her sins.

By the time she abruptly closed the phone, her expression had softened and a veil of sadness momentarily darkened her face.

He says to her, "Go to your father. He's dying. He's not the father you wish you had. But he's the only father you got. So go!"

It was as if he were talking to himself about himself. His father, too, was far from perfect, though not in the depths of depravity as was Senator Schroeder. But Daniel Cuthbert Maynard was the only father he had.

23 – The Press Conference

Next morning, before he had opened his eyes, she was gone. She had taken an early cab to LaGuardia for the first flight out to Arkansas. Perhaps she had wished that at death's door her father would turn around and take one last look at the life he had wasted and the ones he had ruined. Perhaps, in his eleventh hour, in his desire to save his soul, he would confess to a lifetime of fomenting hate and beg forgiveness in the presence of the daughter he had alienated with his bigoted and evil agenda. Perhaps, in a final act of restitution, he would whisper in her ear the whereabouts of his friend, Hamilton, the one who orchestrated the Staten Island murder. Finally, she would beg him to pick up the phone and call off his attack dogs in New York for the sake of her friend. Perhaps then, she could forgive him. But not until then.

But none of those wishes had come to pass, as he would discover when she called from the lobby of the hospice. She said he had already passed into the beyond by the time she reached his bedside and that his face in death was baleful and wretched as it was in life. She said his racist heart was made of stone that would outlast the fires of Hell, for in the facility where people came to die, he had cursed and spat at the Haitian nurse even as she dabbed the morphine on his parched lips. Her mother wasn't there to see him die. Brad had told her his mother was at home too drunk to care.

Her mother in her drunken illogic had claimed her daughter was still a southern gal like her — whatever that meant — but though her daughter had returned to the place where she was born, he knew that in a sense she could never go back. She had traveled too far. She had taught him many things, among which was that a place that had fostered so much hate in the hearts of some, had also spawned a few people of good faith, like the daughter of Senator Schroeder, secret Knight of the Klan.

"So what're you gonna do now, run the wheat farm, you and your brother?" he asked her over the phone.

"No way!" she said, with that enigmatic laugh that likely meant the farm could go to hell as did her father.

"Guess I'll join the Peace Corps after all."

"I wish you the best." With those words he knew he would never see her again.

The telephone rings. It jolts him back to his own sense of insecurity. He braces himself now that his human shield has been lifted. He answers hesitantly. He expects to hear the loathsome, foul-mouthed voice he'd grown accustomed to hearing at the other end. But it's not.

"Mark, my brother, it's Malcolm." The voice bears the high-pitched exhilaration of someone who is about to give a friend good news.

"Your moment has arrived, my friend. We got 'im. We got your killer." The words gush from his lips with unadulterated excitement. Then he seems to hold back and wait for the inevitable question.

Mark jumps to his feet. "You got Hamilton?"

"I'm not supposed to say."

"C'mon, but you are my friend, my brother," he pleads.

"But I'm also an officer of the law. The whole department was sworn to secrecy, Mark. Turn on your TV, the Mayor's gonna make an announcement on the steps of City Hall at one today. This is big, man! Big!"

But Mark, in his pragmatism and anxiety, does not understand the skullduggery in politics, especially in an election year. He expresses his anger in an uncharacteristic burst.

"So why don't the NYPD come out on TV, say they caught the guy and tell us who he is? This is friggin' insane!"

"You don't understand, my brother. The Mayor runs the city. He wants to keep this thing under wraps until his moment of glory. Can't have the police stealing his thunder."

"F'r Christ sake, I've been waiting sixteen years f'r this moment. I want to see his face, to know who the heck he is, to know who the hell killed my father. Plus if they caught the guy the glory belongs to the police not to the Mayor. I say, haul him out o' his friggin' cell and parade him in the public square like in the old days."

He is steaming while Malcolm remains cool and soft-spoken. "That's not how it works. The man is indicted, not convicted. He is sitting in a cell on suspicion of murder, but not yet found guilty by a jury of his peers to be pilloried by you, me or the public."

"Well, it's not your father he killed, Malcolm."

"I understand. If it were my father he killed, damn right I would feel the same way. But you just be there in the square at one o'clock. NYPD will get the credit in due course but not until the Mayor decides. F'r now he wants it all f'r himself. Elections are around the corner, if you know what I mean."

"I'll be there."

He hangs up and immediately places a call to Holyfield. His friend is ecstatic but as a journalist he voices his skepticism. "Mark, it's an election year, the administration needs an arrest. They can't let it fall under another mayor's watch. But about time we caught the summabitch. Who is he, anyway?"

"The Mayor will announce it with a drum roll on the steps of City Hall at one today."

"I'm going."

"See you there."

Carmichael is on the phone with an old Bajan aphorism: "'Boy, day does run 'til night catch it.' They finally caught up with Bruno."

Suddenly Mark is the focus of everyone's congratulations. He feels their elation. They know how much he has suffered the long wait. They vow to be at the Mayor's doorstep later for the affirmation from the lips of the Mayor himself. In his head he writes and rehearses the precise words to deliver the news to his mother. Ermajean will be writing to say, *come home now, you have no more reason to stay.* And she'll be right.

But who could the killer be? Is it Albert Graham from the publisher's meeting, member of the local Ku Klux Klan, who hate all black people with a particular detestation of mixed couples and interracial affairs of which his father had been guilty? Did he commission one of his fellow thugs to do his bidding, killing and raping and destroying everything in his way to keep his identity and that of his fellow members out of the public eye?

Alternatively, were Bruno Giuseppe's suspicions of his father as an FBI informant sufficiently founded to want to commit murder? And were his Mafia affiliates involved? Did one of his Mafioso hitmen leave behind a white cloak to inculpate the dreaded KKK?

Or did Glenn Corbin, the cuckold-husband of Angela Santana, in a fit of jealous rage, pull the trigger, not once, but three times in the heat of passion? After all, not just any man but a black man was thought to be screwing his wife. The police never ran a report on Corbin.

His mind is awhirl with possible suspects and possible motives, lending each name the same weight of culpability before moving on to the next, for each one had his reason to hate, if not to kill. Then the one named Hamilton insinuates himself as the one, but the link to this mysterious character continues to elude him. What reason does he have to suspect this person, other than that his friend Paula believes he should?

High noon finds him across the street from City Hall an hour before the scheduled appearance of the Mayor. New Yorkers from all directions are making their way to

HIS FATHER'S FOOTSTEPS

City Hall Park. Half an hour later, photographers tethered to their reporters are jostling for competitive advantage, squatting, kneeling, creeping towards the stage. At the top of the steps, broadcasters are bustling around the dais, arranging their microphones, clustering them together tightly to capture every word from the Mayor whose voice is known to be thin as a wisp. Each mike has been readjusted downward, accommodated to the five-foot-seven height of His Honor. Never has there been such interest in the capture of a killer since the bloody summer of Son of Sam.

He tears his eyes away from this confluence of television and print media. He is attracted to a commotion across the street where a crowd of black women dressed all in white are assembling in a flurry of excitement, chattering among themselves and scurrying about. Then they settle down and mark off their territory behind the green barriers being erected by a policeman. A man emerges from their midst, head and shoulders above the crowd. He approaches the policeman and gesticulates in the officer's face. The man is none other than the impetuous Brother Sheldon. He has come to hear the Mayor with his flock in tow and will brook no physical interference between him, his people and the Mayor.

As Mark, in his spot, diagonally across from the Mayor's platform, surveys the scene on the opposite side of the street, a disturbing circumstance is taking place right before his eyes. A horde of Klansmen, evidenced by long white robes, is gathering; their swastika banner held high, their cone masks fearlessly flung back to their shoulders revealing bald heads and impassive faces. A motley group of men, they comprise old and young, fathers, grandfathers and children in training, some fat, some scrawny, some visibly fit and ready for combat but, at least for the time being, they are assembling peaceably in keeping with the First Amendment to the Constitution. Nevertheless, they introduce a new tension into the air, the air bursting with expectancy. The atmosphere is electric like a rain-filled cloud that hovers motionless over a city in the moments before a searing flash and the crashing of thunder. Officers with truncheons at the ready are patrolling from one end of the steps to the other, casting wary eyes on the Klansmen, ready to step in to quell any form of confrontation between the self-avowed racists and blacks and people of good faith. The acrimony is palpable.

He spies, farther along on the sidewalk, Ken Holyfield armed with his ubiquitous umbrella on this day when there is no sign of rain. Their eyes meet and they give each other a close-fisted salute. The portly newspaperman unfolds a metal chair on which he plunks his bulk. Holyfield has a tepid fondness for the Mayor, always declaring in his editorials the Mayor can do more to reduce crime and alleviate the suffering of his people in Harlem. His eyes are trained on the door through which His Honor will pass.

Mark feels a tap on his shoulder and is immediately engulfed in a familiar hug. Carmichael has shown up to witness this day of vindication for his friend, Dan. "Boy, is goin' be ruction in Buhbaydus," he says to Mark. "When Bajans read the news in *The Advocate* and *The Nation* people goin' hold their heads and bawl. Rum shops and churches goin' be packed with celebrations and thanks to the Almighty f'r this victory."

But Mark is more interested in the present as he sees the Mayor emerging slowly, gravely, from the building behind him. He is resplendent in a sky-blue suit, white shirt, blazing red tie, colors which the TV cameras will love. A groundswell of applause rises from the street. With a papal wave of his hands he acknowledges the crowd. He moves to the dais, his notes in hand.

"My friends, thank you all for being here for what I hope will not be my last press conference from the steps of City Hall. As you know, in a matter of weeks the people of New York City will be going to the polls to fulfill their civic duty and to decide on the one who will be your Mayor for the next four years and it goes without saying I hope your Mayor fulfilled his …"

He stops midsentence as a voice bellows from the crowd, "Yo Mister Mayor, your honor, we want to hear about the man that killed Dan Maynard. We came here to …"

The voice is drowned in a sudden clamor as the people object to the disrespectful interruption. But the voice persists and rises to a new crescendo. "Yo Mister Mayor, with all due respects, we did not come here to listen to a political speech …" Again his words are lost in the din as competing voices rise in indignation.

The Mayor looks up from his notes as impatience wipes the benevolent smile from his face. A man, supposedly the Assistant Mayor, darts in front of the Mayor and booms through the speakers.

"Sir, His Honor will of course address the matter at hand in due course ..."

"No, no, no! This is not the time for politicking," says the man as two officers draw closer. In that moment Mark recognizes the voice and, on closer observation, the heckler. He is Brother Sheldon.

The Mayor relents. He raises his hands in submission. He snaps his fingers and his inner circle emerges from the doorway to share in the glow of His Honor's shining moment. He introduces them one by one. The Governor of New York, beaming a smile of contentment, leads the lineup. Following is the District Attorney and the Deputy District Attorney for the borough of Staten Island. Their expressions are grim like the faces of warriors not yet reconciled to the end of a war. Next comes Sergeant James accompanied by two arresting officers and two attorneys.

Then to Mark's utter amazement, Councilor Solomon appears on stage. He holds in his right hand his walking cane and, in his left, a wad of papers, presumably the documents which had been buried for years between Mark's mattress and box spring. Just when he thought the Mayor's coterie and his own astonishment were complete, a man with a brown shopping bag steps forwarded from the awning of the City Hall building and stands at the Mayor's right hand. He hands his bag to the Mayor. The man has the look of a retired sumo wrestler in street clothes. He thinks he might have seen him before. But not until the man folds his arms and a green tattooed Shamrock appears on his bulging left bicep, does he recognize him as the Irish bartender of the Hard Rock's Café from sixteen years ago. He is much older now but evidently his memory had not suffered the degradation of time, for clearly he is there to buttress the case against the one about to be named the killer.

The Mayor reaches into the bag and extracts a whitish sheet. He holds it up at one end disdainfully between thumb and forefinger for all to see.

"Ladies and gentlemen, this proves beyond a doubt the work of the Ku Klux Klan who, over sixteen years ago, brought infamy and ignominy from the Deep South to our midst. A young man's father was shot and killed in cold blood and then the killer proceeded to wreak havoc wherever he found peace and harmony between races." He points halfway down the sheet where he claims an infinitesimal spot of blood appears. "This stubborn stain is the blood of Daniel Maynard. The person who spilled his blood is Joe Butts, an eighty-six-old Army veteran who returned from the Korean War with hate in his heart, joined up with his bigoted friends in the Deep South and then made his way to New York. This is the sheet he wore the night he shot Daniel Maynard. He had been wearing it ever since until we tracked him down. This is the standard wear of the Klan. See it for yourself on their members standing there across the street."

With those words he raises a hand to his eyes and squints through the glare of the afternoon sun in the direction of the Klansmen. The men clad in solid-white, street-length robes eerily similar to the white sheet in the Mayor's hand, are standing huddled together in City Hall Park.

With good reason, Mark moves closer to the adjoining street away from the crowd and the tumult, for he sees a formation of dark-suited Black Muslims, judging from their close-fisted salutes, taking up their positions on the other side. They stand stoically, sternly, looking straight ahead, backing the steps, holding hands in a human chain. It goes without saying the Mayor would never get their collective vote, not in his lifetime or in the next. They are simply there in solidarity with the black folk.

Brother Sheldon, who has been quiet for a while, diverts his attention away from the dais to the Klan.

"Yeah, you over there, get out o' my city! Yeah, you haters! Go back where you come from! Yes, I am talkin' to you. You in the white sheets with the cone heads. You haters, terrorists, murderers, rapists, cross burners, shit eaters!"

Of course, this is not the same Brother Sheldon who stands in the pulpit of the Church of Divine Intervention in Harlem in his vestment on Sunday mornings extolling, with a gentle persuasive voice, the incontrovertible truth of the Holy Scriptures. Today he is the civil-rights activist, the defender of human rights, the thorn in the sides of the ruling Party. He ignites the women in his flock. Their shrill voices echo the taunting. "Yeah, we don' need no KKK 'round here. Tell 'em, brother, tell 'em."

HIS FATHER'S FOOTSTEPS

In the blink of an eye, like a giant wave of white foam, the Klansmen are hurdling the green police barriers, pushing them aside, dashing across City Hall Park towards the steps of City Hall to confront the Mayor. The officers are in pursuit, nightsticks in hand. But the Klansmen come face to face with a wall of Black Muslims blocking their ascent. At the topmost tier the Mayor's secret guards are drawing their weapons and encircling His Honor. The Mayor's lineup, from the Governor on down to the lowliest officer, is retreating to the safety of the City Hall building. They had come to receive their official commendations from the City. Some were there to receive their pound of flesh. While the officers hustle the Mayor's coterie back to the safety of the City hall corridors, on the steps below a brawl has been sparked and before long the crowd is on fire.

As Mark retreats in a hurry to Park Row and Vesey Street, he looks over his shoulder and in the distance he sees that a full-scale war has broken out between the various factions; hands flailing, feet and nightsticks flying in the air, men pushing, pulling, screaming, cursing, the dull sounds of bodies thrashing against bodies. He sees people being trampled on the grounds, men wrestling, writhing and rolling on the park lawn. The Klan, the Christians and the Muslims are locked in mortal combat. The melee continues with no sign of abating. As he ducks underground at the Chambers subway station for his ride back to Harlem, he carries a whiff of tear gas and the stench of hate and bigotry in his nostrils.

24 – The Last Kiss

Joe Butts, the homeless derelict, the Korean veteran, the gin guzzler, the drunk, and now the alleged murderer, had been the farthest from his mind and was thought neither physically nor psychically capable of murder. Could he have fabricated the whole thing of being a witness when he was indeed the perpetrator? He remembered the sheet he wore, the so-called poncho, the day he questioned him outside the café. The fabric that day was soiled and discolored, seemingly beyond redemption, yet in the Mayor's hand was a sheet that was almost white but flawed by a spot of dry blood. If indeed the sheet that belonged to Joe Butts had survived sixteen long years and, by some miraculous cleansing agent, had been restored to its original color then the original blood would have also disappeared.

Furthermore, that the police in the beginning had perceived Joe Butts a hallucinating drunk and an unreliable witness and were now prepared to recast the old man as the killer was enough to raise the suspicion that an innocent bystander was being railroaded.

The most distressing conclusion of all was that his friend and brother, Sergeant Malcolm James had allowed himself to be corralled into some Machiavellian scheme by the political machinery that ran the city, powers determined at all costs not to leave unsolved an important crime, a crime highlighted by the Governor and the Councilman and kept alive by Mark Maynard, the letter writer. Suddenly he was filled with shame for having been betrayed by a friend and a brother but then, in his willingness to forgive, he understands that men sworn to secrecy will sometimes forego principle to keep a job and earn a living even at the expense of another man's misfortune.

He attempts to write the long-awaited letter to his mother. But the words about the capture are stuck somewhere between his brain and the hand that holds the pen. The letters that scrawl across the stationery are not his. They are inelegant and crooked and blurred by the tears settling in his eyes. He gives up and dials the number of the Staten Island precinct; he needs to vent his frustration in the ear of Sergeant James; he perceives an injustice at the hands of the police, an injustice that tugs at his own conscience as well as his common sense.

"Can I speak to Sergeant James?"

"Sergeant James is in a meeting, sir. Can I ask who's calling?"

"Never mind."

He feels a need to talk to someone, he needs a shoulder to lean on, a woman's soft sympathetic voice in his ear. Maria is supposedly with her parents in Boston and Paula is a thousand miles away. He can think of no one better than Nakeisha but he is also aware that a thin wall of ice has descended between them since he drifted away in search of a killer. Perhaps she will forgive him now that the hunt has ended and he is now living alone without the obligation owed to another woman under his roof. Sex is not foremost on his mind but if the terms of a rapprochement demand it he will not object.

Minutes later, he is ringing the doorbell in the lobby of Nakeisha's rundown apartment building. He is about to announce himself when the voice of a child playing nearby spares him the effort.

"Mister, the doorbells don' work no mo'. The elevator neither."

Hmm, must be a long time since my last visit, he muses. So he climbs the four flights and strolls down the hallway to her apartment, whose number is etched in his brain. At that moment the thought crosses his mind, he should have brought her a reconciliatory token of red roses but the gesture had escaped him in his urgency to see her. He knocks on the door three times, once, and then two quick raps which used to be their signal that would bring her rushing to the door to take him in her arms. *Silence.* He raps again. Maybe she is not at home; he should have called. Then he hears footsteps, a jangling of keys; the door is cracked open, and there she is. He sees her face and a sliver of a pink negligee peeking from behind the door. Her door is slightly ajar while the chain that restrains it remains in place.

"Mark!" An exclamation of surprise peaks in her voice. "I wasn't expecting you."

"Were you expecting the mailman?" he quips.

"No, but ..."

"Did you hear about the arrest?" he asks.

"Yes, I heard. Congratulations!"

"Thanks, it's been a long time."

HIS FATHER'S FOOTSTEPS

"Yes, it has," she says. "So your white girlfriend was wrong after all. I mean about some fella named Hamilton." She makes no effort to conceal her lingering bitterness. That Paula had been mistaken gives her more pleasure than the arrest itself.

"Only God knows," he replies.

He is standing on the doormat and, throughout the exchange, the door chain is still intact, denying him entry, entry to this nest where he had always been free to come and go. He peers inside and sees two glasses of red wine on her coffee table. A cigarette smolders in the ash tray and two long trouser legs hang down from the sofa but he does not discern a face.

"You have company, I see," he says half-questioningly.

"Yes, Mark, I'm seeing someone. I couldn't wait any longer. I was lonely."

"You could've told me," he says, and then realizes his voice has a pathetic whine.

"If I had told you, you would not have heard me. You were preoccupied with your vendetta."

In his mind he agrees. That he was preoccupied was indeed an understatement. A more fitting word was "consumed". She had been slowly slipping away for a long time but his mind was elsewhere, and the times they had spent together were occasional detours as he headed down that singular track on which he had set himself. Now he must not prolong the conversation. He shouldn't try to explain. What's the use, she wouldn't understand anyway.

HIS FATHER'S FOOTSTEPS

Let her go, let her get on with her new life, he says to himself. But his ego gets in the way. His hurt turns to resentment, then to self-pity, then back to understanding the reason she had left him.

"I was following in my father's footsteps, Keish, to find the one who killed him. That is why I am with Paula. Can't you see that?"

But her eyes, still peering over the door chain, tell him she doesn't buy it.

"Well, goodbye then," he says.

She reaches out the door, puckers her lips and pecks him on the mouth. A parting gift. It will be the last time he tastes her lips.

25 – Closing the Curtain

Next day the press had a field day with the story of the Mayor's debacle of a press conference. The focus was on the melee in City Hall Park. The *News* featured a picture of a wide expanse of governmental property strewn with mangled sheets and swastika banners. Another showed a few hapless men being carted off in a paddy wagon. It was reported that one Klansman was slashed on the arm and the neck by an indentified swordsman. There was no photograph of either the Mayor or the men chosen to be honored. Little mention was made of the indictment of Joe Butts, thus it was unlikely the news of the capture had made it past the borders of the tri-state area of NY, NJ and PA. It was likely the long-awaited news of the arrest had not yet reached the ears of Maria Townsend. She should have been the second person to hear. After all, whereas Mark was the son of Dan Maynard, she was his lover. But she is likely still today in Boston living with and caring for her elderly parents, George and Eva Townsend. He doesn't have her phone number; she was the one who called now and then to enquire about the progress of the investigation. At least it showed she cared; Angela Santana never kept in touch.

The story in *The Times* was more sober in its reporting of the event and even sanguine about the future of the city under its present administration.

The Mayor in his announcement to the public of the long-awaited capture of the Staten Island killer brought to light an even more disturbing development than a single case of murder.

HIS FATHER'S FOOTSTEPS

The case implicated the disreputable KKK organization now laying their roots here in our city and its surroundings.

It has come to our attention that one man's dogged determination to expose this pestilence among us, which if allowed to flourish will spread like a cancer fomenting racial hatred and discord throughout our diverse ethnic communities and eventually do great harm to our city. In the days, weeks and months ahead this newspaper will be watchful and we ask the denizens of this great city to be equally vigilant. We predict that this evil force will bend under the weight of public condemnation.

We therefore laud the efforts of a Mr. Mark Maynard, who at great sacrifice and personal endangerment solicited the help of our Councilor Solomon and the Mayor to blight the growth of the Ku Klux Klan in this part of the country.

Before the newspapers hit the streets, news people were on the phone, salivating, begging for more. They wanted to write about his father and the slaying and the ensuing trail of blood, but he is not about to rehash the past.

"Mr. Maynard, have you thought of writing a book?"

"Yes, I have, Mr. Reporter. Yes I have."

Little do they know he has closed his book and is moving back to the life he had known before.

He is spending the rest of the afternoon setting about to bring his sojourn in America to a close, to lower the curtain on a long and turbulent episode in his life. Somehow he has little feeling of fulfillment; he had anticipated much more when it all ended. But he chalks up the anticlimactic letdown to his overreaching for a morbid and more dramatic ending, like the killer falling victim to a hail of bullets from the gun of a trigger-happy lawman and dropping to his knees as his blood spewed from his body. Such was the fate he deserved, for his father had suffered no less a merciless and excruciating death. Still, in his opinion, old Butts does not fit the mold of the guilty and he is bothered by it.

But now there are friends to be thanked for their long-standing forbearance, for over the years he had been known to bend an ear or two groping for answers. He owes Ken Holyfield a compilation of columns for *The Renaissance*, for throughout his turmoil he seldom put pen to paper to contribute to his worthy newspaper while allowed to remain on the payroll. It was he, Holyfield, who had unwittingly saved his life by arming him on a dark and snowy night when he was set upon on a street in Harlem. There was Benjamin Hanks to be thanked for reversing his devious defense claim and revealing the truth to Councilor Solomon who, in turn, was the one to be applauded for bringing his case to the attention of the most influential and powerful people in all of New York. So many people to thank, so little time to thank them all, before he hits the skies to return to his beloved Barbados.

Then there were the mundane tasks of relinquishing the lease on his father's brownstone, getting rid of possessions he no longer needed, closing accounts and settling debts.

Finally, as a matter of doing the right thing, he must get word to Maria that his mission was complete; that he was going home. After all, she was the one who had written that portentous letter years ago, and had paid his way to America to attend the funeral, and had given him money in the beginning for his subsistence, and had witnessed his passion, his determination to find the killer when he had no idea of the treacherous road he would have to travel.

Yes, he must find her; it was indeed the right thing to do.

26 – Secrets and Lies

Yesterday he paid one last visit to his father's tomb at Trinity Cemetery. For some unearthly reason, yet unexplained, he had gathered up his father's shoes, suits, pipe and pajamas, even his toiletries, stuffed them into an old duffle bag that was his father's. He took them along and placed them neatly, ceremoniously around the perimeter of the sodden grave. After all, as far as he was concerned, his father was a pharaonic figure, loved and idolized by many, hated and envied by some, placed on a pedestal by his children. He had hoped to hear in his mind the words, "Well done, my son!" Instead there was deathly silence.

Then he bought a railway ticket and boarded an Amtrak Acela Express to Boston to convey the news of the capture to his father's lover. As the New England coastline whipped past his window, the view of the ocean took him back to Barbados and the Caribbean Sea. Soon, the monotonous rumble of the train lulled him to sleep. In a dream he was on safer, more tranquil shores sitting on a coral beach, waves licking at his feet, clean white sand squishing between his toes. He had gone for a swim and was resting on the shore, enervated after struggling against the fearsome riptides off the coast of St. Lucy near the Animal Flower Cave. Then he saw a hand reaching down, whereupon he looked up and saw his father and heard his protective voice.

"Get up, son. You had enough o' them high seas. Let's go home."

HIS FATHER'S FOOTSTEPS

He rose and brushed away the wet sand that stuck to his trunks. He and his dad walked home from the sea and he felt an inner peace, a peace he hadn't felt in a long time.

As the Amtrak trundled on farther up the tracks, he awoke and saw that the seascape had been eclipsed by the Connecticut smokestacks, air-polluting factories and the dull clusters of grey housing complexes.

How he misses the sound of the ocean at Maycock's Bay pounding the rugged cliffs of the St. Lucy shoreline, the sweet aroma of luxuriant cane fields, the verdant open spaces, the air laden at night with the fragrance of Jasmine and Lady of the Night, the friendly faces, the human warmth! And once again he longs for the simple life he once had, and on which he had turned his back only because of his father.

He exits the train at the Back Bay station and boards a bus to Boxford, a small conservative town, a bit of a haul outside of Boston, in search of the address Maria had given him a long time ago. On the bus he finds himself an oddity among a load of White Anglo Saxon Protestants, a picture of unsmiling faces and pinched lips. On boarding, he says "Good Evening" and they all stare, frightened as if he had blasphemed.

An hour later he is on serene St. Nicholas Street, where all the houses appear the same, created with elegance but ancient, set back from the street — white brick, multiple floors, towering chimneys, bounteous gardens, picket fences, humanoid gnomes on every lawn — a quiet opulence about them, typical of the conservative class. But the numbers on the houses are tiny or indiscernible, so he walks from one end of the block to the other, his eyes squinting for greater focus.

"Can I help you?" It's the voice of a middle-aged woman poking her head through her parted curtains.

"Looking for Number 16, the Townsends."

Could she think he's on reconnaissance, a professional burglar scoping the neighborhood to return when everyone's asleep? But her next question absolves her of the suspicion and labels her with another.

"Number 16 is across the street. Are you lookin' for yard work?"

He ignores her, crosses the street, opens the gate, climbs the cement steps and rings the bell. He hears a woman's sing-song voice that is unmistakably West Indian.

"Comin', comin', who there?"

She comes to the door, a handsome buxom dark-skinned lady, her corn rows perfectly aligned, dressed in a dowdy black dress with a white deep-pocketed apron. "You come to fix de boiler?" She prejudges him as did the woman across the street.

"No. Is Maria here?"

"Who?"

"Maria Townsend."

She gives him an incredulous stare, then a laugh bubbles up from her belly to her face.

"Chile, we en seen or hear from Miss Maria since 1963."

"How could that be? She phoned me just the other day to say hello and asked how things were going?"

"Not from dis house, she ent. Fourteen long years since we en seen heads nor tails o' de woman. Come in and take a load off yuh feet."

He enters the house; the interior is clean, warm and friendly but lacks the gaiety and vibrancy of young children. He reaches for the nearest chair, for he suddenly feels a weakness in his knees and a sensation that he has been the victim of some grand surreptitious scheme.

"I'm Mark."

"Josephine ... from Barbados, St. Joseph."

"Me too ... from St. Lucy."

"Lord, help us! Another Bajan in Boxford."

"So where is Maria now?"

"Well, my hairdresser in town tell me de girl is livin' with a Jamaican in Hartford. She meet 'im in Ocho Rios two years ago while she wuz on vacation, she and two girls. She en have a t'ing to do with she own kind. Never did. De woman just loves de West Indian man. Always did. She say de African-American man always livin' in de past and hold too much a grudge. West Indian man always willin' to fuhgive and fuhget.

"Want somet'ing to drink? 'Cause you look like you ready to pass out from de heat."

"Water, please." He feels as if he has been struck by lightning. The good news intended for Maria has been knocked clean out of his head.

Josephine leaves and returns with a glass of iced cold water. He remains seated while she is still on her feet.

"Back in New York Maria told me she was going home to take care of her parents."

These words cause the woman to rear back her head and burst out with the most raucous laugh that was at once amusing and bitter. She composes herself and a storm of anger suddenly comes to her face.

"Mister, she mother dead and gone 'long time, eight years ago. She pushin' up daisies all like now. Hear what I'm saying? Maria didn't even go to de funeral to see she mother put down in de ground."

With that she puckers her lips and draws a long Bajan steupse between clenched teeth, the sound of a dry perverted kiss.

"How about her father?" he is afraid to ask, but does.

Again she chuckles derisively. "De medical services agency hired me to take care o' de ol' man years ago, feed 'im, give 'im his meds, wash 'im and his clothes. I cyant tell if I'm his nurse or his maid but de pay is good. He upstairs in his armchair either sleeping or watching TV. Eighty years old, and all he do is drink sweet tea and pee in his pants. He is de one that throw Maria out o' de house."

"Why?"

"Well, she wuz de only chile and he wanted grandchildren to carry on de family name. But not de kind she wuz goin' give 'im."

"What kind was that?"

"She told 'im she wuz gettin' ready to marry a Bajan man in New York and wuz goin' raise a family sooner or later. He wanted a son that look like him ... not like you wid yer brown skin." She laughs.

"Another George Townsend?" he asks.

Her eyes open wide like an owl's. "Who de heck is George? De man name is Hamilton Townsend."

He jerks forward. Water spurts from his mouth and splatters his knees, his shoes and the floor at his feet. He springs to his feet and grabs onto her arm for support. His face is that of a man whose heart has missed one or two beats and he is about to fall, unable to breathe, unable to speak.

She steps back, for she, too, is in shock, surprised at his reaction. "Jesus! Wha' happen? You know Hammie?"

He recovers. "Can I go see him?"

"Yes, follow me."

They climb the padded stairway and enters his room. "En no need to knock, de man always sleepin'. Plus you can make all de noise yuh want, he is deaf as a duppy."

The room is sizeable and fitted with fixtures for the sick and the handicapped. The bed is a hospital type with side rails and a tilt crank at the bottom. The only window offers a view of a little white church with a modest graveyard, an inescapable reminder of the old man's mortality. A miniature Confederate flag hangs above the bed and a print of Leonardo da Vinci's *The Lord's Supper* adorns the opposite wall. The smell of stale urine and sickness permeates the air.

Hamilton Townsend is seated in an armchair facing the TV on his dresser. While the news blares from the tube, the old man is fast asleep, his white-bearded chin resting on his chest. The bifurcated oxygen catheters hang from his nostrils.

"Mr. Townsend, someone here to see you," she yells to the plastic earpiece stuck in his left ear."

"Who?" he mutters, his eyes still closed.

"A gentleman who say he know you."

"Send him away. No visitors today," he mumbles. Mark realizes he has heard this voice before, deep-throated, gravelly, threatening on the phone.

He approaches, lowers his height and shouts into his ear. "Hamilton Townsend, my name is Mark Maynard. My father was Daniel Maynard, a friend of your daughter."

The old man opens his eyes and stiffens. He looks up, directly into Mark's eyes. "Yes, I remember that name, that's the man that stole my only daughter."

"So is that why you killed him?"

"I never saw the black bastard, never touched 'im."

"But you ordered him killed."

"Yes and you can go to Hell too!" he says, then lowers his head and once more closes his eyes feigning sleep.

Mark follows with his eyes the tube that snakes down from the old man's nose past the armrest to a nozzle attached to a cylindrical tank at the back of his chair. With an impulse that surprises both himself and Josephine, he reaches down and with one motion he turns the circular valve shutting off the precious air that keeps the old man alive.

"No, *you* go to Hell!" he says with such force that she is petrified, not only by the act, but by the vehemence in his voice.

Josephine, a strong woman, grabs the arm and tries with all her might to pry away the fingers still gripping the valve. But he is steadfast as an anchor. She hollers: "DONT!" But he doesn't hear. "He's not worth it," she says, "not f'r murder."

With her arms tightly wrapped around his waist, she tries in vain to tear him away from the cylinder but with an inexplicable and sudden surge of energy he is unrelenting, not hearing, not feeling, while the old man coughs and sputters and, in a matter of minutes, turns wan and ashen. He grabs the armrests, coughs repeatedly, stiffens, reopens his eyes and stares as if he is already seeing the flames and feeling the fires of Hell. His head slumps to a side. Cells are fast withering in a brain once wasted in a lifetime of hate. And though the one who is now taking his life knows full well it is not *his* to take, he cannot help himself. Minutes go by before he finally releases his grip on the valve and slumps to the ground. Tears of relief stream down his cheeks. His mission is over. He is bitter and ashamed of having been deceived by Maria, an inveterate liar by all indications: there was never a George Townsend. Meanwhile, the caretaker sits beside him visibly torn between the ethical and moral principles of her profession and sympathy for her own countryman who lost his father at the hands of the one under her care.

"Call the police," he tells her. "I'll give you the number, ask for Sergeant James. This one is not in his jurisdiction but he knows my story. Tell him everything you know, about Hamilton, his daughter and his friends. Tell him he's got the wrong man in prison and help me to set a man named Joe Butts free. And you can tell the police Mark Maynard is the one who killed him. Tell them it was a life for a life, that he killed my father. They can look it up. The year was 1958 outside a café in Staten Island. Tell them the truth and nothing but the truth because you were a witness. Exonerate yourself, tell them you tried to save him, tell them so they can contemplate the irony when they see your face.

"Finally, Josephine, I ask you to do this for me, a brother man from St. Lucy, tell them everything after three o'clock tomorrow when I will be long gone, back to a place where I can heal and beg forgiveness from a merciful God who understands the foibles of mankind and the weaknesses of his flesh and the love of a son for his father, a son who would go to the ends of the earth to avenge his murder, even if it meant committing murder himself."

She rises and for no practical purpose reopens the valve. Precious oxygen surges once again. She closes the window as church bells peal in the distance. She faces a moral judgment but one that is not at all clear.

27 – Closure

As the Amtrak races back down the East Coast, his mind wrestles with the inescapable fact: he has committed a murder. And with every mile of track from Boston to Stratford to Stamford to Penn Station the thought looms more and more hauntingly. He stares at his hands as though they had acted on their own without his volition before he comes to grips with the reality he had willed it from the start. It was the moment he had waited for, to see that the one who took his father's life surrendered his own. All the years of endless grief and terror had built within him a storehouse of revenge that, in that opportune moment, exploded and crippled his conscience. His sense of reason had returned but it was too late, so now he must lay his murder of Hamilton Townsend squarely at the feet of the Klan while he proceeds in his own mind to euphemize the act as not murder, but an execution, for in truth he had not been aware of a single murderous fiber in his body. The notion of an execution gives him peace.

Whatever guilt still lingers in his mind is assuaged when he arrives at Penn station and passes a newsstand where his eyes light on a headline in the *Evening News*.

Man arrested in the Shonelle Solomon case

He drops a quarter on the counter, grabs a copy and tears into the story.

The NYPD has announced the arrest of one Albert Graham for the rape and murder of Ms. Solomon, daughter of Councilor Conroy Solomon. The suspect was found to be an operative in the local chapter of the Ku Klux Klan. A source close to the arrest has said that Mr. Graham was implicated with the assistance of an unidentified executive of well-known Pemberton Publishers along with his secretary. The District Attorney, Mr. Hammersmith, promises to prosecute Mr. Graham to the limits of the law while The Mayor has complimented the Department on the arrest and vows to continue his campaign to rid this city and its environs of this scum of the earth (his words) ...

One more nail in the coffin of the Klan, he says to himself and his spirits rise with the news of the arrest. But his own deed, when discovered, of ridding society of another evildoer, will remain unheralded; as well it should, for his mission was retribution for his father, nothing else. The Klan will live on long after he is gone from this place.

He takes a taxi back to Harlem, back to his lonely house where, hours before, he was percolating with good news for Maria. Now he knows he has been deceived but questions remain. How did she discover her father was the one and when did she know it? Was it her dark secret from the beginning, or did she stumble upon it somewhere along the way, while all the time she saw him suffer and mourn for his father?

His visit to the home of Angela Santana comes back with a lingering curiosity when he had blurted out the name Hamilton, eliciting nothing but blank faces all around, except on the smirking countenance of Miss Santana herself, who perhaps knew more than she claimed but refused to incriminate her erstwhile friend or her father. Did she know the identity of his father's killer all along but chose to protect Maria? Alas, he will never know the answers to these nagging questions. Chances are he will never see Maria Townsend or Angela Santana again.

Whatever the case, he somehow finds it in his heart to forgive Maria. It is likely her love for her father in private was as great as Mark's love for his own, and for that reason she had kept secret her father's crimes. After all, her lover was dead; she still had her father, however estranged they were. He remembers his own father's words of advice to his sons on hard choices: "Boys, remember this, blood is always thicker than water." She had made a hard choice.

Now it is time to go home, time to say goodbye to America. With all her warts and inequities she is still the land of opportunity. But he must go back; they will be looking for him soon. Besides, he had promised his mother he'd return when the mission was over.

No time for letters, he picks up the phone to place an overseas call. She doesn't own a phone but he will call Mr. Babu, the Indian shopkeeper across the street, and he will hurry over to tell Ma she has a call from Amurca, whereupon she and her caretaker will hasten over to the shop.

Ermajean answers the phone. Through the crackling and the static, her voice is bubbly, jittery, breathless. She knows he's coming home. Why else would he call?

"Let me talk to Ma. Put her on the phone, please."

"Son?" His mother's voice is weak and strained. The years have taken their toll.

"I'm coming home, Ma. I'll be home tomorrow."

"Thank God! Bless yer heart, son. 'In everything give thanks, for this is the will of God in Christ Jesus'."

He has always credited his mother for having swallowed the entire bible, for she has a scriptural reference for every occasion, a plaster for every sore. This time her words are words of redemption. She thinks him an instrument of God. He has performed God's will. His soul is at peace again.

"Son, your Ma don' have long to live on this earth. Your Ma will also be goin' home soon." He wonders if these are the babbling words of an old forgetful mind in the twilight of her years.

He repeats the words, "I'll be seeing you tomorrow".

"Son, I want you do somet'ing f'r your Ma when you come home. Promise me."

"Yes, Ma."

"Since you been gone, Ermajean has been takin' care of your ol' Ma, feedin' me, bathin' me', doin' me laundry, takin' me to de doctor, makin' sure I take me medicines. Yes, she has been very good to your ol' Ma all these years. She keep me alive all this time."

"Yes, Ma, I am so very grateful to her," he says, and he means every word.

She whispers in the mouthpiece, "Son, I want you to marry Ermajean".

The words out of his mother's mouth are so inappropriate, so appalling, he lifts the phone from his ear and stares into the receiver as though the signal has become corrupted in the cable that lies two thousand miles on the ocean's floor.

After a second or two of gathering his wits, he shouts into the mouthpiece as if her declining memory needed a timely jolt.

"Ma, Ermajean is my sister. Remember?"

"She is *not* your sister," she yells back. "She is *not* your sister." He hears a thump and imagines his mother stomping the floorboards, which was always her emphatic way of arguing a point.

"She loves you, son, and a woman will never forget de first time, take it from me. And that is why I will never forget yer father," she whispers. She wants him to know she was privy to their "incestuous" romps in the cane fields, he and Ermajean.

He says goodbye and turns his attention to packing a few essentials into his father's valise. Tomorrow, early in the morning, he will take a taxi to the airport for the early BWIA flight to Barbados. But first he will stop on the way at Mr. Goldsmith's pawn shop at the corner of 121st and 7th where he will buy a wedding band with whatever money he has left.

His mother had awakened an old fire that he thought was beyond rekindling. He wasn't conscious of it before, but somewhere in the depths of his innermost feelings, where the subconscious waits patiently, longingly for its own moment of truth, there had always been a special place for Ermajean, a place no one else could fill. Only his mother knew it all along.

ABOUT THE AUTHOR

Enrico Downer was born in Barbados, schooled at various institutions of learning in Barbados, New York, Wisconsin, and Puerto Rico. He first joined Value Line, a NYC publisher, and later was Correspondent with a Division of Airco International in New York and Wisconsin. His writing is steeped in historical fiction and set in places from his early upbringing and travels throughout the Caribbean and North America.

PREVIOUS BOOKS

THERE ONCE WAS A LITTLE ENGLAND, spanning the decade before the Independence of Barbados from Great Britain. Available at Amazon.com, Amazon.co.uk, BN.com, University of West Indies and Days Bookstore, Bridgetown, Barbados.

"Enrico Downer must be congratulated and thanked for bringing to life in this format an incident few living Barbadians will recall and fewer still will have ever heard.

With all the devices at the disposal of only a creative writer Rico fills in aspects of Barbadian hush-hush society that are still very much alive though lying dormant but very easily aroused. All commentators of the Barbadian social situation, as well as some historians, should get hold of this book, and read it, from cover to cover." ... Carl Moore, Barbados.

THE LURE OF AMERICA. True but fictionalized stories of the West Indian immigrant of the 50s and 60s. Available at Amazon.com, Amazon.co.uk, BN.com.

Website: www.caribbeanfiction.com

If you've enjoyed reading this book, please feel free to post your review and comments online at the Amazon.com book site.

Excerpt from "There Once was a Little England"

Chapter 18

Her Majesty's Court

FINALLY! THE day of the trial: February 17, 1956.

When Solicitor Fitzgerald Trotman walked through the portal of Her Majesty's Court on Coleridge Street on that day, he was alone. The look that crossed the face of the officer on guard as he waved him through was one of gratitude tinged with compassion, as one who might look upon another who had fought valiantly on his behalf but was about to be crushed by overwhelming forces. The officer had already admitted a hundred vociferous, excited Bajans now pushing and surging like a rolling sea at the arched door of the courthouse, four or five abreast, waiting impatiently to enter the public gallery. The working-class had turned out in impressive numbers to witness history, to hear the only verdict that would vindicate their true sense of justice and reassure a flagging faith in the decency and fairness of the institution. For months now, they had been chomping at the bit, waiting for this day, constantly querulous about the delay but never taking the law into their own hands. Never before in Barbados had a white man paid with his life for the killing of a black man or woman, though history showed the reverse was never in doubt.

Thornville was represented. Esmay and her husband, Egbert were among the first in line, followed by Sister Innis, the midwife; Mrs. Piggott, the shopkeeper's wife and the domino players from the rum shop; Fitzroy Miller and his woman; Cutting, the butcher and Mrs. Cutting. Carmita Blackman, the tray seller, took the day off from Busby Alley to come down to the courthouse. Marjorie Hinckson and Mrs. Mordecai, the milk woman, were there. The Water Club had temporarily closed its doors; the cooks and servers had taken the day off. Also in line were most of the off-duty *Chronicle* crew. Bajans from far and near converged on the courthouse that morning. Neither Cissy nor Harold was present.

Ben Carson, the octogenarian mortician, also came. Ben still had his doubts about the guilt of a man who had been so generous to him, who had put a roof over his head, provided him with electricity, running water and everything that came with the tool shed. How could he then be capable of committing such an act against a boy almost one-seventh of Ben's age? He was the only person in all of Thornville who could not bring himself to believe that the Englishman had killed the boy. He came to court to make up his mind and to let the Law decide.

The doors swung open. In no time the crowd was swallowed up into the vast interior of the courthouse with all its ornate furnishings dominated by richly polished mahogany tables, cushiony carpeting, shiny banisters and velvet-padded benches. The court was a bold attempt to mimic in miniature Old Bailey in London, which had so often been depicted in post-war British movies. All the minutiae of British court decor were replicated as faithfully as one could expect in this tropical corner of the Commonwealth. One distinguishing feature standing in the foyer was a life-sized Blindfolded Lady Justice, armed with sword and scales, sculpted precisely to detail from a mound of local clay. It was the work of a talented Bajan artist, Carl Brody. It was said that he was practically capable of breathing life into any clump of clay that came in contact with his fingers.

The heat was intense. Despite the efforts of four noisy oscillating fans that looked down from the uppermost corners of the walls, the public gallery was a motion picture of improvised fans: kerchiefs, hats, newspapers, pieces of cardboard, anything that came to hand. Hot, heavy, sultry air lay over the courtroom like a fleece. Only the men in black robes seemed cool and at ease. The accused, flanked by two blank-faced officers, fidgeted, waiting to swear to tell the truth, the whole truth and nothing but the truth. Barrister Cunningham tugged repeatedly at the chain of his pocket watch, anxious to get on with the proceedings. Solicitor Trotman looked peeved and strangely out of his element, perhaps wishing to have had Cissy at his side to bask in the public's favour of her righteous cause. Shafts of bright morning sunlight from the upper windows fell on the white wavy wigs of black men in black robes, a picture that drew giggles of ridicule from some in the gallery. But in truth, these robes and perukes lent an air of order and continuity to the proceedings, for they could be traced to the very provenance of English

Law and these men were sworn to adhere to the highest standards though they sometimes strayed and resorted to courtroom shenanigans.

Three bangs of the magistrate's gavel commanded silence. It was time. The Clerk stepped forward. He exclaimed, "All those having any business before this Criminal Court in the case of the Crown versus Thorne draw nigh and give your attention. 'God Save The Queen.'"

Penelope, brightly dressed in yellow, and her father dapper in a sombre black suit and tie, exchanged smiles as he, now sworn in, stiffened for the inevitable show of assaultive questioning from a white man like himself.

"You are Theodore Augustus Thorne?" asked the Clerk.

"Yes."

"Theodore Augustus Thorne, you are charged with the murder of David Prince on the morning of the twenty-fifth day of September, 1955. How do you plead?"

"Not guilty."

Whispers of "Shameless dog!" and "He ent got nuh shame, doh," could be heard emanating from the back of the gallery. Bang! The gavel at first failed to command silence and the mutterings continued. Then they waned to complete silence as the judge glared at the crowd. Solicitor Trotman shook his head sadly from side to side. Cunningham smiled; perhaps he considered the charge of murder more defensible than manslaughter and that the Prosecutor's aim for the ultimate conviction was overzealous.

Representing the Crown was a white Barbadian-born Cambridge-educated Counsel, Tom Husbands, chosen as much for his dogged tenacity on behalf of the Crown as for the perceived counterweight of colour and erudition between him and the defence attorney. The Counsel was tall, semi-bald, erect and elegant, with one lazy eye which sometimes had a mind of its own and which likely created confusion among some of the jurors as to whether his words were directed to the bench, the dock, or to them. At this moment, however, once the jurors were given their instructions, Counsel Husbands managed to focus both eyes on Thorne to establish that the multiple discharging of a Remington two-inch-bore shotgun, Exhibit A, on the morning of September 22nd 1955, aimed at the head of David Prince by the indicted, were simple facts that were beyond dispute. Neither could it be claimed, he asserted, given the forensic evidence, two spent cartridges, Exhibit B, and a sworn statement by the dead boy's brother and witness to the murder, Nathaniel Prince, that the accused could have been in danger or threatened by the boy in such a manner that could legally or morally justify the deployment of a lethal weapon.

"Had you known the said David Prince, Mr. Thorne?"

"Never saw him in me life."

"Did you know his family?"

"No. Never saw 'em either."

"Mr. Thorne, would you tell the Court what was your motivation for shooting in the direction of a tree in broad daylight on the morning in question when a little boy happened to be in the said tree in the process of recovering a kite that had been caught on one of its branches."

Barrister Cunningham sprang from his seat. "Objection, m'Lawd! My learned friend implies that the defendant had foreknowledge of a boy in the tree in question."

"Sustained. Rephrase the question!" barked the Magistrate.

But the Counsel abandoned the question to pursue the previous answer in which the defendant denied any knowledge of the boy's family.

"Mr. Thorne, you deny knowing the boy's family but is not his mother a friend of your daughter and was she not a frequent visitor to your home as a young girl? Then how can you say you never saw her and you have no knowledge of who she is?"

The Counsel swivelled on his heels, turned his back to the defendant and walked towards the jury rail, fixating his good eye on the jury while his other eye veered lazily. And this for the jury: "I have heard tell she is of such beauty as not likely to be missed."

"Irrelevant questioning, m'Lawd! Objection!"

"Objection sustained!"

And so the proceedings dragged on for an hour and a half with the predictable duelling between Counsel and Defence, objecting and withdrawing, directing and redirecting, attacking and counter-attacking, advancing and retreating; two learned men armed with the weaponry of words and the leveraging of laws, sparring within the latitude set by the judge to score that one irreversible checkmate. When Husbands paced around with his usual histrionics, portraying the Englishman as the antichrist incarnate with no regard for human life, notably the life of poor black people, Cunningham rose to rehabilitate the image of his client with illustration after illustration of his generosity towards the Thornville families and stories of a lavish of affection for their children, and how every year when his daughter, Penelope, was a young girl, he would invite them into his home on Easter mornings. When the Counsel's unruly eye would wander over the jury box depicting a man who would subjugate the life of another human being to his own inviolable property rights, Cunningham would rise again to redirect and restore the image of the Englishman as deftly and as painstakingly as a modern-day artist retouching a discoloured Rembrandt or reassembling a mutilated monument. Meanwhile, the Englishman and his daughter from across the courtroom held each other's gaze with a confidence as palpable as if they were holding hands.

Pastor Gittens was late to the trial, caught up in matters of the church. The court was in session, the main entrance locked. The clergy had its privileges, nevertheless, and he was sneaked in through a side door. Knowing that the parents would not be in the courtroom that day, he had wanted to be their eyes and ears. No sooner had he squeezed himself into the only remaining public space before he heard the voice of Barrister Cunningham. He was about to witness a masterstroke from the ingenious defence lawyer.

"M'Lawd, on behalf of the accused, the Defence wishes to call Superintendent of Police, Captain Foster."

All eyes turned as the Captain strode into the witness box. He who had long ago taken the oath to defend the laws of Barbados from people of all races who would seek to violate them; he who had excoriated the Englishman on the telephone for his inexplicably poor judgment; he who had denied the Englishman the sympathy expected of another white man; he would now be sworn in and be asked to come to the defence of Thorne.

The barrister asked, "Captain Foster, would you tell the Court how long you have known the man before you, Mr. Theodore Thorne." The Superintendent squirmed visibly at the first question; he knew the Defence was aligning his shooting ducks in a row.

"I don' know how long but we are both members of the Barbados Rifle and Gun Club."

"And was it not on a monkey-hunting trip on June 22nd of 1954 in the parish of St. John with the said Barbados Rifle and Gun Club, that you and Mr. Thorne had a conversation about the unfortunate proliferation of capuchins on the island—a capuchin and a monkey being one and the same? And that during that exchange, Mr. Thorne mentioned that hundreds of these primates were destroying his fruit trees, creating havoc on his property, chattering loudly day and night and causing Mr. Thorne and his family much anguish, and that he expressed to you his wish that their population on the island would be decimated?"

"Yes, I do remember such a conversation."

"And did you not on that day of the monkey hunt assure Mr. Thorne that if these creatures were indeed terrorizing him and his family, even to the extent that he saw them in his subconscious, whether asleep or awake, that he was within his rights as a gun owner licensed by the Barbados Rifle and Gun Club to shoot them on sight whenever they appeared on his property? Did you not assure him that to do so was well within his rights?"

"Yes, but ..."

"Thank you, Captain. That will be all."

These questions with the force of negative phrasing were flung into the lap of the Superintendent as though the captain had literally placed the rifle in the Englishman's hand that day. No further explanation from the witness would be allowed to weaken the cornerstone of the defence.

The magistrate had noted a salient point in the barrister's questioning and moved to clarify, asking, "Barrister, did you say that the accused had imagined them, the monkeys, in his subconscious, and that he had described them as such to the witness, as is the testimony of the witness today?" Even the judge seemed to buttress the defence.

"That's right, m'Lawd, that is precisely the case."

Thereafter, the Counsel's cross-examination of the Captain was timid and deferential. No one in his right mind living in a small society like Barbados would choose to shame and discredit the Superintendent of Police without taking into account the certainty of future consequences, notwithstanding the gaping holes in his answers that invited scathing rebuttal. The Crown had done its homework and had been ready to debunk any assertion that there could be live monkeys in the mango trees at that time of the year, but the Superintendent's testimony had closed that loophole with the claim that the monkeys were living in the subconscious mind of the accused. Nevertheless, whereas he would not risk challenging the integrity of the Superintendent, he would not shirk from his responsibility as the Queen's Counsel to defend the dead boy.

"Ladies and gentlemen," he began his summation, facing the jury with his fingers inches away from the Remington two-inch-bore shotgun and with his eyes severely out of alignment. "It is my duty as a servant of the people of this fair land to speak on behalf of one of our dear children who is not able to sit among us today because he was struck down by, not one, but two bullets from this awesome weapon in the hands of the defendant, an accomplished marksman. At the tender age of twelve, David Prince must have wondered what on earth was that sudden massive blow he felt to the head in the split second before he plunged into eternal darkness, while the second bullet from Mr. Thorne's shotgun bore a ghastly tunnel through his delicate body. Needlessly so, for he had already been dead. Ladies and Gentlemen, look at the size of this cartridge! The evidence is clear and cannot be contested." He held up one of the gunpowder casings and some of the jurors seemed to shiver with disgust.

"The only unwitting dispensation of mercy from this murderer was that David's death was swift, though the anguish lives on in the broken hearts of his family. The defendant has admitted — no, I say confessed — to having raised this powerful gun to his shoulder and shot twice into that tree without warning, in broad daylight. I ask you, ladies and gentlemen of the jury, is it at all reasonable to assert, as the Defence would have you believe, that Mr. Thorne would choose to defend his fruit trees at a time when his entire property was about to be assaulted by Mother Nature? And then to claim it was all a case of mistaken identity as if in truth and in fact his racist mind perceived no difference between a little black boy and a sub-human? As if today he sees a parallel between black persons and imperfectly formed creatures of evolution incapable of acquiring even the most elemental rudiments of civilization? Does he not know that to be aligned with monkeys is the damnedest insult you could hurl at the pride of a black man? Or was it the judgment of this racist sadistic killer that the trespassing by black people on his private property was an offence deserving of death?"

These words froze the public gallery; they were like a volley of sharp knives flung from the well of the court to tear into the heart of every black man and woman in the audience. Their eyes were now fixed on none other than their black brother, Barrister Cunningham. His head was bowed. Counsel Husbands concluded his summation with a series of emotional crescendos that riveted the courtroom to stony silence. The Prosecution rested and then it was the Defence's turn.

Cunningham rose and slowly walked over and closed the gap between the table for the Defence and the jury. He scanned each row and peered over his glasses into the eyes of each juror. He would now set out to demolish every shred of defamation hurled at his worthy defendant while careful not to diminish the horror and the misfortune of what he deemed an accidental shooting.

"Ladies and gentlemen," he began, "my heart bleeds for this boy, this victim of such a tragic accident. I am sure it pains each and every one of you, as it does me. But let us assume for the sake of argument that such a crime were *not* an accident. I ask you: What kind of person would commit such an unspeakable crime? A despiser of all children? A depraved beast of prey? A bloodthirsty killer? A disciple of Satan himself? A vampire? A cultist? A racist? A drunk? A fool? What kind of human would stoop to such a heinous crime?"

With a sweep of the arm, he directed the eyes of the jury to Thorne in the expansive way a singer gestures to his accompanist. His client was by now a picture of humility and debilitating grief. At that moment Thorne reached into his breast pocket for his handkerchief and blew his nose loud and vigorously, then dabbed the corner of his eye. Was the court about to witness an exhibition of snivelling teary-eyed mockery?

"Ladies and gentlemen, I ask you, do you see any one of those characterizations of evil in that man? Or do you see a law-abiding citizen of this society, who every year welcomed the children of his estate into his home, who every year gives money to The Nightingale Home for Foster Children, who has welcomed into his family the son of his housekeeper and adopted him as his own, so generous a man that he gave his long-time servant, Mr. Benjamin Carson, who is sitting right here in this courtroom, a wall-house with electrics to live in for the rest of his days? Here is a man who would do anything in his power today to restore life to that boy. I ask you: Is this the kind of man who would, in cold blood, murder a defenceless little boy?"

The jury were eating out of his hands, six whites, four half-whites, and two blacks, all creatures of the twenties and thirties, mesmerized not necessarily by his oratory but by the irony of this tar-black Bajan lawyer, wrapping his arms around the shoulder of this pure-white Englishman, who not five minutes ago was being savaged by one of his own race for spilling the blood of a black boy. These jurors grew up in a time and place when a fault line lay deep and wide as a canyon between whites and blacks. Times were different now; the fracture was still there but now blurred by the rise of the highly educated like Barrister Cunningham, who could today cross the divide to defend a white man, if for no other reason than to proclaim himself a child of the new order in a society in the process of healing itself. The jurors were impressed.

He turned away from the jury and took a moment to look around the court, to survey all in attendance. He was surprised to find one last arrow in his quiver. He hadn't noticed it before the proceedings began. He would now use it to slay the dragon that had been breathing fire down the neck of his beleaguered client, accusing him of callous murder, debasing his good name.

Turning back to the jury, he asked: "Where is the plaintiff in this charge of murder? Where is the boy's mother? Where is the father of the boy? Why are they not sitting here in court next to Counsellor Husbands? I'll tell you why, ladies and gentlemen: it is because the boy's parents are decent fair-minded people. They know full well it was all an accident. They cannot in good conscience come to this court and drive this innocent man to his hanging for an ACCIDENT!" He shouted out the word, banging his fist on the wooden railing of the jury box. He ended softly with: "And for that I applaud their decency and good conscience." He turned to the judge. "M'Lawd, the Defence rests."

Thereupon, Thorne's fate was placed in the hands of the jury. They filed out of the courtroom with pained faces. A pessimistic Solicitor Trotman stomped out of the building in disgust. A soft rain began to fall. He strolled along the streets of Bridgetown, from one end of James Street to the other, up and down Swan Street, down High Street, over to Broad Street and back again. He had greatly wanted Cissy and Harold to be present at the trial, to be exhibits in the courtroom as was the inanimate exhibit of a deadly shotgun entered into evidence; to look into the eyes of the judge and jurors and have them see a reflection of themselves as loving parents. He felt that all his counselling had been for naught; that the two had surrendered before the fight was fought, preconceiving a legal system rigged against them. After an hour and a half of perambulating, deep in thought, from one end of the city to the next and back, drenched with rain and sweat, he decided not to return to the courthouse and in the pouring rain he walked dejectedly all the way from St. Mary's Row through Emmerton and Chapman Lane and back to his home in New Orleans. He would put his legal practice aside and devote all his time and energies now to politics, knowing that only the political will of the masses would champion real change in his beloved Barbados.

Meanwhile, back in Thornville, Cissy had made up her mind to be nowhere near the courthouse that day, reasoning that the carriage or miscarriage of justice did not depend on her presence anymore than it depended on the handling of the truth, but that in the final analysis it rested on the skilfulness of lawyers. If true justice were served that day, she would not be overjoyed, and if it were denied, she would not let the betrayal plunder whatever faith she still had in the basic goodness of people. So she confined herself to the cane-backed chair where she had been sitting the day she heard the two claps of gunfire, and proceeded to pedal the old Singer machine with abandon, as the bobbin whirred soft music in her ears.

Harold had gone to the beach. The beach was his sanctuary. It offered him immunity from all wrongs. On the shore he climbed onto the upended hull of a fishing boat, one of many that were left abandoned under the casuarinas like beached whales. He sat for hours squinting into the glare of the morning sun as it sparkled silvery sequins on the deep-emerald horizon. He surrendered his senses to the smell of the sea, to the white-blue-green gradations from sand to skyline, and to the soothing, soft repetitive lapping of waves. They calmed his spirit and prepared his mind for whatever news would eventually reach him from Her Majesty's Court.

At home, Nathaniel immersed himself in his schoolwork and in the fantasy of his toys. He knew of the court date but had already made his own peace and was moving on. From the first day of the investigation he had not been required, gratefully, to appear as a witness, just to provide a signed deposition of what happened that day on the hill at the wall. The loss of his twin brother had been like the amputation of vital extremities but now he refused to look back and focused only on his own healing.

Back at Her Majesty's Court the crowd anxiously reassembled, waiting for His Lordship and the members of the jury to reappear. A wood-dove found her way in through an upstairs east window, circled the body of the court and then perched high on a rafter directly above the magistrate's bench, upon which she released a pellet of excrement before she flew out in a flurry of white feathers. A chuckle rippled through the public gallery at this whim of the gentlest of birds. Pastor Gittens bowed his head and visibly breathed a prayer. Standing close to the main exit, Jay-Jay Johnson, who was acting that day as Court Reporter for *The Chronicle*, poised with pad and pen in hand.

The jurors returned. The Court Clerk asked the foreman to step forward. The foreman advanced, a stout middle-aged man in dapper brown suit and tie, a person whom everyone recognized as Sonny Clarke, a civil servant. A half-white Bajan, he was perhaps in the context of the case the perfect choice as jury foreman.

"Have you arrived at your verdict?" asked the Clerk.

"We have, Sir."

"Do you find the accused, Theodore Augustus Thorne guilty or not guilty of the wilful murder of David Prince?"

The foreman paused for a breathless second as if to induce an air of drama into the final proceedings and to savour that brief, once-in-a-lifetime moment of command before having to return to his prior irrelevance. Bajans in the public gallery held their collective breath.

"We find the accused not guilty of murder," he answered.

"And that is the verdict of you all?"

"It is."

In the blink of an eye the gallery was empty. Bajans scuttled down the steps and out the door, past the unseeing Lady Justice in the lobby, scurrying in every direction like rats fleeing a burning cane field. The court reporter dashed out and ran down Coleridge Street, back to his typewriter. The Thornville people mingled outside around the courthouse under the watchful eyes of the constabulary. They were all dumbfounded, shell-shocked as if a cannon had gone off in their ears. Ben Carson went home, vindicated. Her Majesty's Court had spoken.

Next morning, Mickey Norris heard a sharp whistle outside his mother's house on Nelson Street, looked out the front window and saw his friend, Harold Prince. He was standing, bareheaded, dripping wet in an early morning drizzle.

"Boy, come in out o' the rain!" he called to him.

Harold climbed the three limestone bricks that served as a front step to this plain weather-beaten, two-roofed wooden house and approached his friend standing in the doorway wearing a smile that beamed the words, "I told you so." Without looking into the eyes of his friend, he plunked himself down in the only chair, a Morris chair with a broken armrest, while Mickey sat cross-legged in the middle of the front house on a large oak steamer trunk with metal clasps that accentuated the antiquity of the room. Next to the window was a settee that declared itself Mickey's bed, the pillows and sheets still ruffled and tangled from the night before; and draped across the back were his street clothes among which Harold spied the garish outfit Mickey wore the day they met on Broad Street. He was still in his purple satin pyjamas. Shards of sunlight fell on rotted floorboards from holes in the roof, evidence that Hurricane Janet had had no mercy on this dilapidated house. The partitions were adorned with wallpaper, a colourful collage of tropical flowers. The flowers, a fair attempt in better times to embellish the house, were now tearing away from the walls like loose scabs.

"Welcome to mah humble abode," Mickey drawled, half-apologetically. "Now you see why ah left mah good job in the States to come back here. To get mah mother out of this rat hole before she kick the bucket. Brother, ah was born in this house and ah'm goin' damn well see the ole lady don't croak in it." And with the same breath, perhaps sensing a tension in the immediate air surrounding his friend, he asked, "How 'bout a drink?"

He reached into the seaman's chest that stored his mother's shiny silverware and fine English bone china teapots and teacups and saucers that had never been used; that were saved for the important guests who never came. His hands reappeared with a fifth of Kentucky Tavern bourbon and two glasses. "No ice … sorry."

But there was something else on Harold's mind, something he needed more imperatively than ice. "I need that gun!" he said abruptly.

A knowing smile dawned on Mickey's face. "Now you're talking, brother," he said. Without questioning, he felt between the two pillows on the settee, produced a snub-nosed silvery .22 Magnum Revolver and handed it to his friend.

"Be careful, it's loaded."

Harold stared at the handgun as if it were the key to right all wrongs and then shoved it in his pants pocket.

"Yesterday could've been a day for true justice but it wasn't to be," said Mickey. "Now justice must be served. The bible says it: 'a life for a life'. The Law is not on your side, brother."

Just then, a voice called from the next room, from behind a white sheet that hung from the top of the doorframe like a stage curtain. "Michael! Who that?" The voice was strained and raspy.

"Ma, it's a friend o' mine."

"Yer friend got a name?"

"His name is Harold Prince. Would you like to meet 'im?"

"Yes, I know who Harold Prince is. He and his family in *The Chronicle*."

Harold followed Mickey into his mother's bedroom and there, propped up on a low ball-poster bed, under a retracted mosquito net, was a frail, fair-skinned woman with thin white hair swept back and tied youthfully with a pink ribbon. Two skeletal feet protruded below the bed sheet. A white enamel po peeped out from below the bed and a bamboo walking cane leaned in a corner. Her face looked as old as Harold had imagined it from the sound of her voice. The dark pouches under her eyes and the fleshy folds were like rings on an ancient oak tree that recorded the passage of time. Yet when she smiled, a gleam in her eyes spoke of happier times, of a youth of self-indulgence that, in spite of everything, was without regret. It spoke of the good fortune to be undeservedly alive and to have cheated death when an earlier demise might have seemed fitting for the hazardous life she had led. Her smile was the smile of one who only looks back as if to look forward would only hasten the end.

"Hello, young man, I am Queen Ramona," she greeted Harold with a toothless grin. "Whew! You's a good-looking chap!" Mickey pointed discreetly to the side of his own head and made a circular motion to suggest that she was "not all there."

A colourful assortment of Cancan skirts, pink crinoline petticoats, skimpy shorts, stringy tops and embroidered bloomers hung from a row of wire hangers on one side of the room. These seductive clothes, like the raiment of some outdated profession, were no longer worn or needed. Given their proximity to the old lady, they took upon themselves garments of historical interest, purposely saved to accompany the "queen" to a royal sepulchre.

Harold was drawn to the countless pictures of Mickey's mother, large and small, framed and unframed, on the partitions, on the shelf, on the dresser, on the nightstand, everywhere. It was obvious to him that she was once an uncommonly beautiful girl in her youth, prized for her good looks, slim and sensuous with eyes that must have bewitched many a sailor in her day. The pictures were of young glamorous Queen Ramona in her glory days, in the red-light district of Nelson Street, posing, dancing, hugging, kissing, drinking, smoking, holding hands with sex-starved sailor boys in their proud whites, wallowing in a life of debauchery. Judging from the galaxy of poses and portraits it occurred to Harold that she must have known the name of every Norwegian frigate and every American warship that landed in Carlisle Bay in the early 1900s. Now approaching her seventies, was it unkind to see her as an old retired battleship herself, full of war stories that were best kept to herself.

"Man, I wuz de queen o' Nelson Street in my day," she said to Harold, smacking her gums contentedly. "Men eyes used to pop when I walk in de club. Soon as they land they asking fer Queen Ramona. Where is Queen Ramona? Nobody else but de Queen. Dem Yankee sailor boys wuz hungry to be wid a real woman, a coloured woman. That wuz against de law back in Amurca, the land of the free. So as soon as they land in Bridgetown, they brekking down de door at de Zanzibar Club. Ask my son 'bout Amurca. God bless his heart!"

"Yes, God bless his heart!" said Harold to himself; "but he was no prodigal son, he left home with nothing and returned to his mother's side with a pocket full of money and a good heart."

He said goodbye to the queen and returned to the front room where the two friends lifted their glasses in a toast to whatever justice remained in the world. Neither man would speak further about the trial nor dwell on the verdict, but Mickey seemed pleased; he had done his good deed.

As Harold stepped onto the street, the rain stopped and the sun broke through the clouds to turn a sombre morning into a sunny glorious day. Walking to the bus stop on Bay Street, he softly patted the pocket that held Mickey's gun as if it contained a living, breathing creature. A warm feeling came over him, the feeling that he was not alone, that he was walking with a friend, and he found himself assuming the same fearless gait that he had observed in the way that Mickey had walked away from him that day on Broad Street. Along the way he drew a few winks and whistles from the short-time girls in the Nelson Street bars. One girl, who said her name was Diana, dressed in a backless halter-top and shorts that clung to her hips like a coat of satin paint, called out to him, "Hey saga boy, what's de hurry?" She would have liked nothing more than to lead him down one of those squalid back alleys, into her workshop and onto her semen-stained mattress, whereupon, with the fire in her hips, she would send his mind soaring on a cloud of blissful indifference. But his state of mind was implacable, far removed from Nelson Street, and his heart was most definitely in a different place.

The only voice resounding in his head was the voice of a middle-aged, well-dressed stranger, who approached him on the beach the evening of the trial. He said his name was Moses and that he had come directly from the courthouse to the beach because he knew he would find him there. He said the words, "Dey say de white man not guilty!" then shook his head and walked away.

Made in the USA
Middletown, DE
14 April 2017